# OUT OF TIME

## SANDS OF TIME TRILOGY

## C.J. PETERSON

ISBN: 978-1-952041-44-0 (Paperback)

ISBN: 978-1-952041-45-7 (Ebook)

# CONTENTS

# DEDICATION

This book is dedicated to my loving husband and dear family who love and support me. You all mean more to me than you will ever know. Thank you! I love you!

This trilogy is also dedicated to my mom, **Sue Mann**. We lost her in January 2021. She never hesitated to take other kids under her wing to guide, direct, and pray for them. She was a prayer warrior and an encourager until the end! Her legacy of praying the family through all our good times and bad will never be forgotten. I only hope to continue to grow in my prayer life to be as strong as she was! Mom, you are loved and missed, but we all know you're up in Heaven making sure to keep an eye on all of us!

A portion of the proceeds from this series go to:
www.daretodream-dallas.org
**Their mission:** To pick up the broken pieces of the lives of wounded youngsters in group homes, shelters, detention centers, and orphanages by providing life-skills education and ministry through role model speakers, cultural experiences (art, music,

and dance), and one-on-one mentoring. **Who they serve:** Youth between the ages of ten and eighteen, living in shelters, foster homes, group homes, detention centers and orphanages. Many have been abused and neglected and do not have a father present in their lives. Partnerships have been developed with Juvenile Departments, State Youth Commissions, youth shelters, group homes and orphanages.

To learn more about C.J. Peterson, you can find her online at:
http://cjpetersonwrites.com/
'While the stories are fiction, the journey is real!'

# SUMMARY

With the Maine Facility teens released and the Willow Bend teens safely tucked away, the next phase was to rescue the kids from the Wyoming and Oregon Facilities.

Colby is driving Holly, Blake, and Adam to the Wyoming Facility. Meanwhile, Wyatt is driving Deanna, Eddie, and Freya to the Oregon facility. Both teams are unaware The Professor is waiting for them with plans in place. With both facilities in lockdown, will the teens be able to rescue their siblings? Will Hope pull through from the damage inflicted by Professor Roth? Are the Willow Bend teens, Gemma, Bells, and Hope safe all the way over in Philadelphia, or are they still a target? Everyone has to be ready for this mental chess game. Moves and countermoves are being made. Calculations are continuously changing. Who will come out the victor? Will it be The Professor or the teens? Can the teens succeed, or are they *Out Of Time*?

**1 Peter 5:8** – "Be sober, be vigilant; because your adversary the devil, as a roaring lion, walketh about, seeking whom he may devour."

**Jeremiah 29:11** – "For I know the plans I have for you,"

declares the Lord, "plans to prosper you and not to harm you, plans to give you hope and a future.

**"Time slips through our hands like grains of sand never to return again. Those who use time wisely are rewarded with rich, productive and satisfying lives." Robin Sharma**

# CHARACTERS

<u>**Characters In The Sands Of Time Trilogy & Series:**</u>

Holly  Blake  Deanna  Adam

Charlie  Eddie  Freya  Gemma  Isabelle

The Gifted Maine Teens

Shawn  Mac  Colby

Lindsey  Megan  Tanya

Willow Bend Teens

# ONE STEP AT A TIME

**"For the present is the point at which time touches eternity."**
**C.S. Lewis**

"Pull over here," Blake instructed.

"Your wish is my command," Colby said. He pulled the van into a rest area and put it in park.

"This is a good place to rest for the night," Adam agreed.

"I have to go to the bathroom," Holly said, getting out of the van.

"Let's all go together. Holly, stay in the bathroom until we call for you," Blake said. "We don't want you waiting outside by yourself. It's not safe."

"Agreed," Colby said, taking her hand into his as they walked.

She looked up at Colby with a smile and gave his hand a gentle squeeze.

"Do you think the others are okay?" Colby asked.

"They're going to drive through the night," Adam said. "They'll be fine as long as they keep moving."

"What about the Pennsylvania crew?" Holly asked.

"Gemma and Bells will take care of Hope," Adam encouraged. "They won't let anything happen to her."

"What about the Willow Bend teens?" Holly pressed.

"Let's just pray The Professor doesn't know where they are," Blake said, going into the bathroom with Adam behind him.

Taking both of her hands into his, Colby said to Holly, "I'm glad I'm able to be with you this time. Waiting around to hear something was killing me. I don't have a gift that connects me to you."

"Yes, you do," Holly said. When he shook his head in confusion, she explained, "We have the gift of the Holy Spirit connecting us. Know God is with us in this. He gave us the gifts to get this done and the prayer power of the other teens to survive this. He put everyone in place at just the right time."

"For such a time as this," Colby said in understanding.

This time Holly shook her head, bewildered.

"*For such a time as this* refers to Mordecai's words to Queen Esther in the Bible," Colby explained. "You see, she was put into a position to help her people, the Jews. However, she had to go before the King to do so. Anyone who went before the King without being called could be put to death. Mordecai had to remind her that she was a Jew as well and would not escape the punishment the King would inflict on the Jews. He told her she was in that place, at that time, for such a time as this. She stepped out in faith after three days of fasting and prayer by her people and was able to plead before the King – therefore saving her people."

When Holly shook her head, he continued, "We're all put in these places – Wyoming, Oregon, and Pennsylvania – for such a time as this. God placed everyone where they are for a reason. If we're all to survive, He had to get everyone in the right place at the right time."

"Gotcha. So, you're saying…"

"We're where we are supposed to be, just as everyone else is where they're supposed to be. And the only way we'll all survive this is if we all stay focused on Jesus and our specific goals," he said and then kissed the top of her head. "Understand?"

"I do."

"Good!" He tapped her behind. "Now, go to the bathroom, so we can get out of here. I don't like hanging out in rest areas."

Holly laughed as she walked into the bathroom. Her smile quickly faded when she walked into a man in the women's bathroom. "Um," she looked at the closing door before looking back to the man. "Wrong restroom."

"No," he said and slammed her into the wall. Feeling his breath on her face, she froze. "I'm in the right place. You and I are going to have some alone time," he said, running his hands down her body. He grabbed both of her hands and held them above her head.

"No! Stop!" Holly shrieked.

He slapped her and hissed, "Shut up!"

Holly stared at him, wide-eyed. She suddenly felt a burst of confidence, and knew it had to be from Blake or Adam. *Help was coming!* Heart racing, she kneed the man in the groin. He swore as he dropped to his knees. She thrust her hands forward, sending him back, knocking his head against the sink. He fell to the ground, unconscious.

Not caring if he was alive or dead, she ran from the bathroom, right into Colby's arms.

"Where is he?" Adam demanded.

Holly could not form words. She only pointed toward the bathroom. Adam and Blake ran inside as Colby kept ahold of Holly.

"What happened?" Colby asked. "My heart started racing,

and then a split-second later, Adam and Blake said you were in trouble." Bracing her with his hands on her shoulders, he crouched to look directly into her eyes. "What happened?"

Holly shook her head and hugged Colby. Colby protectively wrapped his arms around her, keeping an eye in every direction.

"Are you hurt?" he asked.

"No. She's just scared," Adam said, walking out of the bathroom.

"Your *friend* is tied with his hands behind his back by his belt to a bathroom stall," Blake said. "He's still unconscious. Did you go to the bathroom?"

Holly shook her head.

"Colby, take her into the men's room to go to the bathroom so we can get out of here," Blake said. "We'll keep an eye on our *friend* until she's ready."

Colby escorted Holly into the bathroom. Between the smell of the men's room and the emotional mess she just faced, she ran into a stall and threw up.

"Holly?" Colby stepped into the stall with her. He held her hair while she vomited again. "That's okay. You're going to need to get it out of your system. We have a lot we still have to process."

When he knelt behind her, she leaned back against him. "I was by myself," she said, body and voice trembling.

"You are never by yourself. You have us. Those with mind gifts, in this case, Adam and Blake, are with you, too. My heart started racing, and just as I was about to say something, both of them looked at each other in panic, saying you were in trouble. Then they bolted."

"I-I'm okay," Holly said, wiping her mouth.

"Okay. Can you stand? This isn't the cleanest place. Try not to inhale."

Holly shuddered as she scrunched up her nose. "It smells like urine."

"I know. Doesn't look like the owners care too much about this rest area. Sorry."

He helped her up. When she was balanced, he stepped out of the stall so she could go to the bathroom. Afterward, she washed her hands and then swished water in her mouth and spit it out a few times to clean her mouth as much as possible.

"Pretty sure we have some gum in the van," Colby assured her. "Are you okay to walk?"

She nodded. Wrapping his arm over her shoulders, he escorted her from the bathroom to outside.

Together, the group of four went to the van, with Blake and Adam on high alert for anyone else in the area.

"Sorry we didn't know he was there," Adam said. "I don't know why we didn't feel him."

"I was concentrating on the outside area, not the bathrooms," Blake said.

"I was, too. I guess we were on the same page."

"Being the non-gifted person in the group, I'm not one hundred percent sure how this works," Colby said. "Is there a way you guys can check with each other so we don't run into this again in the future?"

"Fair enough," Blake said as they loaded up into the van.

"I don't know about you, but I'm too much on edge to sleep," Colby said, starting the van and heading back out onto the highway.

"Agreed," Adam said. "But let's get closer before we stop to rest."

"What if we stop in Cheyenne? It's only three or four hours from Creston," Holly suggested. "We can get some rest there before going to the facility near Creston?"

"There's a military base there," Colby warned. "My mom was in the Air Force. She was at Warren Air Force Base in Cheyenne for a few years."

"Good to know," Adam said. "That may be a safer place than

you think. The Professor won't think we'll stay somewhere with a military base. He'll expect us to stay in some out-of-the-way place to stay off-grid."

"Ooo! Good point!" Colby said. "I like it! Let's head to Cheyenne."

⟐⟐⟐⟐

THE WILLOW BEND teens played another game of Texas Hold 'em while a movie was playing on the TV in the background.

"I have a concern," Mac said.

Shawn flipped the cards, called the flop. "What's that?"

"Dang it!" Megan threw her cards in the center. "I fold. Shawn, you seriously suck at dealing cards."

Shawn chuckled. "Sorry."

Megan pouted. "You're fired."

"I'll tell you what," Shawn said, "you can deal whenever it's my turn from now on, so you won't have to have such a sucky dealer anymore."

"You don't think I'll take you up on that, but I'll take that deal," Megan said. "I don't know what you do, but it's sincerely horrible."

Lindsey rolled her eyes and sighed.

"Lindsey?" Tanya raised an eyebrow. "Why did you just roll your eyes?"

Shawn furrowed his brow. "What's wrong now?"

"You've been sucking up all day," she said to Shawn. "It's annoying."

"So, you get mad at me when I'm honest and get mad at me when I'm trying to get along? I can't win with you," Shawn snapped. "Geesh!"

"Can't you two just get along?" Megan scolded. "Just pretend she's your sister."

"Like a sister I never wanted," Shawn growled. "I've tried. She's not giving me an inch."

"Stop trying and just be," Lindsey explained. "When you try, you're not yourself."

"Oh, stop acting like you care."

"Enough!" Tanya said loud enough to be heard over the bickering. "Do I need to separate you two again?"

"*Nope*," Shawn said, popping the *p*.

Lindsey waved her off. "I'm good."

"Maybe we should just stop and watch a movie?" Mac suggested.

The others agreed and moved the table back to where it was supposed to be. Mac and Shawn pulled the bed out of the couch and laid down, while Lindsey was on one of the beds, and Megan and Tanya were on the other.

After everyone was settled, Mac suggested, "What if we boys sleep here on the sofa bed?"

"Why?" Lindsey asked. "We have the door."

"We've also been here for quite a few days," Mac pointed out. "It wouldn't even take someone as powerful as The Professor to find us at this point. I would sleep better being in the same room, hearing what's going on so we don't potentially miss something."

"I would feel better," Megan admitted.

"Me too," Tanya agreed.

"If you think that's best, then that's what we'll do," Shawn said.

"Seriously!" Lindsey crossed her arms. "This Mr. Congeniality act is getting old."

"Lindsey, you need to relax," Tanya snapped. "He's not even doing anything."

"No. He's being fake. I would rather he be his genuine jerky self."

"Lindsey!" Megan sat up abruptly. "Now who's not being kind?"

She clicked her tongue. "At least I'm being real."

"I'm giving myself a time out," Shawn said, getting off the sofa bed. He stormed into the boy's room, closing the adjoining door between the rooms. It did not take long for them to hear a movie being played on his TV.

"All righty then," Mac said on a sigh. "Tanya, please start the movie? I don't think he's coming back anytime soon."

"I don't either," Tanya said, starting the movie. "These next few days are going to be a barrel of laughs."

⬤⬤⬤⬤

ALEX PACED HER OFFICE. Hearing a gentle knock, she called out, "Come in."

Kendrick Holmes, one of her guards walked in. He did not say a word. He just sat down on the couch, arms crossed, with his blue eyes watching her pace the office.

After a few moments of pacing, she finally stopped and asked, "Is there a reason why you're here?"

"Yep."

"Care to elaborate?" she asked, feeling a twinge of annoyance.

"Well," he sighed. "Seems you're in here stewing. You've already gone off on the supervisors, and the facility is in chaos. Everyone is anxious and worried. What's going on?"

Alex leaned against her desk. Shoving her hands in her pockets, she explained, "Daddy called. He wants the facility locked down indefinitely."

"What? Can he do that?"

"He can do whatever he wants. The rest of the world has to follow. We're just his puppets. He doesn't care that people have families. He doesn't care how much stress he puts on people. All he cares about is his precious *subjects*."

"Okay. I don't particularly care for the man. We've already discussed that aspect on the plane. However, he's in Oregon, right?"

"Right."

"And you are in charge of this facility. Correct?"

"Yes."

"And since you're in charge of this facility, and your father is at least fifteen hours away in Oregon, you can do what you want, correct?"

A smile slowly formed on her face. "Correct."

"So, Alex, what do you want to do here? Are you going to follow Daddy's orders or are you going to be your own woman? C'mon. You're how old now?"

"Thirty-seven."

"When are you going to lead your own life?"

Alex cocked her head. "What do you mean?"

Leaning forward, Kendrick rested his elbows on his knees and interlaced his fingers in front of him. "I'm pretty sure I'm going to get fired for this, but –"

"Not necessarily. I didn't fire you guys for the conversation in the airplane."

"Right. This conversation will go a bit further. I'm going to cross employer-employee lines here."

"What are you saying?" Alex asked.

He got up, running his hand through his sandy-blond hair. "Alex?" he asked. "Do you like me?"

"Of course I like you. If I didn't, you wouldn't be here."

Crossing his arms again, it was his turn to pace. "That's not what I meant."

"What did you mean?" she pressed.

"*How* do you like me?"

"You're cute, but you're also my guard."

He stopped and looked at her. "What if I wasn't?"

Alex pondered his question for a moment. "If you weren't my guard...If you weren't working for my dad...If you didn't work for the facility...If all of that didn't happen, we would not have met."

"What if we did? What if we met outside of the facility?"

"You're my confidant."

"Exactly. What would you do if I wasn't here?"

"Probably go crazy." She rolled her eyes. "Without you to talk to, I would have shut off from the world a long time ago."

"And you're that for me," Kendrick said. "To me, it's not a brother-sister type relationship. What about you?"

"I feel it's deeper," she confessed.

"Agreed."

"How did we get here?"

"Time." He shrugged. "What would you do if you were free from this facility and The Professor. Don't think of him as your dad. Think of him as your boss. Don't think of us as employer and employee. Just think of us as you and me. No work." When she shrugged, he asked, "Do you realize you're just as much a prisoner as those children?"

"I am not." She squared her shoulders. "I have the freedom to come and go as I please."

"Do you?" he challenged. "Are you really free to come and go as you please?"

"Of course I am."

"When they took the kids, what did you do?"

"Went to Daddy."

"Then what?"

She sighed. "I started packing because I knew I would be leaving."

"Okay. Let's stop there and analyze," he said, taking a few steps toward her. "Why did you go see The Professor as soon as the kids were taken?"

"To see what he wanted to do about it."

"And why did you start packing?"

"Because I knew he would send me elsewhere."

"Did he call you to his office?"

"No."

"Did he tell you to pack?"

"No."

"Why did you do those things?"

"I already explained that."

"You explained you did them because you knew he…dot, dot, dot," he said. "In other words, you knew what he wanted you to do. You tend to be emotionless at times. Did you ever think it was because your life isn't yours? It's his."

Alex reeled backward, struck by his words. "I-I never thought of it like that."

He closed the distance between them and rested his hands on the sides of her face. He looked deep into her dark-brown eyes. She did not pull away. "Alex, you have a good heart. I've seen it. When you do bad things, you're operating on automatic mode. You do them because they're expected of you…by him. You're thirty-seven. When are you going to live your life for yourself? When are you going to make choices for yourself?"

"I see myself as the dutiful daughter."

Kendrick chuckled. "I promise you are a force to be reckoned with. That man is controlling you, just as he has all your life. When are you going to stand up for yourself? When are you going to take control of your own life? You owe him nothing. He's your father. He does not own you."

"He could kill me."

"You mean he would have you killed."

She shrugged. "Same difference."

"No." He shook his head. "He never does his own dirty work. He either sends you or one of us to do it."

"What do you mean?"

"You have to understand he will not hurt you directly."

"He doesn't have to; he has people to do that."

Kendrick growled in frustration and then sighed. "Alex? Do you want to live forever as a slave to him? Or do you want to live your life to its fullest, potentially losing years of your life, but living free? He's abusing you, just as much as he abuses those kids."

"He doesn't hurt me."

"He doesn't have to. Mental abuse is just as volatile as physical. The bruises from physical abuse heal in time. Mental abuse is more difficult to get over. I suffered both growing up. The mental abuse took a whole lot longer to work through."

Tears formed in her eyes. "How do I do this? Am I strong enough?"

He laughed. "Alex, you are seriously fierce when you want to be. You're strong with everyone except The Professor. Use that feistiness inside of you, and make a plan. He's fifteen hours away. You are in charge of this facility. What are you going to do?"

◈◈◈◈

Bells and Gemma sat in Hope's room at the hospital, one on each side of the bed. Bells finally came out of Hope's head. "I'm tired," Bells admitted, resting her head on her crossed arms.

"Get some sleep. I'll keep watch," Gemma suggested.

"If you keep watch now, I'll keep watch so you can get some sleep later?"

"That sounds like a plan."

"Let me take a look around the minds on the floor and see if anything is up," Bells said, closing her eyes.

Standing in the white room of her mind, Bells concentrated on the surrounding voices. One by one, she heard phrases pop up in different voices: *BP is low... Need morphine... Too much pain!... Make it stop!... Fight this!... I'm tired... Hopefully my shift will be over soon... When is the nurse coming?... I can't believe I'm still in here... When am I getting out?... I miss my mommy... I want to go home... Why won't they let me just die?*

Convinced there was no one with a bad motive toward Hope in the area, Bells came out of her mind room.

"That was fast," Gemma said.

"It doesn't take me long to sort them out anymore."

"How was it with Hope?"

"Heartbreaking," Bells said. "She was in a black room. I thought –"

"Black? I would think her mind room would be white?"

"I'm sure her mind room is white. Her escape room is dark. It's black. She's hiding in there."

"What do you mean she's hiding?" Gemma asked, tucking a strand of her light-brown hair behind her ear.

"How can I explain this?" Bells said, tapping her chin. She snapped her fingers. "Got it! It's like she's hiding from whatever is trying to kill her – the poison. She's staying in the darkroom, in order to escape the poison until she's strong enough to combat it."

"I see," Gemma said, understanding. "Okay, if everyone has good intentions around here, then get some sleep on the couch. I'll keep watch."

"Yes, ma'am." Bells saluted. She laid down on the sofa in the room. Covering herself with a blanket, she lay her head on the pillow. Huddled under the covers, it did not take long for her to drift off to sleep.

While she slept, Gemma kept an ear out for anything out of the ordinary. As she held Hope's hand, she quietly talked to her. She spoke quietly so she would not disturb Bells. "I know you don't know me, but I'm one of your children's siblings. Guess that sort of makes us related. Blake showed us some memories of you guys as a family. I would have loved to have been raised by you and Ben. I hope we can still enjoy some time with you once this is over."

Gemma sat there for a few moments in silence before she explained, "I always wanted a mommy. Daddy was brutal, but we had to respect him or he would hurt us. If I didn't do what he said, he would hurt Freya and vice-versa. To be honest, Freya is stronger than me. Just don't tell her I said that. It will go to her head. She's a few minutes older than me too. I'm glad I'm the one here. They need Freya more than me. They need our strongest to rescue the others. While I do have power, I'm not anywhere near as powerful as the others. I know it. They do, too. Anyway, I would love to tell them you're awake. Please open your eyes?"

When she asked that, there was a sudden alarm on the monitor. A nurse came running in, and Bells sat straight up on the couch. "What's going on?" Bells asked.

"I-I don't know," Gemma stammered, moving out of the way when more people flooded the room. "What's happening?"

"Stand back," the nurse ordered. There was a sudden halt to the beeps on the monitor, and it turned into one long, continuous beep.

Wide-eyed, another nurse yelled, "Get the crash cart!"

"Code blue. ICU room 312. Code Blue. ICU room 312," came over the loud speaker.

Bells grabbed Gemma's hand and pulled her to the corner of the room. She whispered to Gemma, "If we're quiet, they'll forget we're here."

Gemma nodded in response, and the pair locked arms, watching every move the medical staff made.

◁◁◁▷▷▷

WYATT, Freya, Deanna, and Eddie drove for what Wyatt knew were hours. He drove a lot over his lifetime, but the amount of

14

driving he did over the last few weeks was more than he wanted to do for the rest of his life. "So, tell me something good," Wyatt said to the trio. "I've heard all of the bad. I know what a prig that man is. Tell me the good between you guys."

The trio debated for a few moments. Finally, Freya said, "Gemma and I have always been close."

"Like inseparable," Deanna added. "It's almost like they're one person at times."

"They complement each other well," Eddie added. "Sometimes even finish each other's sentences."

"They also like to play jokes on people," Deanna said with a smirk. "Adam usually caught them before they did it, so they stayed away from us."

"Well, you could kick our behinds, and Adam could beat us pretty well if he wanted to," Freya explained.

"What did you do?" Wyatt asked.

"Oh, you know." She shrugged. "Sugar and salt in the beds."

"Hiding our stuffed animals," Eddie said.

"Oil in the doorway, so when the nurses came in, they slipped," Deanna continued.

"Syrup on the toilet seats," Eddie added.

"We like to have fun," Freya said in her defense. "If we didn't, you all would have died of oppression a long time ago."

"One time, they somehow got ketchup inside the doughnuts," Eddie explained.

"We had help with that one," Freya confessed. "The nurse knew we wanted to add a little spice. My idea was hot sauce, but Gemma felt bad, so she suggested ketchup."

"Gemma's the nice one," Eddie said and winked at Freya. "Freya's the ornery one."

"I prefer the word fun," Freya said with a mischievous grin.

"So, there were fun times?" Wyatt asked.

"When we were left alone in the room and had free time, we

were able to relax and bond as a group," Freya explained. "Sometimes, we could get the guards to join in with us too."

"They're just little boys with big guns," Deanna said.

Wyatt chuckled. "We tend to be little boys in big bodies."

"I like guys with a good sense of humor," Freya said. "I hope my husband has a great sense of humor. I can see us playing practical jokes on each other all the time."

"God help your children!" Deanna rolled her eyes to everyone's laughter.

"Seriously! Have you ever thought about what your husband or wife would be like?" Freya asked. "To have someone who loves you for who you are? Someone who will cuddle with you at night? Someone to travel with. Who will hug you when you need it, or who will hold your hand when you go out. Someone to enjoy doing regular everyday life with. Someone who you can raise children with. Did you ever think about what your kids would be like? Gemma and I always talked about our future families. I want to have four kids, but she only wants two. She likes the idea of pairs. I do too, but I know life happens. We've seen too much violence to neglect that aspect of life. Something could happen to one of my kids, and then I'll still have three. Plus, with four, each kid has a best friend."

"Kind of a morbid way of looking at life," Wyatt pointed out.

"Morbid is more Deanna's realm," Freya said, looking over her shoulder toward Deanna.

"Really?" Wyatt raised an eyebrow. "Classic teenage angst?"

"No. She's always been that way," Freya said.

"Not true!" Deanna defended herself. "I'm quiet. Not morbid."

"Violent," Freya countered.

"Not violent. Rebel," Deanna offered.

"That, I'll agree with," Freya conceded.

"In her defense, she always seemed to be The Professor's vent," Eddie explained.

"What does that mean?" Wyatt asked.

"He seemed to have it in for her. It's like he knew she was strong-willed. Since she was little, he made it his personal mission to break her before she got older."

"He never did," Freya said. "She may have bent, but never broke."

"Nope," Deanna agreed. "I didn't."

"Good girl," Wyatt said, glancing in the review mirror at her. Her head flinched back slightly. So, he explained, "Strong-willed people are difficult when they're little, but they're the ones who will ultimately change the world."

"What do you mean?" Eddie asked.

"Strong-willed people tend to be the changemakers. They buck the system. Those who rule by power hate them because they can't control them. They also tend to be leaders of revolts. You, Adam, Holly, and Blake led the way on this one. Do not think for a minute The Professor doesn't know who's leading this. I may be a driver, but you four are the driving force."

"I guess I never thought of it that way," Deanna admitted.

"Holly's always been an in-your-face strong-willed person. Meanwhile, Blake will not say anything. He'll just do what he feels is right, whether you know or not. He doesn't care."

"So, there are two types of strong-willed people?" Deanna asked.

"Yep. And both can be used for good or bad. The heart dictates which one is going to rule the soul," Wyatt said. "You and The Professor are a perfect example of strong-willed gone good and bad. You are using your strong will for good. You're using it to save your siblings. The Professor is using his to control every aspect of his world. Right now, his world is unraveling."

"That means he is too," Eddie said.

Wyatt nodded. "Which means y'all need to stay on your toes.

When a strong-willed person loses control of their world, things get dangerous."

⟨⟩⟨⟩⟨⟩⟨⟩

IT TOOK them longer than either Gemma or Bells wanted, but medical team finally got a pulse. It was faint, but it was there. With a breathing tube inserted, the machine breathed for her. The dialysis machine continued to cleanse her blood of the poison. The catheter continued to relieve her body of fluids, while the IV continued to push them into her body.

"I'm sorry we don't have better news, but she's slipped into a coma. It's up to her what comes next. I wish I could be more positive. We'll keep a close eye on her," the doctor said before leaving the room with several nurses.

Still linked arm-in-arm, Gemma and Bells slowly made their way over to Hope.

"What do we do?" Gemma asked.

"I don't know. I can't go into her mind; she's in a coma. If I go in, I'll go into one too, and I don't know if I can pull out of it."

"What if we call the hotel?" Gemma asked.

"Is that safe?"

Gemma shrugged. "The hotel is pretty close to the hospital. I'm sure we're not the only ones calling the hotel from this hospital."

"Good point," Bells agreed.

Gemma dialed the phone while Bells searched the minds of the doctors and nurses for more information on Hope's condition. "I don't know what else to tell you," Gemma said into the phone after she explained what happened.

"Just keep us posted," Tanya said. "In the meantime, we'll be in prayer."

"Sounds good. You have the room number here, correct?"

"Yes. If we hear anything, or if you do, go ahead and call," Tanya said.

"I will," Gemma agreed. "Any information is welcomed, whether good or bad."

"Agreed. Be safe."

"You too. Bye."

"Bye," Tanya said and hung up the phone.

"What's going on?" Lindsey asked. "We didn't catch much."

"Go get Shawn," Tanya said to Mac.

It took a few moments of convincing before Shawn reluctantly came over. He leaned on the doorway between the rooms, fully intending to go back on his own after the news. He crossed his arms as he leaned against the door.

"Hope's in a coma," Tanya said. "We need to pray."

Mac furrowed his brow. "What happened?"

"They really don't know. Bells just finished doing some memories with Hope to keep her focused on fighting. She was exhausted, so Gemma told her to take a nap. While she was asleep, Gemma was talking to Hope, and Hope flatlined."

"Flatlined?" Shawn stood. "There's a difference between coma and flatline."

"She flatlined," Tanya said. "The doctor and nurses brought her back. She's intubated. There's a machine breathing for her, a machine trying to clean her blood of the poison, and a machine monitoring her and giving her saline. The machines are keeping her here until she can fight for herself."

"She's young, strong, and has a lot to live for," Lindsey pointed out. "And if God's not done with her, she's not going anywhere. If He is, He'll call her home."

"This sucks!" Shawn said and left for his room.

After the door closed behind him, the others looked at each other.

"Who's going to go after the wayward son?" Mac asked.

"No one yet," Tanya said. "He needs a bit of time by himself. Maybe he and God can come to an understanding."

"In the meantime, I think we need to pray for Hope," Megan added.

"Agreed," Tanya said.

Together, the group paused the movie and prayed for Hope, as well as the others out traveling. They prayed for God to give the doctors wisdom in Hope's case and for the safety of the others.

# TIME AFTER TIME

**"A brother may not be a friend, but a friend will always be a brother." Benjamin Franklin**

"How are you driving without sleep?" Eddie asked from the second seat. Deanna was asleep on the seat next to Eddie, and Freya was asleep in the passenger's seat.

"How are *you* not asleep?" Wyatt asked.

"I already took a nap." Eddie shrugged. "When we get closer, I'll take a power nap while the others are awake. I don't sleep very long when I do sleep. I used to practice my gifts when everyone was asleep, and I guess my body just got used to functioning on little sleep."

"Interesting. Well, in my line of work, I've learned how to do extended times with no sleep if I have to. Those times are few and far between the older I get, but I can do them. A little energy drink helps in situations like this," he said, holding the can up with one hand before setting it back into the cupholder.

"I see. That's not exactly healthy."

"Ring! Ring! Hello, pot? This is kettle," Wyatt said, tongue-in-cheek.

Eddie shook his head, confused.

"Sorry. Basically, the saying is, *that's the pot calling the kettle black.* What it means is you shouldn't criticize someone else for a fault you have yourself. You said my staying up using an energy drink as a way to stay awake isn't healthy. Well, I would counter with you functioning completely on power naps, and no extended period of deep REM sleep isn't healthy either."

"Oh. I see. I'll file that one for later. Thank you."

"No problem. There'll be a lot of phrases y'all will need explaining."

"I'm sure. Living on the campus all of our lives didn't allow for much exposure to the real-world ways," Eddie pointed out.

"I can only imagine. Actually," Wyatt changed his mind, "I wouldn't want to imagine that. I like my freedom."

Eddie rubbed his chin in thought. "What's it going to look like when we go to Texas?"

"I think that's something we'll have to look at when we have a final count."

"What does that mean?"

Wyatt raised an eyebrow. "Really? This is from the guy who calculates like mad to find all the angles? As angry as Professor Roth is, do you really think everyone will come out alive? Neither sets of kids in Wyoming or Oregon are close to anyone rescuing them. They may not even think they need rescuing. They may try to fight you instead of going with you willingly."

"Good point," Eddie agreed. "My plan is to link with those who have the mind gift and have a chat with them before we breach."

"What are you going to say?"

"I don't know," Eddie admitted. "I was just going to go with my gut on this. While we were raised thousands of miles apart, we were raised by the same man."

"This is true."

"Have–have you considered adopting some of us?" Eddie asked hesitantly.

"Yes," Wyatt said. "As it is, whether Hope comes through or not, Blake and Holly are mine. I helped raise them."

"I see."

"I have a couple thoughts in mind for the rest of you. Why?"

"I guess my question is, well, I'm broken," Eddie explained. "I'll be a lot more work than the average sibling."

Wyatt glanced in the mirror at Eddie before looking back toward the road. "Eddie, I don't think you're more work. Your chair is just your mode of transportation. That's not who you are. I know I've said it, and a couple other kids have said it – you're the strongest one here. Do you realize that? You are the strongest one here," Wyatt enunciated the last sentence.

"I guess I don't see myself that way."

"You don't have to prove anything to me. Even if you didn't have your gifts, you could run circles in intelligence around any one of those teens. Well, except for Megan. She's pretty smart."

"She is!" Eddie chuckled. "She's feisty! I like her!"

"She's super sweet most of the time. She sure put Shawn in his place!" He laughed.

"That she did."

"Eddie, I'm going to make you a personal promise. I have not and will not promise this to anyone except you, Holly, and Blake."

"Okay," Eddie said, uneasy.

"I promise you, if you and I make it out alive, I will adopt you. I don't want you worrying if there will be a home for you. I will be your dad. A real dad. Like a dad you should have had all your life."

Eddie swallowed. Looking up at the roof of the van, he blinked away the few tears that threatened to come down. Once he got control, he said, "Th-thank you. I-I don't know what to say."

"Nothing to say. I am making you a promise. I give you my word. You will have a home under my roof with me. All you have to do is make sure we both make it out of this alive."

"We will," Eddie said confidently. "We will."

"Good man," Wyatt said, focusing back on the road.

⬦⬦⬦⬦

"I'LL BE BACK." Mac got off the bed. He walked into his and Shawn's room, closing the door behind him.

"What's up?" Shawn asked, pausing the movie.

Mac plopped down on the bed next to Shawn. "What's going on with you? Why are you hiding out here?"

"Because it's a lot more pleasant in here than it is in there with Lindsey," Shawn pointed out. "You cannot tell me different."

"I'm not going to argue that fact. However, we're supposed to look after and protect those girls. It's a bit difficult when you're locked away in another room."

"Well, you seem to have it all under control." Shawn shrugged. "I don't hear any arguing when I'm pulled out of the equation."

"I would rather you joined us."

"Not until Lindsey chills out."

"I'll handle that. Are you willing to come back if I can get her settled?"

"I can do that," Shawn agreed.

"Fair enough. I'll be right back," Mac said and went through the adjoining door to the girl's room, closing the door behind him. Sitting on the bed next to Lindsey, he picked up the remote and paused the movie.

"Hey! We were watching that!" Lindsey objected. "And it was at a good part, too."

"We need to talk," Mac said sternly.

The girls all sat up on the bed they were sitting on.

"What's up?" Megan asked.

"Lindsey and Shawn," Mac said. "We can't have this much discord in this group. Shawn feels singled out by Lindsey. He says the other two, meaning you two," he said to Megan and Tanya, "are fine." Then he turned back toward Lindsey and added, "But you and I have a problem."

"What kind of problem?" Lindsey asked, picking at her nails.

"A friend problem. You are both my friend, but you basically attacked him while he was trying to be a good guy."

"That's the point. He was trying. He wasn't behaving like himself," Lindsey argued.

"So, pretty much he's toast either way. He's caught in a catch-22. If he's a jerk, you nail him. If he's over-polite, or just trying to have fun, you nail him. Do you see the problem here?"

"Now I feel attacked."

"Probably because you attacked him first," Tanya said. "You owe him an apology. Yes, he can be a jerk. However, he wasn't a jerk at the time you attacked him."

"Fine!" Lindsey huffed as she got up. "I'll apologize."

Megan grabbed her arm. "Not with that attitude."

Lindsey threw her hands in the air, exasperated. "I don't understand what y'all want?"

"You need to go with the proper heart attitude," Tanya pointed out.

Lindsey rolled her eyes. "Oh, Miss High and Mighty now says I can't go without the proper heart attitude!"

"Okay," Megan got off the bed. "I'm going to go join Shawn. Tanya and Mac can come too. But, Linsey…" She shook her head. "You need to work on your heart attitude before you come over."

Megan went through the adjoining door to the boy's room, closely followed by Tanya.

"And when you clean up that heart attitude toward Shawn, you may want to consider apologizing to Tanya too," Mac said, standing up. "That was uncalled for. In the meantime, here's Who you need to spend time with," he said, handing her a Bible from the nightstand before he went next door with the others.

When she heard a movie playing in the next room, Lindsey let out a long sigh. "My heart attitude," she huffed. "I guess I can do it the unique way," she said, opening the Bible. She closed her eyes and flipped through the pages. Shoving her hand into the pages, her finger landed on a verse. "Proverbs 17:22 – *'A joyful heart is good medicine, but a crushed spirit dries up the bones.'* Yeah. Okay. That actually applies. Not the normal way to do devotions, but that one is applicable." She sighed. Looking up at the ceiling, she admitted, "I like him, Lord. I just feel like we're thousands of miles apart right now." When she did not hear anything, she closed her eyes and searched again. "It worked last time." Opening her eyes, she found herself on Philippians 4:8. "Okay. *'Finally, brothers, whatever is true, whatever is honorable, whatever is just, whatever is pure, whatever is lovely, whatever is commendable, if there is any excellence, if there is anything worthy of praise, think about these things.'* Hmm. That's another good one. This way is actually working for once." She shrugged. Then, looking toward Heaven, she asked, "It is me. Isn't it? I'm the one who is hurt and who is acting out of hurt. I'm not thinking of Heavenly things or good things. I'm being selfish and thinking only of myself. Okay. One more time," she said and repeated the process. "Colossians 3:17, *'And whatever you do, in word or deed, do everything in the name of The Lord Jesus, giving thanks to God the Father through Him.'* Yeah. Okay. Don't need to hit me in the head with a two-by-four, God. I got it. I screwed up. Please forgive me?" When she still did not hear anything in her heart or mind, she said, "I'll give this one more shot." Finding Matthew 5:30, she read, *"And if your right hand causes you to stumble, cut it off and throw it away. It is better for you to lose one part of your body than for your whole body to go to hell.'* Should have stopped while I was ahead." She chuckled. "Now, I *am* going to stop. This could lead me down a very dark path. There's a reason why we're not supposed to do it this way." Looking toward Heaven, she admitted, "Despite the sick joke of the last one, the other verses do apply. I get it. My thoughts and heart are not in the right direction. Shawn hurt me, and I have been hurting him back. What he did was so wrong, though!"

Matthew 7:1-2 crept through her mind, *'Do not judge, or you too will be judged. For in the same way you judge others, you will be judged, and with the measure you use, it will be measured to you.'*

"I get it. I get it," Megan said aloud. "You are the judge. Not me. I know he did the same thing I did…well, almost the same thing. I didn't go that far. What I don't understand is why it's okay for a guy and not a girl. Why are there different standards?"

1 Corinthians 6:18-20 shot through her mind like a reprimand, *'Flee from sexual immorality. All other sins a person commits are outside the body, but whoever sins sexually, sins against their own body. Do you not know that your bodies are temples of the Holy Spirit, who is in you, whom you have received from God? You are not your own; you were bought at a price. Therefore honor God with your bodies.'*

"Okay. So, you'll handle Shawn, and I need to handle myself. I get it. Stay in my own lane and keep myself pure. Wait! That last one does apply. I've been offending you with the way I have treated my body. Okay," she said, looking toward Heaven, "here it goes. I'm sorry. I have been treating my body like a weapon or tool to get what I want. However, my body is not my own. It was bought with the price of Jesus' blood. He sacrificed, not so I could just give it away. It's not mine to give away. When

I accepted Jesus' gift of forgiveness and salvation, I gave Him my life in exchange…and that includes my body. I will be more conscious of that fact and will clean up my act. I'm sorry. Please forgive me?" She sighed. Glancing toward the closed door, she then looked back toward Heaven. "I'll do what You want me to do, and you'll take care of Shawn. I get it."

After a few moments of silent reflection, she headed over to the other room. When she walked in, Mac paused the movie. "Can I talk to Shawn for a minute?" Lindsey asked.

"Oh no!" Shawn shook his head. "You lambasted me in front of the group. Anything else you have to say to me, you can say it in front of the group as well. I want witnesses."

Lindsey put her hands up in surrender. "You're right. I screwed up. I was hurt and hurt you in return."

"What do you mean you were hurt?" Shawn asked, sitting up on the bed. "How did I hurt you? We were all playing cards. As far as I know, Megan was the only one I hurt with my dealing?"

Megan rolled her eyes. "Ain't that the truth!"

Lindsey took a few brave steps toward Shawn. He was on the bed next to the window, which had the table at the end of his bed. She leaned against the table, bracing herself for the conversation she had dreaded for years. "I, um," she nervously cleared her throat. Looking toward Heaven, praying for the right words, she said, "I really do like you, Shawn. Well, I like the you that you used to be."

"What does that mean?"

"You've changed…a lot. You may not see it, but you have." She sat down on the chair next to the table. "You see, you used to look after us but not try to control us. You used to be kind, caring, and considerate. Lately, you're more arrogant, obnoxious, and quite frankly…a jerk."

Shawn raised an eyebrow. "Is this supposed to be an apology?"

"I'm getting there," she said, tucking a portion of her hair behind her ear. "I'm sorry for holding you to the standard you used to be. I'm sorry for taking my frustration out on you. That's not fair. You used to be an amazing guy. You used to enjoy the Bible and talking about Christ. You used to be a good witness for Christ. Then, you started doing really well at the rodeos. Once that happened, it's like fame went to your head. You did a one-eighty. I guess I miss my friend. I really miss the guy I liked."

"Honestly? Me too," Megan admitted.

Tanya raised her hand. "Me three."

"I'm working on changing to be more like I should be, but I'm not there," Mac said. "I know it would be easier if you came back as well."

Shawn sat back on his pillow and crossed his arms. "I thought this was supposed to be an apology, not an intervention."

"It is an apology," Lindsey said. "I'm explaining my heart first. Now, I am sorry for behaving the way I have lately. There is no excuse for me lashing out at you. You're behaving how you want to. That's on you. I'm behaving poorly. That's on me. I'm sorry. I have also been treating my body as a weapon or tool, and it's not my body. It belongs to Jesus. Our bodies are the temple of the Holy Spirit, and I have been using it to get what I want. I promised God that I will do my best to think more on the things God wants me to think on, and not what Lindsey wants to think on."

"If you stay focused on what God wants you to think on, the two may blend together," Tanya added.

"Oh! And, you?" Lindsey said to Tanya, who looked at her wide-eyed. "I'm sorry to you too. That was uncalled for. You have a kind heart. You do your best to guide us in the direction we're supposed to look. When you love darkness rather than light, the brightness of the light hurts. I want to live more in the light. It'll take time, but I'm willing to do the work."

"Do you need an accountability partner?" Tanya asked.

"Can you handle my sarcasm?"

"Ha!" Tanya laughed. "Is that a trick question? I grew up in a half-Latino home. Passion and sarcasm reign there."

"I would appreciate it," Lindsey said. "I know our breakfast times have helped me out. At first, I resented them. Now I look forward to them."

"I know I'm excited to join them. That's another reason why I don't mind being in the room with y'all," Mac added.

"What breakfast time ritual are you talking about?" Shawn asked.

"We take turns reading a Proverb before we eat breakfast, and we talk about it while we eat. Then afterward, we pray for the safety of everyone and for clarity of mind, and for God to guide our steps," Megan explained.

"How do you know what to read?" Shawn asked.

"It really doesn't matter," Megan said with a shrug. "There's wisdom in all of the Bible. However, we use the daily method, where you read the Proverb that matches the date. There are thirty-one Proverbs, and the longest month has thirty-one days. So, whatever the date is… you read that chapter in Proverbs. Make sense?"

"Yep."

"Then, in my own alone time, I'm reading through the Bible in a year," Megan continued. "Right now, I'm in Second Kings and John."

"That's ambitious!" Shawn said, impressed.

"It's not the first time," Megan explained. "This is my third time through."

"Doesn't it get boring reading the same thing?" Mac asked, sincerely curious.

"No. Depending on what I'm going through will depend on what stands out. Quite honestly, the Kings are quite violent. You guys would probably like them." She smiled. "I read some chapters from the Old Testament and some from the New Testament. It's nice to get a balance. If I don't get something from the one, I get it from the other. It's rare that I don't get something from both."

"That's kind of cool," Mac said. "Can you show me how to do that?"

"I'll tell you what. Why don't you do them with me for a bit?" Megan offered.

"I would really like that," Mac said. "Thank you!"

"No problem. It sometimes helps to have an example to go by."

"Let's back this love fest up a bit," Shawn interrupted. "I want to go back to the lambasting of Shawn that Lindsey did while trying to apologize for the original slaughter. While I appreciate the apology. The way you did it seems pretty backhanded."

"What do you mean?" Lindsey asked.

"You pretty well assassinated my character and then apologized for attacking me," Shawn pointed out.

"I said that hoping you would consider making changes," Lindsey admitted.

"You want me to change for you?"

"No. I want you to change for you and Jesus," Lindsey countered.

"What if I don't want to change?" Shawn asked, leaning back on his pillow. "What if I'm happy just the way I am?"

"Then, I feel sorry for you," Lindsey said. "However, I won't be rude toward you anymore…unless you're rude to me."

"Um, okay. I think," Shawn said.

"I really am sorry for being rude earlier. Please forgive me?"

"I forgive you."

"Thank you. Please join us again?"

"Okay. Tomorrow, I'm going to take some *me* time, though," Shawn said. "Not because I'm mad. I just need some space through the day."

"May not be a bad thing for all of us to do that," Megan

pointed out. "I know I'm not so good when I don't get a break from people. Being an only child, I'm not used to constant company. It can wear you down if you're not used to it."

"I didn't think about that," Tanya said. "I guess I'm just used to people all the time."

"You have like three brothers and two sisters," Mac said. "I can't imagine alone time is a thing in your house."

Tanya laughed. "It's not."

Just then, the phone rang in the other room.

"Got it!" Megan jumped off the bed and ran for the other room. The others slowly followed as Megan answered the phone, "Hello?"

"Megan?" Gemma asked.

"Yep."

"Hi. This is Gemma. Do you think we could trade places for a bit? We have gotten zero sleep since being here."

"I can understand that. What if we switch out one of you for one of us and then reverse it? That way, there is at least one there who can somehow give us either a heads-up that someone is coming or defend us?"

"I think that's a brilliant idea!" Gemma said, pleased. "I think Bells'll stay here first. She has at least slept on the couch for like twenty minutes, getting a power nap. I haven't gotten any."

"Okay. Wyatt told us to stay here. How are we going to do this?"

"Oh, crud! You're right," Gemma groaned. "If you're here, you'll be on video. I forgot. Hmm."

"We could disguise ourselves if you can get us in?" Megan offered. "We have hats, glasses, and makeup."

"If you guys are comfortable with that, we could do that for just two nights. Like, I'll come tonight to sleep, then come back in the morning. Then tomorrow night, Bells can come sleep at the hotel and then come back that morning."

"I think that's fair," Megan said. Looking up at the group,

Megan asked, "Who wants to switch places with Gemma and stay the night with Bells so Gemma can sleep?"

"I'll go," Shawn said, raising his hand. "I can take the trolly to the hospital if Gemma can meet me downstairs and take me up?"

"I can go with you," Mac suggested. "Then I can come back with Gemma so she won't have to be on the trolly by herself."

"I think that's a good plan," Megan agreed. "Did you hear that, Gemma?"

"I did. And I agree. Thank you all so much!"

"We're in this together," Megan said. "Give Mac and Shawn a bit to ride the trolly over there."

"Okay. I'll meet them downstairs. See you soon!" she said and hung up.

"Okay. Time to disguise y'all," Megan said to Mac and Shawn.

⧫⧫⧫⧫

"This isn't exactly the most spacious of hotels, but it'll work," Blake said as they walked into their room. "Holly, why don't you take one bed, and I'll take the sofa bed, leaving Colby and Adam for the other bed?"

"What if you and I switch?" Colby suggested to Blake. "For two reasons. Number one, a sofa bed isn't the comfiest. I may have to drive, but you have to get your rest so you can fight. Number two, I'm bigger than you. Poor Adam won't have much of a bed if I share with him."

"What if I take the sofa bed?" Holly offered.

"Same reason as number one," Colby pointed out.

"I think that's a good idea," Adam said. "Colby on the sofa bed, Holly on one bed, and Blake and I on the other."

Colby nodded. "I agree. Thank you."

"All right," Holly said, heading into the bathroom. "After she changed, the boys took turns changing in the bathroom before all four went right to sleep. No movie…just sleep.

⬡⬡⬡⬡

IN HER DREAM, Holly went into the bathroom at the rest area from earlier, only to come face-to-face with Professor Roth. He slammed her into the wall, and she saw stars. "You have been a thorn in my flesh since you were born. Your aunt was a pain when you were born too. I actually considered killing her, but she learned her lesson."

"What did you do?" Holly asked, wide-eyed.

"I sent a few of my men to warn her about coming back to the clinic or pushing the issue of seeing you or your mother's bodies."

"What do you mean?" Holly demanded.

The Professor got into her face, and she gasped. "I will shut you up, too, if you become too big of a pain," The Professor warned.

"What will you – no!" Holly shouted at him. "You will do nothing to me!" She thrust her hands forward, shoving The Professor back without even touching him.

He whipped a dart gun out of his jacket and shot it at Holly.

Holly looked down, seeing the dart empty into her system. She looked back up at him but only saw her reflection in the mirror. Blood came from her eyes, nose, mouth, and ears…and then she dropped to the ground.

"Holly!" Blake shouted. Holly continued to scream in her sleep. "Holly!" Blake yelled again. "Adam! Help me!"

Adam ran over to Holly's bed and took her hand into his. The next thing he knew, he was standing in a bathroom at the rest area with Holly. Holly was on the ground with blood coming from every open orifice on her head. She was not moving.

"Holly!" Adam ran over to her and gently shook her. "Holly, you're in a dream. You need to wake up!"

"Adam. My boy!" The Professor said, standing up.

Adam jumped to his feet. "What did you do?"

"She wouldn't listen." The Professor shrugged. "So, I taught her a lesson."

"You killed her!" Adam shouted. "How could you?"

"She wouldn't listen."

"You are a sorry excuse for a human being! I pray the Lord will avenge all of us!"

"The Lord? As in God? Are you serious? I am god! I created life! I created you! I created each one of my subjects."

"Subjects?" Adam took a step back. "Subjects? We're your children!"

"Don't you worry. You'll be brought back soon enough. I know where you are. I know where all of you are!"

Adam ran over to Holly and placed his hands on the sides of her face. "Holly, look at me. We need to wake up. You have to fight this! Use that tenacity I know is in you! Use that temper and fight!"

Holly shook her head to clear it. "I–I…what?"

"Wake up! We're in trouble!"

With blood still coming from every orifice in her head, she sat up and looked around.

"It's just a nightmare. You have to wake up," Adam coaxed. "You have to wake up now!"

Holly closed her eyes. When she opened them, she was in the room with the guys. Blake was shaking her shoulders while Adam held her hand, and Colby paced the room. "What happened?" she asked, wiping her face, relieved to not see blood.

"We need to get out of here," Adam said. "He knows where we are."

Colby stopped pacing. "How do you know?"

"He told me in the dream. He has a creepy gift. He can infiltrate dreams," Adam explained. "He would torture us in our dreams if we had a particularly rough day behavior-wise."

"Are you serious?" Blake asked, stunned. "Do the others know this?"

"Those from Maine. Yes."

"I have to call the hotel and warn the others," Blake said.

After calling the Willow Bend teens, they quickly changed and left the hotel. Stopping at a gas station to get coffee or energy drinks, they took their time moving forward.

"We cannot sleep," Adam explained. "If we sleep, he could hold us there."

"He said I have an aunt," Holly said. "Do I really have an aunt?"

"It's possible," Blake acknowledged. "We have to check the file."

"It's true. It's in your mom's file," Adam said. "She's a few years older than your mom was. They were the only children. They were also orphans."

"So, I am literally the only family she has?" Holly asked.

"According to the file, yes," Adam said. "I'm sorry."

"She doesn't even know I'm alive."

"As far as she knows, you died during delivery with your mom."

"I don't know what to do with that," Holly admitted.

"If you stay there, then he'll win," Colby said.

"What do you mean?" Holly asked.

"If he can get you distracted, being the strongest one in this group, then wherever we raid, they'll get us," Colby said. "You need to snap out of it, or he wins."

⬦⬦⬦⬦

"He can infiltrate dreams?" Tanya asked, horrified, hanging up the phone. Turning to Gemma, she demanded, "Did you know this?"

"Yes," she admitted.

"Why didn't you warn us?" Mac asked.

"I didn't think he was going to bother with all of us in dreamtime. I thought he would be more concerned with keeping his precious children safe in Oregon."

"Gemma, this is something we needed to know," Megan said calmly.

"That's how he isolated the gene. He has it himself. That's the main reason why he seeded the experiments," Gemma clarified. "He knew what gene he needed to manipulate, and he knew he already had it."

"If you go to sleep, can he find you?" Lindsey asked.

"Yes."

"Is there any way you can stay awake until they raid the facilities?" Mac asked.

"How are we to know when that is?" Megan asked. "She's already been awake for over twenty-four hours. How long can we honestly expect her to stay awake?"

"What if he gets her in a nightmare and uses her against Freya?" Mac asked. "You have to understand my concern is for everyone."

"I do. I get it. That's my fear as well. I think that's why I haven't slept," Gemma admitted. "I don't want him to find me and use me against Freya. He did that enough growing up."

"Then, is it a good thing for you guys to switch out to sleep?" Megan asked. "Can't he find all of us if we sleep?"

"I'm exhausted," Gemma admitted.

"Trust me. We understand," Megan said. Sitting beside her on the bed, Megan took Gemma's hand into hers. "I know you want to sleep, but should you right now?"

"Probably not," Gemma said, looking down.

"What if you just relax with all of us. We'll stay up with you. We can play games and watch a movie," Tanya suggested.

"I think that will work," Gemma agreed. "Then do the same with Bells tomorrow night."

"This is going to be a very long time to stay awake. We need to brace for what that's going to do to our systems," Megan said.

"Let's not focus on that right now," Tanya suggested. "Let's take it one movie at a time."

"I think that's a good idea," Mac said as they settled in for the night.

# RIGHT PLACE AT THE
# RIGHT TIME

**"You cannot always wait for the perfect time. Sometimes you must dare to jump." Yasmeen Bleeth**

"So, how did I get you as my babysitter tonight?" Bells asked Shawn.

"Well, probably because I needed some breathing room," Shawn admitted.

"Why?"

Shawn admired Bells. Her dark-brown hair and fair skin allowed for her beautiful chocolate brown eyes to stand out. To Shawn, it gave her a soft look. "Lindsey's a bit much lately. Besides, I don't mind the company."

Bells smiled as she blushed. "Thank you, but I don't know you that well."

"Then, let's get to know each other. I could use a friend."

"A friend?" Bells' eyebrows rose in surprise. "Just a friend?"

"At this point. Yes. That's all I can handle right now."

"Then, I accept," Bells said, shaking his hand.

They talked and laughed for over an hour. Shawn talked more, telling stories about the rodeos and some of their antics during youth outings or at school. Meanwhile, Bells filled him in on some of the past of the Maine teens and what growing up with The Professor was like.

After one story about Shawn and Mac winning a rodeo, Bells asked, "What are you trying to prove?"

"What do you mean?" Shawn asked, taken off-guard. "That question came out of nowhere."

"Shawn, you do remember what my gift is?"

Shawn smiled, looking down as he nodded. "Yes. I guess there's no hiding anything from you."

"No. Not really."

"All right. Yes. I often feel like I have to prove my self-worth. I may seem confident on the outside…"

"But you're still that terrified little kid on the inside," Bells finished.

"Yeah."

"Why is that?"

"When I was younger, I was at one of the rodeos. I got lost. I couldn't find my family or Mac. I ran into another rodeo rider. He pulled me aside, and we talked for quite a while before he showed me a bull up close. He told me that only a man's man would ride a bull. He said team roping was a good option, but bull riding is where you get the ladies. He said you not only get the admiration of women but also of the men. My dad works a lot. He's a good man, just works a lot. He's not home that often. He never goes to my rodeos or sports events. He never congratulates me. I often wonder if I were a bull rider, if he would take notice."

"So, you would put your life on the line to get your dad's attention?"

"That about sums it up. Yet, I can go to school and have a girl on each arm as soon as I walk in. Or if I go to a rodeo, I only have to snap my fingers, and there's a buckle bunny by my side in seconds, ready and waiting."

"For what?"

"What do you mean?"

"What do you do with these girls?"

"What's expected of me."

"What does that mean?" Bells asked, wide-eyed.

"If I don't keep up my reputation, then I may as well hang up my rope."

"So, let me see if I have this correct," Bells said, lining things up in her mind. "Are you telling me that you will do anything to get your dad's attention and stay in the spotlight at rodeos and at school?"

Shawn furrowed his brow. "That's an odd way of putting it."

"Is it true?"

"Yes."

"So, what's the big deal about getting attention and recognition, if you have to be someone you're not to get it?"

"Ouch!" Shawn cringed.

"Is it true?"

"Yes, but –"

"But, what? Why do you act like someone you're not, just so people will accept you? Why not act like yourself and let them figure out if they like the real you or not?" Bells asked.

"That's a good question."

"Do you have a good answer?"

"It's one I've been struggling with since this whole thing started," Shawn admitted. "I've heard how that man treated you. And I use the term man loosely. He's not a man. He's not even a boy. He's an *it*. He's an *it* that preys on people he thinks are weaker than him. However, what he doesn't understand is just how powerful you all really are. I don't know too many people who would give their lives just to rescue someone else."

"You all gave up your lives for your family," Bells pointed

out. "All of us on this venture are giving ourselves for someone else."

"*Greater love has no one than this: to lay down one's life for one's friends*," Shawn quoted.

"What is that?"

"That is John 15:13. It's one of my favorite verses."

"Why is it one of your favorite verses?"

"Because it reminds me to think of others before myself."

"But do you think it meant for you to think of others so much that you lose yourself?"

"What do you mean?" Shawn asked.

"You're trying to be something you're not, so others will notice you. That doesn't sound like you're thinking of others. That sounds like you're being selfish, trying to impress people to get the spotlight. I've picked up a lot on this Jesus and Bible thing you all hold dear. I've been curious since Hope had such a strong desire to keep such a painful memory of Ben just so she would know he followed Christ before his death. From what I understand, you are created to be an individual. This God gives you a purpose for your life."

"He could be your God too."

"Not sure if I want that yet," Bells admitted. "I have a lot of questions."

"Then, my lady, enough about me. Ask your questions."

⬦⬦⬦⬦

"It's actually nice and quiet without Shawn here," Lindsey said with a smile.

"That's not very nice," Megan chastised. "You're the one being mean. Why is it he has to go for you to enjoy yourself?"

"Because he irritates me."

"Is that because you like him?" Mac asked.

"I used to like him," Lindsey corrected.

Mac shrugged. "If you used to like him like you say, then he shouldn't bother you."

"No. It's because I know he's better than he's behaving."

Mac raised an eyebrow. "So, you're his conscious now?"

"Why am I on trial here?"

"Because your behavior is affecting the entire group," Tanya pointed out. "By being irritated by Shawn behaving how Shawn wants to behave, you are making the entire group tense."

"No, I'm not. He left."

"Because of you!" Tanya snapped. "That's not cool."

Gemma raised her hand. When everyone looked at her, she said, "I realize I'm new here, but can I make an observation?"

"Sure," Megan said. "Everyone's opinion is welcome."

"Well, it seems to me that Lindsey is angry with Shawn regarding his behavior, but from what I've heard, he was trying to change when Lindsey got angry again?"

"Not angry," Lindsey corrected, "just frustrated."

"Frustration is a form of anger," Gemma pointed out. Lindsey nodded in understanding. "Because of Lindsey's anger, not Shawn's behavior, the group has been in turmoil."

"You make it sound like I'm the reason we've had such a rough day!" Lindsey said defensively.

"It sounds like it is," Gemma said. "Is it not true?"

"No! It's his fault!"

"No," Tanya interrupted. "It's yours. Gemma's right."

"So, do you want me to leave?" Lindsey asked.

"No. We want you to do a self-check and figure out why you're being such a brat," Mac said, snacking on chips.

"Such a brat?" Lindsey's face went bright red. "Such a brat? I am not a brat!"

"Really?" Mac questioned. "Throwing a temper tantrum is a sure sign of a brat."

When he said that, Lindsey huffed as she crossed her arms.

"That's still a temper tantrum," Mac said nonchalantly.

Before popping another chip in his mouth, he said, "Welcome to Hurricane Lindsey, Gemma."

Lindsey narrowed her eyes at Mac. "How dare you!"

"How dare me?" Mac's eyebrows arched in surprise as a smile crossed his face. "You're the one pushing everyone. You got upset at Shawn for basically doing what you wanted him to do. I call you on it, making a point to let you know what you feel like, and you said, how dare me? Ha!"

"You can be such a jerk! You and Shawn are like two peas in a pod!" Lindsey shot.

"No. They're not," Megan stood up for Mac. "Mac's been working on his walk with Christ. He's also making some changes of his own volition. Shawn's not sure why he needs to make any changes. They are in two completely different boats."

"Then just let Shawn sail away!" Lindsey threw her arm through the air dramatically.

"Let me get this straight. You want us to send the lost sheep to the wolves?" Tanya asked.

Lindsey rolled her eyes. "No need to put it quite so dramatically."

"That's what he is," Megan said. "He's a lost sheep. He needs to find his way to the Shepherd again. However, you keep pushing him further and further away. How is that helping? Besides, what happened to you changing your heart attitude?"

Lindsey sighed. "I'm working on it."

"May want to work on it a lot more," Megan said. "Your mood swings are giving me whiplash."

"Fine!" Lindsey huffed. "I'll be nicer."

"That would be appreciated," Gemma said. "I'm a little jumpy due to The Professor's actions. When you yell or get angry, I hate to admit it, but it really gets to me. I can't imagine it'll be different for Bells. She's more sensitive than me."

"It's probably the same for all of you," Megan said. "It'll

take time for you guys to relax and stop looking over your shoulder."

Gemma shook her head. "We won't be able to do that until that man is dead."

⁜

"DADDY, you don't seriously think they'll come here first, do you?" Alex asked The Professor on video chat.

"I think we need to be ready. The last time I was in contact with any of them, they were in Wyoming," he warned.

"Here? Really?"

"I don't know how many, but yes. It's at least Adam and Holly."

"Why do you go poking around in people's dreams?" Alex asked, rolling her eyes. "It's honestly kind of creepy."

"You're just jealous."

"No. Not really. It's handy because you can let us know where someone is when you make the connection."

"That's the trick. Making the connection. I can't always make a connection. That's how we found Hope, or Grace, or whatever her name is now, way back when they first kidnapped Holly and Blake. Holly is usually strong, so I normally cannot connect with her. For some reason, she was vulnerable tonight. When their fear levels are up, it's easier for me to find them."

"So, something happened to her," Alex said, thoughtfully tapping her chin.

"From her dream, it looks like she was attacked," The Professor explained. "The point is, they're in Wyoming. That's your backyard."

"What about the others?"

"I don't know…yet. Give me time. I'm looking for all of them. Hope is strangely off-grid as well."

"You have no idea where she is?"

"Again, not yet. I have my people looking for them." The Professor rubbed his chin. "I wonder if they're separated?"

"What do you mean? I thought you said there was no way they would separate."

"If they didn't separate, then you're first. I think I may head out to the east coast to see if I can find Hope. Everything here is pretty secure. I also don't like that she got away…again."

"She got away, but she may not have lived. You gave her Belladonna," Alex pointed out.

"It was actually a little more than just Belladonna," The Professor admitted. "It's my own personal concoction."

Alex furrowed her brow. "What do you mean?"

"Well, you know me. Always a scientist. I added a little something that will adjust her DNA."

"Like you did with the kids?"

"Yes. Chances are… if she's alive, her body is going through a transformation."

Alex anxiously ran her hand through her hair. "Did you just activate the gene, or did you change her DNA to generate the gene?"

"In order to activate the gene, she has to have it," The Professor said, wiggling his eyebrows.

"You did it to generate the gene."

"Yes. If it generates, I would be really curious to know if I could activate it, or if it will activate on its own."

Alex narrowed her eyes at The Professor. "Daddy? Did you ever do that to me?"

"No, my dear. You are perfect just the way you are. You are the spitting image of your mother."

Alex mulled over his words for a moment before she asked, "I am a product of the both of you, right?"

"Sort of," The Professor said cryptically.

Rubbing her chin, she asked, "What do you mean by that?"

"You are exactly like your mother in every way, shape, and form."

"Meaning?" Alex pressed. "C'mon, Dad. I'm a big girl."

The Professor cleared his throat before he admitted, "You, my dear, *are* your mother. You are her clone."

"Her...*what?*" Alex sat up, stunned. "I'm her what?"

"You are Anastasia's clone. I tried to generate the gene in the first two cloning experiments and lost the subjects. With you, I just created a straight clone. You are her clone, my dear. You are the spitting image of my love."

"So, did she actually die in childbirth?"

"Unfortunately, no. She passed in an accident. Before she passed, we were both researching the gene. We tried it on a few of the clones during formation, but they did not make it through. Then, she died in a car accident. I was so heartbroken, I just wanted her back. So, I created you in her image...exactly. Your carrier died during childbirth."

"So...okay." She took a deep breath. "I think I need some time to process this."

"Alex, love, you are my child. I raised you. I created you. You are my firstborn. You are my daughter."

Alex rolled her eyes. "Now you're acting like you are a god or something."

"I am a god!" The Professor pounded his fists on the desk. "I created life! I created a new form of human! That puts me in the same category as a god! I created those kids. They are mine, just as you are mine."

"While I understand why you're angry the older group was taken, don't you have the other two groups you can work with instead?"

"Alex." The Professor dropped his head. Shaking it, he sighed. "Just as I cloned and created you. I did that with the others. I need the older ones to have a pure form of DNA to produce the clones. A copy of a copy will eventually fade and will affect the cloning process. I need pure DNA. I also need them to teach the younger ones to be stronger. Dream with me for a few moments. Each one of those children is a weapon. They are all strong. How strong will they be as adults if they're this strong as children?"

"I'm not sure I want to know. That's pretty powerful."

"Exactly! Now, when they're a little older, I'll make even more. The older ones can train the younger ones, making the group stronger with each consecutive group. I'm going to create my own army! Can you see it? A group of gifted can help any country win a war! I have the recipe to make me the most powerful man on this planet!"

"Daddy," Alex said, shaking her head. "Look, I gotta go. If the kids are on their way here, I need to brace my guys for impact."

"Alex?"

"Yes, Daddy?"

"I love you, my child. You are my daughter…no matter how you were created. I love you."

"I hear you. Love you too, Daddy," she said and hung up.

Once it was disconnected, Alex got up and paced her office, trying to process what she just heard. "A god? He thinks he's a god?" She shook her head.

She stopped short when a thought hit her. "Did he try it with Ben too? Is that why he died so quickly?" She slammed her fists on the desk. "Why him? I actually liked him." Looking toward the ceiling, a tear crawled down her cheek as she demanded, "Why?"

Sitting in her chair, she dropped her head into her hands. "A clone?" She sighed. "I'm a clone?" Lacing her fingers under her chin, she said to no one in particular, "He created those kids to make a gifted army. He killed Ben and possibly Hope, hoping to generate the gene in them. He even created me…a clone. Is he delusional or a madman?"

# CENTRAL TIME

**"There comes a time when you have to choose between turning the page and closing the book." Josh Jameson**

t five o'clock, Colby, Holly, Blake, and Adam pulled over about a half-mile away from the facility in Wyoming, just south of Creston. "You'll be safer if you stay here," Holly told Colby.

"What if you guys need an immediate evacuation?" Colby asked, panic laced through his words. "What happens if big guys with guns come after you and I can't get to y'all on time? What happens if you guys get captured? What happens if –?"

"Shh," Holly said, putting her finger on his lips. "I love you. I trust you. I know you'll be in prayer. Don't let your feelings get in the way of the Spirit's guidance. You'll also have Blake or Adam to keep you posted in case we need you to come closer. Remember, Adam can contact you a little better than Blake. Blake's more short distances for now. Be listening for Adam in your head."

"Okay," Colby relented. "I love you. Please be careful?"

"I will. I love you too." She sat up in her seat. "We have a job to do, gentlemen."

Adam turned to Blake and asked, "Are you sure you don't want to handle your eternal security before we do this? You kind of skirted getting killed in the last one. Do you really want to chance it with this one too?"

"Blake!" Holly said, horrified. "You're not a follower of Christ yet?"

"I want it to be my choice, not one made out of pressure," Blake grumbled.

"No pressure, brother." Adam put his hands up in surrender. "Just concern."

"I'll make the decision when I'm ready," Blake announced, "and not a moment before."

"Fair enough, friend," Colby said. "Just know we're all praying for you but cannot pray you into Heaven with us."

"I understand."

"Are we going to pray before we go in?" Holly asked.

"I think that's a great idea," Colby agreed.

Everyone joined hands. They took about five minutes to pray for safety for the groups, for success in their mission, and for the younger ones to not fight them.

"Okay. Are you ready?" Holly asked Blake and Adam when they finished.

Blake took a deep breath. "It's now or never. They're all depending on us."

"Us, and the other team. They're getting into position as well."

"You guys have twenty minutes to get yourselves into position," Colby said, tapping his watch.

Holly leaned over and kissed Colby's cheek before she got out of the van. Standing outside the van for a moment with the door open, she said, "Keep my seat warm for me."

"Always," Colby said with a wink.

"Be listening for me," Adam said. "We may need you to scoop in and rescue us."

"You got it."

"And keep praying for us…all of us," Blake added before getting out, closing the door behind him.

"Always," Colby said, watching the trio walk briskly down the road toward the facility. "Lord, keep them all safe, please?"

"WHO'S GOING to talk to them?" Holly asked as they walked.

"I will," Adam said.

Adam multitasked while Blake and Holly kept an eye out. The small group maneuvered closer to the facility in the shadows of the trees.

*Are there any children with a mind gift that can hear me?* Adam thought.

*Who is this?*

*Who is this?*

*I asked first!* snapped the young female.

*My name is Adam.*

*You're the first one!*

*Yes. You've heard of me?*

*Yes. I'm Sydney. You're from the Alpha group. We're the Gamma group. There's another in Oregon called the Beta Group. We're in hiding. They knew you were coming and split us up.*

*We figured as much.*

*We? How many are there?*

*Enough.* Adam thought, not wanting to give her too much information. *Listen, we're on our way to get you guys out of there.*

*Why?*

*Are you not tired of getting punished by Daddy?*

*We are, but we're also scared. He said if we try to escape, he'll kill us.*

*Is he here?*

*No. His daughter is.*

*Alex?* Adam asked.

*Yes.*

*What gifts do you guys have?*

*There are mind gifts, some telekinesis, super hearing, persuasion –*

*Persuasion?* he cut her off.

*Yes. There are also a few who remember everything they read, and some can control emotions.*

*What do you have?*

*I have mind gifts and can control emotions. I can also remember everything I read and can take a really good guess at what someone will do before they do it.*

*Okay. So, you are the same as me. Do you have super hearing too?*

*No. But we do have a few here who do.*

*Where are you?*

*We're in the basement.*

*What are you doing in the basement?*

*They've had us locked in the metal rooms for days. They took the kids who have telekinesis to a different part of the building. I can't reach them.*

*Do you want out?*

*Yes!* Sydney practically shouted in Adam's head.

Adam grunted in pain. Grabbing his head, he winced.

"What happened?" Holly asked.

"They're scared and seriously want out," Adam said, getting his own mind back under control. "She kind of screamed in my head."

"Can you calm them down?" Holly asked.

"Blake, I may need you to help with the others while I calm

Sydney down," Adam said. "She seems to be their leader, but even she's seriously upset. They've been locked in the metal rooms for days."

"Days?" Holly asked, wide-eyed. "Those poor babies! They're only ten!"

"Calm down, Holly," Blake warned. "I can't keep you calm and calm everyone else."

"You don't need to calm me down!" Holly snapped. "I'm angry! This facility is about to find out what happens when they mess with children!"

Blake and Adam had to walk faster to keep up with Holly. While they walked, Blake and Adam connected with the others who had the mind gift. There were five. They were all only ten years old, so the trio had to be cautious in getting all of them out without anyone getting hurt.

⊙◁◁▷▷⊙

COLBY LOOKED at his watch as he nervously drummed his thumbs on the steering wheel to a worship song. He figured it was the best way to stay calm. "Lord," he said aloud, "I know You're here. I know You already have this all sorted out. Please keep them safe? Please don't let Holly do something she will regret for the rest of her life? She has a tender heart but also a fiery temper. You know that because You created her. Give her strength and courage to do the right thing. Please keep Blake, Adam, and the other kids safe as they get them out? Please let it all go according to Your plan?"

⊙◁◁▷▷⊙

"ARE THEY READY?" Holly asked as they crouched out of sight of the guards behind some bushes.

"Yes," Adam said.

53

"More than ready," Blake said. "They're terrified and have been separated for days. The mind gift kids are the only ones who know if the other mind gift kids are okay. They haven't been able to connect with the other three. They said they're blocked."

"Are they sure the kids are all down there?" Holly asked. "What if they separated them? What if they have half downstairs and half upstairs? And how does someone block the other three from the mind gift kids?"

"Okay. Too many questions. What if we hit this two different ways?" Blake asked.

Holly shook her head. "I don't think we should separate."

"I didn't say to separate. I said we need to come at it two different ways," Blake reiterated. When Holly nodded, he continued, "I think we need to get the five with the mind gift from the basement first. At that point, when we're closer, we can probably hone in on the other three easier. Then we get them all out."

"What if you get the five out and to the van once we get them from the basement?" Adam asked to Blake. "Then Holly and I will get the other three. That way, we know for sure those five are out. Plus, my hearing will help us find the other three."

"Once we get those five, alarms will go off," Blake warned.

"Then, you'd better run fast!" Holly shot. "Leave the other three to Adam and me. We'll get them free."

"Fair enough," Blake relented. "We have a plan."

"Good." Holly glanced at her watch. "Because it's time to go."

The trio silently made their way through the area within the trees. Unfortunately, the tree coverage thinned the closer they got to the facility. The three-story brick building looked like it had seen better days. Holly knew it was a lot older than ten years old. It looked to be more than twenty years old by the architecture. Her best guess was that it was built around the turn of the century. The ivy climbing the side of the building, the stains on the windows, and the rust coming through the painted railings told her that maintenance was not a high priority during the last few years.

"There," Holly whispered as she pointed to an entrance.

Blake shook his head. "There are two guards there."

"Give me a minute," she said. Using her gift, she picked up a decent-sized rock and tossed it in the opposite direction from where they were. It made a loud *crack!* as it landed on other river rocks.

"What was that?" one guard asked.

"Dunno. It came from over there. I'm going to go check it out," the other guard said.

As the second guard came off the concrete stairs, Holly slipped his ID badge off the clip and dropped it onto the ground, out of sight of the other guard. She moved it next to a bush.

"Nice!" Adam whispered.

"Now for the other one," Holly said and threw a rock closer to them with her mind, but in the opposite direction from the other guard.

"Miller!" the guard at the door yelled for his partner. "Miller!"

Holly picked up another good-sized rock and used it to knock Miller unconscious.

"I love your gift!" Blake whispered as Miller dropped to the ground. "What about the other one?"

"Give me a minute," Holly whispered. She tossed another rock in the direction she sent the second rock again.

"Miller!" the first guard growled. When Miller did not answer, the first guard stomped off the steps in the direction where Holly tossed the two rocks. When he was close enough, Holly knocked him out as well.

"Great job!" Adam said, patting her shoulder.

"Well done!" Blake encouraged. "Now, let's head in."

"Slowly," Adam cautioned. "There's a guard just inside."

"Is that something you can take care of?" Holly asked Adam.

"Hmm," Adam said. Closing his eyes, he focused on the security guard at the desk. Hearing him answer the phone, he found out his name. Once he hung up, Adam thought, *Officer Chen?*

"What?" Officer Chen asked aloud.

*Aren't you tired? Maybe you should go get some coffee?*

"I can't go – who said that?" Officer Chen looked around, confused.

*You did. This is your conscience.*

"Who? Are you one of those brats we have down in holding?" Officer Chen growled. He got up from the desk. "When I get ahold of you..." his voice trailed as he stomped off down the hall.

"We need to hurry," Adam said. "He thinks it's one of the kids from downstairs. He's heading there now."

"Then, let's go," Holly said.

Together, they got up and ran toward the building. Scooping the card off the ground, Holly used it to access the building.

"Which way?" Holly asked.

"This way," Adam grabbed her arm, tugging her with him, with Blake taking up the rear to make sure they did not get caught off-guard.

They ran down the hall in the direction the guard went. Instead of getting in the elevator, the trio ran down the stairs. At the bottom, they heard Officer Chen yelling at the kids, hitting the doors with his cane, threatening them.

Holly unlocked the hall door and swung it open with her mind. She stood in the doorway, fists clenched to her sides. "Leave them alone!" she demanded.

He laughed. "And who are you?"

"I don't have time for this," she said and slammed him against the wall, knocking him out.

"Way to go, sis!" Blake said as he and Adam ran past her.

Adam grabbed the keys off the wall and started unlocking the doors he knew someone was behind. When he opened the door, he was slightly taken aback. The little boy looked like a miniature of Blake! "Get to Holly. She'll protect you," he ordered, shaking off the creepy feeling.

"Come on, guys. We have to hurry. Do you know where the others are?" Blake asked.

"We don't know," a little girl said, who looked like a little version of Bells.

Blake knelt in front of her. Placing his hands on her shoulders, he asked, "What's your name?"

"Yvette," she said.

"And what is your gift?"

"More like a curse." She rolled her eyes. "But my gifts are super hearing, the mind gifts, and controlling emotions."

"Okay, Yvette. Is your closest sibling one of those with telekinesis?" When she nodded her head, he asked, "Who is it?"

"It's Xander. He's my twin," she explained.

"Brilliant!" Blake smiled. "Since he's your twin, you have a stronger connection with him. Great! Can Adam use you to connect with him?"

Yvette nodded, so Adam came over and crouched in front of her. He held her tiny hands in his and closed his eyes. "Think on Xander. Try to reach out to him," Adam said quietly.

When she did, Adam saw a small boy in a room. He was blindfolded, and his hands and feet were bound.

*Xander?* Adam thought.

Xander looked around, anxious.

*Xander, this is Adam. We're in the basement with Yvette, Sydney, and the others. Can you think, don't say it out loud, but think where you are?*

*We're in Alex's office. It's on the second floor.*

*Okay. Just relax. Those down here are getting evacuated right now. We're on our way up.*

*Who is we?*

*Do not say anything. We'll get to you as soon as possible. Thank you.*

"Okay. You guys go," Adam told Blake. Turning to the children, he said, "Go with Blake. Listen to him and Colby. You'll know who Colby is when you see him. Holly and I will go get the others. Stay by him. Understand?"

"Yes, sir," the kids said in unison.

"Be careful," Blake said sternly to Holly and Adam.

"I will protect her with my life," Adam promised.

"And I will do the same. He's my brother. Those kids up there are our brothers and sisters. We *will* get them out of there," Holly promised.

"Let's just pray it doesn't come to that," Blake said.

"Get out of here before those guards wake up," Holly warned. "The coast is clear for now."

"I'm going," Blake said and left up the stairs with the kids.

Adam and Holly went upstairs. They made sure Blake and the kids got out the front door before heading back to the stairwell.

"Is it me, or did those kids look –"

"Yes!" Adam said, cutting Holly off. "How did he do that? They are like carbon copies of us! It's really creepy!"

"I haven't seen a *me* yet. I wonder if she's upstairs."

Adam thought for a moment. "What if we go up a different way?"

"Such as?"

"Is there any way besides the stairwell or the elevator? Like an outside window?"

"Probably, but we don't have a lot of time. Those men are unconscious, not dead," Holly pointed out.

"Okay. I guess a surprise attack is out. Let's go," Adam said, and together, they headed up the staircase.

"Let's do this the easy way." Holly grabbed his arm and

pulled him up with her. Landing on the second floor, she said, "Next?"

Adam took a deep breath. Putting his hand on the doorknob, he stopped. Turning toward Holly, he whispered, "They're not on this floor."

"Where are they?" she asked.

He looked up at the next level and then to Holly. She nodded and lifted them to the next level.

Walking in, he put his finger to his lips to tell Holly not to talk. She nodded again, on high alert.

Adam pointed toward a door three doors down. They quietly went down the hall. The door was locked, so Holly unlocked it before opening the door. Inside were three children, blindfolded, with their wrists and ankles zip-tied, as they sat in the dark.

"Which one of you is Xander?" Adam whispered.

"He's the one on the left," Alex said, flipping the light on. Standing beside her was a young man of about thirteen, along with another man who looked to be a little older than Alex. "Didn't know I was here? This is Justin. He protected me from being found by you," she explained. "He's from Oregon."

Adam gasped. He found himself staring into the eyes of a thirteen-year-old child who looked just like Charlie! Had Charlie survived a few more years, he would have looked just like Justin! He gulped. Adam felt like he was staring at a ghost!

"Wonderful," Holly said, rolling her eyes as she crossed her arms. "You're here."

"We need to talk," Alex said.

"Who?" Adam asked.

"Holly. You can stay here with Justin and Kendrick to make sure nothing happens to the kids," Alex said. Walking by Holly, she looped her arm through hers, and they headed out into the hall. Alex closed the door behind them so they would not be overheard. "Justin has sound-proofed us. There's no way anyone in there will hear or know what's being said out here."

"What do you want?" Holly demanded.

"Hostile much?"

"You're holding three ten-year-old children hostage, and you're calling me hostile?" Holly shot.

"Look, believe it or not, we have a lot in common."

"Don't try your pop-psychology on me. It won't work."

"Holly," Alex put her hands on Holly's shoulders. Looking into Holly's eyes, Alex said, "I was in love with Ben. I'm sure you know that if you really think about it. Also, I just found out that I'm actually a clone of my mother."

Holly's eyes widened at the second piece of news.

"Finally, some sort of surprise," Alex said on a sigh. "Have you figured out yet that the others are clones of the first group?"

"What?" Holly asked, stunned.

"Your clone is in that room. Look, I just found out all of this today. He wants to create some super army of gifted people. He's not in Oregon. He's going to the east coast to find your mom."

Holly took a step back, uncrossing her arms. "I hope this is some sick way of ticking me off, and you're not serious!"

"Why would I tick you off?"

"To make me angrier and stronger."

"I'm not trying to make you angry. Holly, if the rest of your crew is going to Oregon, they're walking into a trap. Dad has the other seven. They're not at the facility."

Holly's face went pale. "How did he know?"

"Dad has this creepy gift. He can infiltrate dreams. When he connects, he can figure out where you are. He gave me a heads-up that you, in particular, were in Wyoming with Adam. That's what started our conversation."

Holly's jaw dropped. "That was real?"

"That's how he figured out so long ago that Hope and Ben were in Texas. He connected with Hope when she was having a nightmare shortly after they left with you guys."

Holly shook her head. "Unbelievable."

"I used to think he was some brilliant scientist," Alex admitted. "Now I know different. He's trying to change Hope's DNA. It didn't work with Ben. Dad mixed something with the Belladonna he gave them to change their DNA. He's trying to generate the gene and activate it in adults. He seriously thinks he's a god! He has to be stopped! To prove to you that I am being honest, and I'm on your side, I'm releasing those three to you. I know your brother already has the other five. They're probably in the van waiting for you."

Holly narrowed her eyes. "You know about that?"

"Oh! For someone so powerful, you're still such a child." Alex stated in frustration. "Do you seriously think there aren't cameras for miles around this place? You don't think I would only have three guards for you to get past, do you? Don't you think it was a little too easy? I wanted you to come here and get the kids. If I made it way too easy, you would run. I want those kids to have a better life than I did. I honestly used to think Dad was amazing. He was handsome, charismatic, and the ladies loved his accent. However, all these years with you guys down in Texas, I learned a new way to live. I know you don't believe me. I know you don't understand this. Honestly, you can walk out with these kids. I am doing this for me as much as I am doing this for all of you. I feel betrayed by him. I need to get out from under him. He's paranoid and delusional. He literally thinks he's a god. He thinks the world revolves around him."

"Do you know he killed all of our moms?" Holly asked.

"I'm sorry. I was naïve when you guys were born. I knew something happened to them, but I thought it was a product of the experiments he was doing. He didn't kill the actual moms of the second and third group – he killed the carriers."

"Carriers?"

"Basically, he cloned you guys and put the clones in the women. He had children with the gene. Now, all he had to do was replicate it. He wants you guys to teach the younger ones to be stronger. He also wants an army of gifted people. He said with an army of gifted, he would be the most powerful man on this planet."

"He would be!"

Alex started pacing the hallway. "I'm sorry. I should have seen it sooner. He's seriously mad! He's hoping to generate and activate the gene in Hope, so he can trigger and activate the gene in other adults. He wants to create superhumans."

"What?" Holly took another step back. "Are you serious?"

"I just found all of this out today. I'm sorry, Holly. I really am. I hope everyone gets out of Oregon okay, and he doesn't find Hope."

Holly felt like her world was spinning out of control. *The others were in serious trouble – both in Pennsylvania and Oregon! Would Hope survive counteracting the poison and her DNA getting messed with at the same time? Was Alex telling the truth? She was right. It was too easy to get to everyone in Wyoming. They expected a lot more guards...Clones? Every one in the younger groups were clones of them?* She shuddered. *What was she going to do now?*

"Holly, take the kids. Get ahold of those in Oregon if it's not too late. Then get back to wherever you are all staying on the east coast to stop him!"

"I-I don't know if we can," Holly stammered. "How do we do this?"

"Come with me," Alex said, taking Holly by the arm.

They went down a floor to Alex's office. "Call your friends on the east coast," she said, offering her cell phone.

She shook her head. "I'm sorry. I can't."

"Justin," Alex said aloud. She then added, "He's one of those with super hearing." Then, looking back toward the ceiling, she said, "Justin, please bring Adam, Kendrick, and the others down to my office?" Looking back to Holly, she added, "They'll be down in a minute. I'm sure. Justin was the only one who heard everything."

After a few minutes, there was a knock on the door. Adam, Kendrick, the three kids, and Justin walked in. Holly did a double-take at the little girl who was the spitting image of her as a young child. "I-I can't –" She shook her head. "I'm having a hard time processing this."

"What's going on?" Adam asked.

Turning to Adam, Holly asked, "Can you shield us from being heard if we step out into the hallway?"

"Of course. I do it all the time."

"We'll be right back," Holly said, dragging Adam out into the hall with her. Closing the door behind them, she explained, "We have a problem…a couple, actually."

Adam crossed his arms. "What's going on?"

"Okay, when we go back inside, I need to you figure out if Alex is telling the truth. Have Justin drop the shield. If she's telling the truth, she won't care if he takes it down."

"Just a sec," he said, closing his eyes. Focusing on Alex, he was able to look into her mind and read what was going on. His eyes flew open, distress evident. "Oregon's a trap?" he whispered. "Do we even have a way to get ahold of them?"

"There really isn't any way. The only way we were able to communicate at all was because you and Eddie connected in your minds on the way out of town," Holly pointed out. "I highly doubt he'll try to connect right now. And even if he does, I seriously doubt he can do it multiple states away. He's powerful, but even Eddie has limits."

"True. What are we going to do about Pennsylvania?" Adam asked.

"She said she would let me use her phone. However, my concern is once I call the hospital or the hotel, then they can easily find them. But, if I don't call and he finds them anyway, and we had time to warn them, how would I feel?"

"That's why you wanted to talk to me," Adam said in under-standing.

"Yeah. What do we do?"

"Well, if it's any consolation, she's telling the truth. She's quite ticked off at The Professor. Frankly, so am I. I understand her anger. Seriously? She's a clone? Those kids are our clones? Well, I mean, it explains why two of them look like Bells, and a couple look like others. He wouldn't know which ones would take for the pregnancy." Adam shuddered.

"You got all of that in a matter of seconds?" Holly asked, amazed.

"It's like a download on a computer. I'm trying to sort through it right now. How did you?"

"No idea. But that doesn't matter. What are we going to do?"

"Do you have the hospital number?" Adam asked.

"I do. Can we trust she won't call her dad and give him their location?"

"Is there a way to use a cell phone and delete the data?"

"I don't know. I could try. Can we take the risk?"

"It's either trust her or potentially risk everyone's life. As it is, Deanna, Freya, Wyatt, and Eddie are in trouble. If we call and warn the Pennsylvania group, then we can take these eight, along with all of us, and get to Oregon to get them out," Adam suggested. "As I said, she's pretty ticked at her dad."

"Ticked enough to betray him?"

"She already did that by giving us these eight. We can use them, along with those of us here, to track down the Oregon group. We can use Justin too, if he knows and is angry enough."

"Ooo! Good point! Is he?" Holly asked.

"Don't know. He's shielding himself."

"Don't blame him. Okay, let's go talk to them and explain to them what's going on," Holly said, putting her hand on the doorknob. When Adam put his hand on her arm, she asked, "What?"

"You call Pennsylvania. I'll fill in the others with Alex. Come out here so I can block you from everyone else."

"Good idea."

They went back into the room. Alex freely gave her cell phone to Holly, who went back out into the hall to call the hospital, while Adam and Alex talked to the others.

"So, as you can understand, we need to get to Oregon, and y'all need to get out," Holly said to Shawn.

"I can get back to the hotel and gather everything. Our car is still here. My concern is Hope. She's not doing well at all. Do we leave her unguarded?"

"Can you guys stay put but stay on guard and have a plan?" Holly suggested. "At least until we can get back to you?"

"I think we can do that. I'll leave Bells here and go back with the others. Then, I'll come back and fill her in."

"No one can sleep," Holly warned. "He will find what state you're in if you sleep, and he connects."

"Are you serious?"

"Better make a massive pot of coffee and keep it on an IV until we get back. We're not sleeping either."

"Fair enough. Gemma hasn't slept at all since y'all left," Shawn pointed out. "And Bells got a little, but not much."

"I'm sorry. I know this'll mess with y'all's psyche, but you have to keep each other awake. You will get irritable and possibly have hallucinations, but you cannot sleep! Understand?"

"Got it. I'll take care of it."

"Thank you, Shawn. We're heading toward Oregon."

"Be careful!"

"Be in prayer!" she said and hung up. She deleted the number in the recent numbers list, as well as cleared any and all recent numbers in Alex's phone. That way, Alex knew Holly deleted it and wouldn't try to pull it back up. Then she turned the phone off before turning it back on again. "That should do it," she said and headed back into the office.

"Are you serious?" Justin shouted angrily. "I've been here with you, and he took the others? He said they would be safe if I came here and did my job!"

"Justin, I had him bring you here because you were the strongest in your group," Alex explained. "I knew you would help them in finding their friends, and –"

"You mean our other brothers and sisters," Justin corrected her.

"Yes. Bear with me here. I'm doing a complete mind shift in this whole thing," Alex said.

"Her stress levels are high," Adam pointed out. "And it's not because she's lying."

"Technically, she's our sister too," Holly said, coming into the room. Handing the phone to Alex, she added, "I deleted all recent calls, so don't bother trying to pull it up."

"I wouldn't anyway." Alex shrugged. She put the phone on the ground and smashed it with her heel. "Not a problem."

"This is a completely different look for you," Holly observed.

"Well, you did just put things in a completely different perspective. You are all my brothers and sisters," Alex said.

"So, what are you going to do?" Adam asked her.

"I'm going with you guys," she said, putting the smashed phone into the trashcan.

"I'm going too," Kendrick said.

"No." Alex shook her head. She pulled him over to the side and explained, "I need to do this for me."

"I've stayed here for you. There's no way I'm abandoning you now," Kendrick said. "You have to know how I feel."

"I do. Trust me. However, I need to do this. I put these kids in this position. I was a crappy big sister. I have to help them."

"You can. Just bring me with you. I'm sure you could use the muscle."

"Yes, but space will be limited," Alex explained. "I know

your phone number. Please go back to the Maine facility. Don't say anything. Just act like Daddy told you to go back. Understand?"

"I can do that," he agreed.

"I'll come back for you once this is over," Alex promised. "You stood by me all these years. Let me stand up for myself and my siblings now. I need to know I have the guts to do this."

"All right," he agreed.

She kissed him on the cheek before turning toward the others and announced, "We need to get the others out."

"Looks like we're all cramming into one van," Holly said. "Let's go. We may need you as a screen, Alex."

"Not a problem." She waved her off. "Let's go."

# PACIFIC TIME

**"Do what is right, not what is easy nor what is popular." Roy T. Bennett**

"I have to admit I'm nervous," Freya said. "What if I'm not strong enough?"

"Just do the best you can," Wyatt encouraged while driving.

"What if they don't want to come with us? What if –?"

"Freya, we just need to do our best," Eddie said. "The rest will sort itself out. You could *what if?* yourself into a panic attack."

"I'm not going to have a panic attack. I'm just really concerned."

"That's understandable," Wyatt said. "Even after being a police officer all these years, I still have that twinge of anxiety when I head into unknown situations."

"Really?" Freya asked, relief evident as her body relaxed. "I thought it was just me."

"This is the first time you've been off-campus," Wyatt

pointed out. "Your twin sister is across the country. You're heading into a dangerous situation with a ton of unknowns. It's justifiable to be on high alert with some anxiety. You need to focus on one step at a time. The variables will constantly be changing."

"Not sure if that makes me feel any better," she said, nibbling on her nails.

"You have to make a choice. It may not be easy, but it's the right thing to do," Wyatt said.

"Freya," Deanna said in her seat beside Eddie, "You're strong. You may not have mine or Holly's temper, but you do have a calculative mind. You tend to get anxious before testing days, but you pass with flying colors. It's like once you're in the situation, a calmness comes over you, and you do great."

"Thanks."

"Just stay focused on our goals. Our brothers and sisters are counting on us."

"Got it!" Freya nodded her head, determination etched on her face.

"There ya go!" Wyatt encouraged.

❦❦❦❦

"OKAY, Y'ALL ARE UP," Wyatt announced, pulling up beside a fence that bordered the facility's land. "Are you sure I can't get you closer?"

"This is as close as we dare let you," Deanna said. "Don't worry. We'll take care of Eddie and get him in there."

"I'm more worried about you guys wearing yourselves out," Wyatt pointed out. "Having to maneuver Eddie through the grass cannot be easy."

"I can get myself through there." Eddie shrugged. "I'll just levitate."

"No." Deanna shook her head. "We need you strong. Freya and I will get you there. You need to be at full strength."

"Fair enough," Eddie agreed. Then, looking at his watch, he said, "Time to go."

"Remember where the cameras are," Wyatt cautioned. "I'll meet y'all back here."

"Got it. Thank you," Freya said, getting out of the van. Opening the sliding door, she added, "See you in a few minutes with some more siblings. Let's go!"

Eddie got out first, followed by Deanna. Wyatt got out, cut the fencing with wire cutters, and then got back in the van. "God be with you all," he whispered. As they ducked out of sight, he added, "Please protect them, Lord."

✦✦✦✦✦

WITH DEANNA BEING the stronger of the pair, she is the one who kept Eddie about four inches in the air as they crossed the lawn, keeping out of sight of the cameras. While they navigated the campus, Eddie got a strange feeling in his stomach. The hair on the back of his neck stood on end. "I gotta bad feeling about this," he said after a few minutes.

"You too?" Freya asked. "I thought it was just me. I mean, I know my body is on edge, but shouldn't there be guards or something? We haven't seen anyone at all."

"I agree," Deanna said. "Eddie, can you use some of those super mind powers of yours to find some people and figure out what's going on?"

"What if we duck behind those trees over there, and then I'll do it?" he asked. "It's kind of unnerving hoovering in the air."

"No problem," Deanna said.

When the trio was tucked into a wooded area, Eddie closed his eyes. He searched high and low in the facility, unable to

71

connect with anyone. Opening his eyes, he said, "Something's not right."

"Is there anyone you can connect with?" Freya asked.

"No. That's the problem," Eddie explained. "There are plenty of cars here, which tells me there are people here. I can feel them, but I can't read them."

"Someone's blocking you," Deanna said in understanding.

"Let me try one more time," Eddie said and closed his eyes. *Anyone there?*

*Who's this?*

*Who is this?*

*Mitch.*

*Are you the reason why I can't read anyone's mind?*

*Yes.*

*Why are you stopping me?*

*Daddy told me to.*

*Mitch, my name is Eddie. We're here to get you all out of there.*

*No one's here except me. They took Justin to Wyoming, and Daddy took the others with him somewhere else. He said I had to do this or he would hurt the others.*

*Where are you?*

*They have me in the Security Office.*

*Are you alone?*

*No.*

*If we come and get you, will you come with us?*

*Definitely! I haven't seen my brothers or sisters for days! Can you help me get Justin?*

*I'm pretty sure he's already being helped.*

*Good. Daddy's been especially cruel lately. He said it was the older subject's fault.*

*Of course, he did.*

*What does that mean?*

*It means he doesn't take responsibility for his actions,* Eddie thought. *It also means he tried to turn you against us. We're not the bad guys. He is. He beat us and the sibling we were closest to for years. He would also lock us in the metal rooms.*

*You too?*

*Yes.*

*Eddie, this is a trap,* Mitch admitted.

*What do you mean?*

*He knew you were coming. It's a trap. Those in Wyoming are walking into a trap too. Get out of here. It's not safe here.*

*We're not leaving without you.*

*You have to. There are a lot of guards in here, and they're all armed. They're waiting for you.*

*We're not leaving you behind!*

*You have to! They'll kill you! They were told to capture you. However, if you were getting away, he gave instructions to kill.*

Eddie gasped as his eyes flew open. "Oh!"

"What's wrong?" Freya asked.

"They have orders to capture us, or if we resist to kill us," Eddie said.

"Then, let's get out of here!" Deanna went to get up, but Eddie grabbed her arm. "What?" she asked.

"There's still one in there. He's got a powerful mind gift. There's another one, Justin, in Wyoming. The others are with The Professor somewhere else."

"Oh no!" Deanna groaned. "Adam, Blake, and Holly."

"They know by now," Freya said. "It's time for us to figure out what to do here. Do you know where he is?"

"His name is Mitch. He's in the Security Office, but he's got a lot of guys on him," Eddie explained.

Deanna shook her head. "We can't leave him."

"It's going to take all three of us coordinating. We have to hit them in three different places so they scramble," Eddie said, thinking over the logistics.

"Agreed," Deanna said. "What if I take the front? Then,

Eddie, you take that door over there? And Freya, why don't you take the back door?"

Freya nodded. "Got it."

"I'll stay connected with you two," Eddie said. "Get into position, and I'll say when to go. Everyone okay with that?"

"Definitely!" Freya said. "I'll follow your lead."

"Who's going for Mitch?" Deanna asked.

"I will," Eddie said, determined. "You two keep the others busy."

With that, the trio broke up and headed toward their assigned doors. Knowing they were walking into a trap made things a little easier but still caused massive anxiety. However, they could not and would not leave Mitch in there by himself.

*Ready?* Eddie thought to Deanna and Freya.

*Yes,* they both replied.

*Go.*

Eddie went in through his entrance, only to be met by several guys with guns.

"Seriously?" Eddie said, hands in the air. "I'm in a wheelchair! Why do I need six guys with guns coming after me? You guys seriously need to get a life or a boss with a brain!"

The head guy cocked his gun.

"I'm sorry, guys," Eddie said. A few furrowed brows, eyebrow raises, and baffled looks later, a slow smile crossed Eddie's face.

"W-why are you doing that?" the head guy asked nervously. "Why are you smiling?"

"Scared?" Eddie asked, wiggling his eyebrows. "You should be. I may be in a wheelchair, but I'm the most terrifying of the Alpha group!"

With that, he separated the men from their guns with one hand while he lifted them in the air with his other hand. When the head guy reached for the gun on his hip, Eddie said, "Tsk! Tsk! Tsk! I thought we had an understanding."

With both hands, he threw the men against the wall as hard as he could. Then, as they all crumpled to the ground unconscious, Eddie wheeled toward the stairwell. He threw the door open with his mind and wheeled through. *What level?* he asked Mitch.

*Three.*

*Be there shortly.*

*Thank you!*

Eddie lifted himself to the third floor.

⟨⟩⟨⟩

DEANNA WHIPPED the door she was assigned open to find six guys with guns aimed directly at her. "Really?" Deanna said, rolling her eyes. "Only six? No contest!"

Flailing her arms left and right, she slammed the guys into each other and the wall until all were unconscious.

"Unbelievable!" she said on a sigh. "Did he really think that would work?" Shaking her head, she maneuvered her way through the maze of bodies to the stairwell. *Eddie?* she thought.

*Yeah?*

*What level?*

*Three.*

*Coming!* she thought and headed up the stairs.

⟨⟩⟨⟩

FREYA WALKED into eight guys with guns. Fearing what happened to their co-workers would happen to them, one got off a couple rounds. As soon as he did, in fear, the others blindly shot toward Freya.

"I…" Freya's voice faded. She dropped to the floor, covered in blood. "I'm sorry," she said and thought at the same time.

*What?* both Deanna and Eddie asked at the same time.

Freya swallowed. She originally felt searing heat penetrate all over her body. As she lay there for a moment, her body went numb. Looking toward the Heavens, she said, "Jesus, if you can hear me, please forgive me?" Tears crawled down her cheeks. "I'm so sorry!"

⬥⬥⬥⬥

"FREYA!" Gemma breathed out, suddenly sitting up on the bed as they were watching a movie. She grabbed her chest.

"What's wrong?" Megan asked.

"She's…gone," Gemma said in shock. "I-I don't know what…" Looking toward Megan, who was in the bed with her, tears streamed down Gemma's cheeks as she asked, "How do I live without her?"

Megan did not say a word. She just hugged Gemma while she cried.

⬥⬥⬥⬥

SHAWN HUNG UP WITH HOLLY.

"Shawn?" Bells said when she felt it. She put a hand on her stomach and her heart, as the pain was intense. "Shawn!" She cringed.

He knelt beside her. "What's wrong?"

"It's Gemma! She's in terrible pain!"

Putting his hands on her shoulders, he faced her toward him. "Why? What happened to Gemma?"

Bells gasped. "Freya."

"Wait! What? What happened to Freya? Do I need to call the hotel?"

Tears slowly crawled down her cheeks. "Sh-she's gone! She's gone!"

"Gone? As in –"

"Gone," Bells said, shaking her head, moving both hands to her chest. "Freya's gone. Gemma felt it, and I can feel Gemma's pain. It's so strong! It hurts."

Getting on his knees in front of her, Shawn wrapped his arms around Bells. "Shh," he said, "It's going to be okay. Not now, but it will. It will be okay eventually. I promise."

"No!" Bells looked up at Shawn. "I hate that man! It's all his fault!"

"It is his fault, but it's not good to hate, Bells. You have a good heart. Don't let this harden it."

"I don't-I don't know what to do," she said, trying to catch her breath. "There is so much anger and hurt."

Shawn put both hands on the sides of her face. Making sure she was looking at him, he said, "You will do what you are supposed to do. You will protect Hope. *We* will protect Hope. I'll call the hotel and have them send Mac. I'll fill him in, so he can fill the others in. I won't leave you."

"Promise?"

"Not unless God takes me."

"Thank you," Bells said, still clutching her chest, breathing heavily.

⬩⬩⬩⬩

*"I'M SO SORRY!"* Freya's words momentarily echoed in both Eddie and Deanna's heads.

"Freya," Deanna breathed out. With her hand resting on the third-level doorknob, she leaned her head on the door frame. *Eddie? Are you okay?*

*No,* he admitted. *However, Mitch needs us.*

*I know. Gemma must be crushed.*

*She will when she finds out.*

*She knows,* Deanna thought to Eddie. *She already knows. We all felt it. It was the same when we lost Charlie.*

77

Eddie did not think anything for a few moments. He looked toward the sky, angry, and whispered, "I thought you were supposed to love and protect us? That's what I read on the other's minds. What? Did you give up on Freya? That's it! You may say that revenge is yours, but I will avenge Freya and the others! Do you hear me? I don't need you! They don't need you!" he said louder to the Lord. "I will avenge them!"

*Eddie?* Deanna thought after not hearing anything from him. *Are you ready?*

Eddie took a deep breath before he returned back to Deanna. *You know it's a trap. They just killed Freya. They will do their best to –* Eddie stopped mid-thought. Mitch released the minds of those in the facility to Eddie. There were ten in the hallway and several more with Mitch in the room. The guards who shot Freya were on their way to the staircase in one of the other corners from Eddie and Deanna. *Deanna, we have our work cut out for us.*

*Give me a moment to clear this room,* Mitch interrupted their thought conversation. *I have the gift of persuasion.*

Deanna furrowed her brow. *Wait! What?*

*Let me get them all into the hall. Those who killed our sister are almost to the third level,* Mitch explained.

*Fair enough,* Eddie thought. *Dee, we can take them all out at once and then get out of here.*

*Your call,* she thought.

In the Security Office, Mitch stood.

"What are you doing?" Officer Shultz asked.

"You will go out into the hall and leave me in here alone," Mitch said confidently.

"Why would –"

"You will all go out into the hall and leave me in here alone. While you're out there, you will shoot your co-workers for betraying The Professor. Understood?"

"Yes, sir," they said in unison.

As soon as the door closed behind them, Mitch heard gunfire erupt.

*What's going on?* Deanna demanded.

*They're shooting each other. Just a minute.* Mitch thought to both of them.

The gunfire slowed and then picked back up again when the group who shot Freya burst through the door. Once silence reigned, Eddie opened the door in front of him with his mind and wheeled in. There were bodies and blood everywhere.

"Crap!" Eddie exclaimed, looking around. When he heard a gun cock, he saw three of the guys still standing, aiming their guns at him.

Deanna opened her door at the opposite end of the hallway. "Leave him alone!" she shouted. "Enough already!"

Before she could do anything, Eddie lifted all three into the air. He snapped their necks and then let them drop to the ground in a pile. "We need to get Mitch and Freya, and get out of here."

"Freya's gone," Deanna pointed out.

"We are not leaving her here!" Eddie insisted.

Deanna put her hands in the air in surrender. "Okay. Okay."

Mitch opened the door of the Security Office.

Both Eddie and Deanna's jaw dropped. He looked just like a thirteen-year-old Eddie, only not in a wheelchair.

Eddie swallowed hard. "Are-are there anymore?" he asked. He shook his head to clear it.

"No," Mitch said, staring at Eddie, equally stunned. "That's all who was left here. I-I don't understand. I look like you. How is that possible? And, you!" he said to Deanna. "Piper looks just like you! I don't get it."

"I don't either," Deanna said, shaking her head.

"Guess we'll have to figure that out later." Eddie spun back toward the staircase he just left. "Let's get out of here before more decide to come, or someone decides to figure out what all the gunfire was about."

"Good idea," Deanna said as she and Mitch walked toward the staircase Eddie was in. Deanna carefully made her way over to Mitch. Instead of wading through the maze of bodies, and slick blood, she simply levitated her and Mitch over to where Eddie was waiting. They all stood at the top of the staircase.

"Count of three?" Eddie asked.

"Yeah," Deanna agreed. "I have Mitch."

"For what?" Mitch asked as she wrapped her arms around him from behind. "What are you doing?"

"Trust me," Deanna encouraged. "We trusted you. You need to trust us."

"Okay."

"One, two, three," Eddie said. He levitated off the ground, over the rails, and went down first.

"Seriously?" Mitch asked.

"Hold your breath. It isn't so bad," Deanna said before lifting him in the air.

"Whoa!" Mitch panicked as he clutched onto her arms. "It wasn't that bad from the office to here, but this? There's nothing around us!"

"Calm down," she said, lowering them to the bottom level.

Once on the ground, Mitch shuddered. "Have never done that before!"

"I'm sure it won't be the last." Deanna shrugged. "Hang with us long enough, and you'll get used to it. We can be fun."

"A little on the violent side, but fun," Mitch said, as he smiled weakly.

The trio made their way to the other side of the building where Freya's body lay in a bloody mess. Deanna gasped and then sprinted to Freya. "Oh, Freya," she said, shaking her head as she knelt beside Freya's body. She rested her hand on the side of her face. "She didn't have a chance. Look how many times they shot her! Animals!" Deanna growled, feeling like she would explode in anger.

"Then, let's go hunt them down," Eddie said, narrowing his eyes. He lifted his hand in the air. Freya's body lifted at the same time, landing gently on Eddie's lap. He cradled her body in his arms. "Little help?" he asked Deanna.

"You got it," she said.

They slowly made their way outside the building and down the stairs. When they were halfway across the grounds, Eddie stopped. "Just a second," Eddie said, and Deanna lowered him to the ground.

"What?" Deanna asked. "There's no one alive in there."

"No, but the research is in there," Eddie pointed out.

"What are you going to do?" Mitch asked.

"What I should have done in Maine, and we should make sure to do in Wyoming. I found what I needed before the last one died. Stay quiet for a moment," Eddie ordered.

He closed his eyes, searching the facility for the various objects he needed. It was almost as if he was flying through each hallway like a ghost. When he found a few oxygen tanks, he noted them. When he found a nitrogen tank, he noted it. When he found the lab, he noted its location. Finally, he found what he was looking for in the boiler room. He super-heated the boiler until it reached the point of maximum. Then, he gave it one last shove, and it ignited.

Deanna and Mitch gasped as an explosion in the basement set off a chain reaction. The boiler ignited the lab, which ignited the oxygen tanks, which ignited the nitrogen tank. The chain reaction explosion only took a moment to combine and engulf the entire building.

Deanna pushed her hands forward, protecting the small group from any flying debris. She stood her ground for several long, painful moments as Eddie sat there with his eyes closed.

Mitch looked at the devastation wide-eyed. His jaw dropped when all of the flames seemed to get sucked into the building and then thrust up into the air before everything landed in one huge pile of fiery debris.

"Finally," Eddie said. "Next is Roth himself."

The small group continued across the campus to where Wyatt waited in the van. After seeing the explosion, Wyatt was terrified if he would ever see them again. However, when the door opened, Wyatt was not sure where to look. Freya was in Eddie's arms, coated in blood. There was also a young man who was the spitting image of Eddie. "What happened?" Wyatt demanded, getting out of the van, coming around to the trio. "The ground shook, and flames were seen everywhere. And now you are holding Freya in your arms?"

"They killed Freya," Deanna said, jaw clenched.

Wyatt looked up at them stunned. He then leaned down, brushing Freya's blood-soaked hair out of her face. Feeling her neck for a pulse, he shook his head when there was none. "We don't have anything to wrap her in," he said. "What if we lay her on the floor in the back until we can get to a few different stores to get what we need?"

"That'll work." Deanna nodded before slowly lifting Freya's body off Eddie's lap, floating it into the van, and then lowering it gently onto the floor of the back seat. Then, Deanna climbed into her seat in the second row of the van. Mitch climbed into the passenger's seat, while Eddie lifted himself into the van. Once everyone was in, Wyatt closed the door. He wiped the tears out of his eyes as he went to the driver's seat.

Getting in, he started the van. "Is this a quick getaway, or…?"

"No. There's nothing and no one left," Eddie said flatly.

Wyatt gulped before turning around on the road, and heading toward the highway for Pennsylvania at a normal rate of speed.

# MOUNTAIN TIME

**"Time is free, but it's priceless. You can't own it, but you can use it. You can't keep it, but you can spend it. Once you've lost it you can never get it back." Harvey Mackay**

*W*yatt's mind was spinning. He wanted to ask what happened, but then again, maybe he did not want to know. The less he knew, the better. He could plead ignorance. After all, all he did was drive.

Knowing Freya's lifeless body lay on the floor in the back pained his heart. During their drive, he got to know her since she was in the passenger's seat for the duration. He found out her favorite color was purple. She shared funny stories about the things she and Gemma did as they grew up together, playing tricks on the nurses. It helped that they had the same gift. She admitted her gift was stronger than Gemma's. However, Gemma's heart was bigger. Freya was a matter-of-fact person. Gemma led with her heart and emotions. Sometimes Freya wondered if Gemma was empathic too. She said Gemma would tell her what each doctor or nurse was feeling all the time. Freya used this to their advantage. She was the mastermind of the pair.

The van was silent, except for the radio playing Christian music from Wyatt's iPod. Finally, as they crossed into Idaho, Eddie spoke, "You know, I once heard a quote from Harvey Mackay that says, *Time is free, but it's priceless. You can't own it, but you can use it. You can't keep it, but you can spend it. Once you've lost it, you can never get it back. Time.*" He glanced behind him toward Freya before looking back to Wyatt, "I wish we had more time with her. I wish we had more time with Charlie. I can honestly say without a shadow of a doubt that I truly hate that man!"

"I don't blame you," Wyatt said. "He's on my crap list too. Here's the thing. None of you can hold onto that anger. It will eat you from the inside."

"What are you going to do if Hope dies?" Eddie challenged.

Wyatt gulped. "She could already be dead. We haven't heard from anyone. However, I know I will see her again in Heaven when it's my turn."

"Why is this so important to everyone?" Deanna asked. "This Heaven?"

"Well, when we die, there are one of two places we are going to go – no doubt. It's one or the other," Wyatt explained. "There's Hell. As in real Hell. Not a living hell that some refer to here on earth, but an honest and true real Hell. There will be wailing and gnashing of teeth. There will be a lake of fire. There will be demons. There will be people who will have skin hanging off their bodies, but they will never die. They will be tortured and tormented for all eternity."

"That's horrible!" Deanna said, stunned.

"That's Hell. You see, Satan, also known as the Devil or Lucifer, runs Hell. He knows that's his eternal punishment, and he wants to have as many join him as he can. He'll try to distract you long enough that you die before accepting Christ. Or my personal favorite. If you're one of God's, he'll try his best to trip you up, get you angry, or get you so busy you stop spending time with God, and then he's got you. He'll start throwing things left and right at you until you throw your hands in the air and curse God."

"Nice guy," Mitch said, tongue-in-cheek.

"Yeah. Not so much. Then, there's Heaven. In Heaven, there are streets of gold. There is a mansion where those of us who are children of God are all going to have a room. There will be praise and worship. There will be no more tears. No dying. There will be peace and celebration. There will be eternal life with the God Almighty."

"Okay, such a stark contrast. What's the appeal of Hell?" Mitch asked. "I've heard some of the nurses talking or seen them watching television. They make a joke out of Hell. One even said if they ever set foot in a church, God would strike them with lightning."

Wyatt chuckled at the way Mitch said it. "It's a joke the way they said it," Wyatt explained, "but it's not really funny when you understand what they're saying. You see, a long time ago, God spoke the world into existence. After He created the world, He created the first humans – Adam and Eve. He gave them only one rule. They were allowed to eat from any fruit in the Garden of Eden, except for the Tree of Knowledge of Good and Evil. When Satan heard this, he used it to his advantage. He asked Eve why they couldn't eat the fruit. Her response was that God said if they did, they would die. He said they would not die but be like God. So, he pushed her to try it. When she tasted it, she found out how good it was and gave some to Adam, who ate it as well. It was at that point that sin entered the world."

"Just because they ate fruit they weren't supposed to?" Deanna asked.

"Yes. Before that point, humans, meaning Adam and Eve, could talk directly to God. When God found out what they did,

He cursed men to have to work for their food. He cursed women to have pain during childbirth. He also cursed the snake, that it would always crawl on the ground and be underfoot of man. The worst part of it was direct communication with God was cut off. They would have to offer sacrifices to make up for sin, instead of talking directly to him."

Mitch crossed his arms in a huff. "All because they ate the fruit."

"More like, because they disobeyed the one rule God gave them," Wyatt countered. "You see, God created humans with this thing called free will. We have the free will to make choices. We know the difference between right and wrong. He wants us not only to choose right but also to choose Him."

"What does that mean?" Deanna asked.

"When each person is born, they are born into this sinful world. An extremely long time ago, God and Jesus got together and figured out a way to fix what Adam and Eve did."

"Great!" Mitch exclaimed.

"Not great when you find out the cost."

"What was the cost?" Deanna asked.

"The cost was the life of Jesus Christ." When Wyatt said that, a silence fell over the van for a few moments. "Remember when I said when they sinned, they had to make a sacrifice?"

"Yes," Mitch said, and Deanna nodded.

"Well, the sacrifice for sin had to be an animal. There had to be a shedding of blood. Not just any animal either. It had to be perfect. It had to be the best of the lot. Well, Jesus is the Son of God. He willingly sacrificed Himself to save everyone in this world. He is the ultimate sacrifice. The kicker? He would have done it even if it was just you."

"What happened to him?" Mitch asked. He glanced toward Freya's body and then back to Wyatt and gulped.

"Back in those days, there was this horrible way to die called a crucifixion," Wyatt started. "Only, when it came to Jesus

Christ, they took extra pleasure in seeing Him die because He showed them up time and time again. The Scribes and Pharisees thought they knew the law of God, but Jesus knew God Himself. They challenged Jesus left and right, but He won every time. So, they got one of the closest in His circle to betray Jesus…with a kiss."

"No way!" Mitch said, appalled. "Are you serious?"

"Yep. So, when Judas kissed Jesus on the cheek in the garden, they arrested Jesus."

"I would have put up a fight!" Deanna said.

"Oh! They did. One man cut off another's ear. Jesus told them to stop. He healed the ear and went with them willingly… knowing exactly what they were going to do to Him."

"What did they do?" Mitch asked.

Pleased Deanna and Mitch were so into the story, Wyatt continued, "They took Him back to the governor at the time. The governor tried to get Jesus released. He knew Jesus did nothing wrong, but the people wouldn't have it. They even chose to have a murderer released over Jesus."

"For real?" Deanna asked, surprised.

"For real." Wyatt nodded. "That's not the worst of it, though. You see, once the decision was made, they whipped Him with this torture device called a cat o' nine tails. Look that up when you get a chance. They beat Him until the bone was showing."

Deanna gasped.

"Also, back then, purple cloth signified royalty. They teased Him, calling Him King of the Jews. He was King of the Jews, but they did it in a mocking way. They took a purple cloak and placed it on Him when His skin was still wet and bleeding. They also shoved a crown of three-inch thorns on His head. Once His blood was dry, they ripped the cloak off."

"Ouch!" Mitch cringed.

"Exactly!" Wyatt said. "Then, if that wasn't bad enough, they made a game out of who got the cloak. They made it into a lottery."

Deanna huffed. "That's so not right!"

"Oh! I'm not done," Wyatt said. "When it came to the day of His death, they made Him try to carry His own cross. The cross was made of two heavy logs. He was supposed to carry it all by Himself."

"Even after everything they did to Him?" Deanna asked.

"Yes. He was so weak, they pulled someone else to finish carrying the cross. They made their way to the hill where they crucified men. Once there, they laid the pieces of wood on the ground in the form of a cross. Then, they nailed Jesus's hands and feet to the cross with three-to-four-inch spikes."

"What did they do next?" Mitch asked.

"They tilted the cross up and literally hung Him until He died. It took a little while. The people jeered and ridiculed Him the entire time. His mom was even there."

"How horrible!" Deanna said, imagining what it must have been like.

"Here's the thing," Wyatt continued. "He did die on the cross that day. As a matter of fact, they buried Him in a tomb. And, to make sure no one stole His body, they placed guards outside the tomb and sealed it with a massive boulder."

"Why?" Mitch asked.

"Because Jesus told people multiple times through His thirty-three years He would raise from the dead after three days."

"Did He?" Mitch asked.

"He did!"

"No way!" Mitch said, waving him off.

"Yes! You see, it was customary back then to anoint the body with oils and spices after three days. They did things a little differently back then. After three days, the body would smell something awful!" Wyatt said, scrunching his nose. "So, three women went to Jesus' tomb on the morning of the third day. They were not prepared for what they found."

"What was it?" Deanna asked.

"Well, the massive boulder they placed in front of the tomb was moved. The guards were also passed out. And, to top it off, there was a real-life angel sitting on the boulder!"

"No way! Are you serious?" Deanna asked. "How is that possible?"

"Remember when I called Jesus the Son of God?"

"Yes."

"With God, all things are possible," Wyatt said with a twinkle in his eyes. "Now, just so you don't think I'm messing with you, there were over five hundred people who saw Jesus after His death."

"Wow!" Deanna said, surprised.

"Exactly! Now, while Jesus was here, He did some incredible miracles. He healed the lame, made the blind see, helped those who couldn't walk before to walk again. He even raised His friend from the dead after he had been dead for four days."

"That's insane!" Mitch said, amazed.

"That's Jesus," Wyatt said. "And so we wouldn't be left alone, just before He went to Heaven, He thought enough of us to make sure we had a guide. He left the Holy Spirit. When we trust in Christ as our Savior, the Holy Spirit comes and lives inside each of us. He guides and directs us. He helps us stay in the will of God if we listen to His still small voice."

"That's pretty cool!" Deanna said. "Is it all true?"

"Very true!" Wyatt assured her. "I can show you in the Bible after this is all over."

"So, you said we only have to trust Jesus as our Savior?" Mitch asked. "Savior of what?"

"Not *of* what, but *from* what," Wyatt corrected. "Remember when we first started talking about Heaven and Hell?"

"Yeah," Mitch said.

"Do you also remember when I said after Adam and Eve ate that fruit, sin entered the world and that we are born into sin… meaning we'll go to Hell if we don't choose Jesus?"

"Yes," Mitch said.

"Well, when Jesus died, He created the perfect sacrifice. He was the only One in this world Who was born without sin. He was, is, and will always be the perfect Son of the Lord God. When He died, He paid the penalty for everyone's sin. In doing so, He fixed the communication between God and man. Here's the key to this. Remember that free will I also talked about?"

"Yes," Deanna said. "You said it was the free will to choose right from wrong."

"Right. I also said we need to make a choice to follow God. Jesus coming back from the dead after three days, bringing with Him our salvation from Hell, gives us the opportunity to have a choice. If He didn't make the choice to die on the cross the way He did, we would still be sacrificing animals."

"I see," Mitch said, lining things up in his head.

"So, are you saying we have to make a choice to follow Christ?" Deanna asked.

"Yes…and no. Yes, you have to make a choice, but it's not only just to follow Christ," Wyatt clarified, "but you also must believe He is the Son of God and that He is the only way to Heaven. You need to ask Him to forgive you of your sins. There is no way on this planet you will ever be good enough to work your way to Heaven. The only way is through Jesus. What He did is a gift to you. If you choose to accept His gift, then all you have to do is pray and talk to Him. You have to give Him control over your life. He has an amazing plan for your life. You just have to ask. The only thing He asks is you take time to have a relationship with Him by reading the Bible – which is God's love letter to you. He also asks you to tell others, just like I'm telling you right now."

"That doesn't sound like it's a tough decision," Deanna said. "Especially knowing the difference between Heaven and Hell."

"It's tougher than you think. Humans are strong, independent people. We don't like being told what to do," Wyatt pointed out.

"So, why did you do it?" Mitch asked. "You seem like a strong guy."

"And very independent," Deanna added.

"Well, while my life was good, I always felt like there was something missing. I tried chasing the things the world told me I needed. Status? I am the County Police Chief. There are many people who know me. Girls? Tried that. I always felt empty. Food? Tried that too. Had to change my eating habits drastically for my health. Speaking of health, the drinking didn't help either. It took me years to figure out what was actually missing. It was Jesus. Once He and I got together, I finally felt whole. After a few years, He led me to Hope, and I felt twice blessed! And look now! I have more family than I know what to do with when it comes to all you kids!"

"So, you're saying –"

"Once I followed Christ, I never looked back, and I never wanted for anything," Wyatt said, cutting Deanna off. "Now, just because I'm a child of God, it doesn't make me immune to pain and suffering. On the contrary, it's usually worse because Satan's trying to get me down. However, I know Satan did the same thing to Jesus, and Jesus stood against him and won. I also know Satan can never touch my soul. So, when I get down, angry, upset, or any other number of emotions, I stop what I'm doing, pop my headphones in, and play this music we're listening to now."

"It's really peaceful music," Deanna observed. "The music behind it has great rhythm. It's the words. They make me feel at peace."

"Same with me," Mitch said. "It's like, it lifts my spirit."

"Exactly!" Wyatt said. "It makes my soul happy to sing to the Lord. When I'm alone, I'll sing the words with the song."

Deanna smiled. "Nice!"

Eddie crossed his arms. "With everything going on in this world, consider me a cynic."

"There's a lot of dark in this world," Wyatt admitted. "However, there's also a lot of beauty. I once heard a quote from Oswald Chambers that says, *'Seeing is never believing; we interpret what we see in the light of what we believe. Faith is confidence in God before you see God emerging; therefore the nature of faith is that it must be tried.'* You'll see what you want to see. Trusting in God takes faith. Try Him. Trust Him."

Eddie sighed. "Let's talk reality. Our sister is dead on the floor. We don't know if the other group is dead or alive. And we don't even know if The Professor has found those in Pennsylvania yet."

"Okay, Mr. Sourpuss!" Deanna grumbled. "Can you be any more positive?"

Eddie looked at her out of the corner of his eye. "I'm positive I will kill The Professor myself!"

"Eddie, what if you and Mitch switch places so we can talk?" Wyatt suggested.

"Fine," Eddie said in a huff.

Mitch unbuckled and then went behind his seat to Eddie's wheelchair and sat until Eddie lifted himself and levitated to the front seat. Then, Mitch got in the seat beside Deanna. They immediately started talking about what Wyatt said.

"Wanna dump some of that?" Wyatt asked once Eddie was settled.

"Dump some of what?" Eddie asked.

"Some of what you're carrying. It doesn't take someone with some of those gifts y'all got to figure out you're ticked off."

Eddie sighed. "I am."

"Well, talk to me, son."

"I'm not your son. I'm *his*," Eddie said, snidely emphasizing the word his.

"Not for long. I told you when we get back to Texas, no matter how this turns out, I'm adopting you. For all intents and purposes, you are my son. So, talk to me, *son*."

Eddie sighed heavily again. "All right. I'm really angry they killed Freya. She didn't have a chance. As soon as we felt it, I dove into her head. She literally walked into a firing squad. Why would He do that? What's wrong with Him? Had Deanna and I not been so strong, we would be dead too!"

"Do you want to tell me what happened in there?" Wyatt asked. "You said there was no one else alive."

"That was my fault," Mitch spoke up. "I did something bad."

"No. The Professor put you in a bad position," Eddie corrected. "What kind of man puts his kid in a room with a dozen men with guns and sends over eighteen more after his other children?"

"He did–Wait! What?" Wyatt shook his head. "What happened?"

"We each had about a half dozen guys with guns trained on us as soon as we set foot inside the doors," Deanna explained. "Eddie and I disposed of our six or seven pretty quickly. Everything happened too fast to warn Freya. She expected it, but she didn't have a chance to react."

"Then, I was being held in the Security Office with the head of security and a dozen other men," Mitch added. "I have another gift, it seems, the Alpha's don't have."

"What's that?" Wyatt asked.

"I have the gift of persuasion."

"The gift of what?" Wyatt asked.

"Persuasion," Mitch said again. "Basically, I can make people do what I want them to do by being assertive."

"Blake can kind of do that. He does it mentally, not verbally," Wyatt said. "When we feel pressure to do something, we look to see if he's around and do the opposite. It's not easy, but we can tell when it's him."

"Yes." Mitch nodded. "I tell them. They don't have a choice. They have to do it. They cannot resist."

"I see. So, what did you do?" Wyatt asked.

"I told them to go into the hallway and to shoot the others for betraying The Professor," Mitch admitted. "I-I'm sorry. I really didn't know it was wrong. The Professor made me make people do things all the time. Sometimes even cruel things. I didn't want to. Then, when Eddie said he and Deanna were there to get me out, I got excited. Then, I knew one of my sisters was gone. I felt the blow to Eddie and Deanna. I got angry too. I made them kill."

"Then, I went in and finished off the last three by snapping their necks," Eddie added. "I'm not ashamed of it. They already killed my sister. What was going to stop them from killing the rest of us?"

"This is true," Wyatt said. "You used the only weapon you had to defend yourself. It was your life or theirs. The Bible does say *thou shalt not kill,* but it also says you can to protect yourself. I would consider using your gift a different way in the future. And, if you can do it without killing, that would be more ideal."

"Really?" Deanna asked. "It talks about that?"

"Yep. In Exodus 22:2, it says, *'If a thief is caught breaking in at night and is struck a fatal blow, the defender is not guilty of bloodshed.'* Granted, you guys were not at home, but you get the point. Pre-meditated is a completely different issue," Wyatt explained.

"Not in regard to The Professor," Eddie said sternly. "That man killed all of our mothers. He killed Ben. He killed Freya. He killed Charlie. He must pay."

"Vengeance is mine sayeth the Lord," Wyatt reminded him.

Turning toward Wyatt, Eddie said sternly, "I will avenge the lives taken. I don't think God made me this strong if I wasn't supposed to look after others. I know I will be the one to kill him."

"Eddie, just think about it…for me?" Wyatt asked.

Eddie clicked his tongue. "You would pull that card. I'll tell you what, if he is not in the process of hurting someone else I love, I'll just knock him out. Fair enough?"

"Fair enough," Wyatt agreed. "And thank you."

⁂

DURING THEIR DRIVE, Wyatt stopped at three different gas stations which had stores in them. He picked up a shovel and gloves at one, a tarp at another, and a couple rolls of duct tape at another. At the store where he picked up duct tape, he also picked up flowers, as well as seeds for perennials, so Freya would always have flowers where she lay.

As they were going through Idaho, he turned off on a road that led to the middle of nowhere. He marked the spot on the paper map in case any of the siblings, especially Gemma, wanted to come back. While they were there, Wyatt went to dig a hole, but Eddie stopped him. While Eddie worked on the hole, lifting the earth into two piles, Deanna lifted Freya's body off the ground with one hand and wrapped the tarp around her body with her other hand. She held it in place while Wyatt put the gloves on and secured it with duct tape. Knowing how to secure it well after being at enough crime scenes, Wyatt took care but secured her properly. Afterward, Deanna set Freya's body back down on the ground and helped Eddie continue to pull the dirt out with their telekinesis. All in all, it took a total of thirty minutes to complete everything.

After the hole was dug, Deanna lifted Freya's body and then lowered it into the ten-foot deep by six-foot-long hole. Wyatt held the flowers while he spoke, "Freya was taken way too fast.

95

They say the good die young. In her case, this was completely true. She didn't get the chance to live a full life. I know she will be sorely missed, especially as her siblings experience real life. I pray at some point on this trip, she accepted Christ as her Savior, and we will be able to see her again in Heaven when we get there. Lord," Wyatt looked toward Heaven, "only You know the answer to that. I pray if she goes to Heaven, You will welcome her with open arms and show her the love she never got on this Earth. Amen." Afterward, he tossed a white rose on top of her body.

Deanna stepped forward and took one of the roses from Wyatt. "She was a twin, but one of a kind. They could fool the nurses and staff, but not us. There was a definite difference between the pair." Looking toward Heaven, she wiped her tears as she said, "Lord, if You're really there, I ask you to be with Gemma. I ask You to comfort her and let her know she may have lost her twin, but she has many siblings. She will never be alone." When finished, she tossed her rose into the grave.

Wyatt handed Eddie a white rose. "I'm mad," Eddie started. His bottom lip trembled as he fought his emotions.

"Just tell her how you feel or say what you feel you need to say," Wyatt encouraged.

Eddie looked toward the sky as he wiped a tear. Then he looked back down at the hole, with Freya's body wrapped in a tarp, and said, "You didn't deserve this. Being in an unmarked grave is not fair, but I understand. You were supposed to be with us, Freya. Why did you not know they would be there? I'm sure you felt us fight. Mind gifts aren't your thing, but you and Gemma always seemed to be a half-step ahead of the rest of us when it came to reading the room. Why didn't you see them?" He pounded his fist on the arm of his wheelchair. "Why didn't you know?" Eddie sighed, looking toward Heaven. "Why didn't You tell her? You're supposed to be God. You're supposed to be all-knowing. Why? She was sweet and innocent. She was strong and powerful," he said loudly. Then quietly, he added, "She was my friend." He tossed the rose into the grave with the other two.

"What about you?" Wyatt asked Mitch.

Mitch shook his head. "I didn't know her."

"But she was your sister."

Mitch thought about it for a moment before accepting the rose. Standing at the edge, he said, "I'm sorry I didn't get the chance to know you. I'm sorry for not stopping them before you were hurt and killed." A few tears escaped down his cheeks. He wiped them away as he said, "I hope the rest of us make it through this. I will do my best to be the best brother to Gemma. I will personally look after her with everything I have."

Wyatt put his hand on Mitch's shoulder. "I'm sure you will, son. I'm sure we all will."

With that, Mitch tossed his rose into the grave.

"Whether you are a Christian or not, please bow your head while I say a prayer over her," Wyatt said, not giving them a choice. When all heads were bowed, Wyatt started. "Father, we commit her body and soul to You. We pray she was one of Yours. We ask You to have mercy on her if she was not. We know there is only one way to Heaven – through Jesus. We also know you are not without mercy and grace. We ask You to continue to direct our steps and protect us as we go back to Pennsylvania. We ask You to protect those who are in Wyoming in a miraculous way. Losing Charlie so young, and now Freya, I don't know how much more hurt and loss this group can take. I ask You to bring those to You who are not followers of Christ. I ask You to protect their hearts, souls, minds, and bodies until this is over and they can make a knowledgeable choice. Thank You, Father, for those who have made it through. Please keep us all safe. Also, please bring justice for Charlie and Freya. Please do it, so no one will feel the need to carry that burden. Thank you, Father. In Jesus' name, I pray. Amen."

Eddie did not say a word. He lifted his chair a few inches off the ground and levitated to the van, waiting for the others.

"He's not happy," Mitch said quietly.

"I know," Wyatt agreed. "It'll take time."

"Wyatt, when we get back on the road, can I sit in the passenger's seat?" Deanna asked. "There are some things I want to talk to you about."

"Definitely! C'mon," Wyatt said, picking up the shovel and gloves.

Before they left, Deanna took her hands and brought the two large piles of dirt together. When she did, the piles of dirt on either side of Freya's grave cascaded in over Freya's body.

"*And the dust returns to the earth as it was, and the spirit returns to God Who gave it,*" Wyatt said, quoting Ecclesiastes 12:7.

Once all the dirt was back in place, Deanna smoothed it by waving her hands over it so it did not look like it was freshly laid. After that, Deanna then took several packets of perennial seeds. As per Wyatt's instructions, the packages were opened. Then Deanna levitated the seeds, so that when they fell, they would lay evenly on the ground. She then waved her hands, spreading the dirt lightly over the seeds.

"Too bad none of you can control the weather," Wyatt remarked. "Those seeds need water. That will have to be up to God."

With that, they returned to the van. As they were loading, light rain fell around them, slowly picking up to a steady rain.

"He answered," Deanna said with a sad smile as lighting shot across the sky, then rumbled the ground around them.

Wyatt smiled, starting the van. "That He did!"

Wyatt spun the van around and headed back to the main highway. Eddie was silent. Wyatt did not need anyone's gift to know Eddie was brooding. He prayed in his head for his soon-to-be son's heart and soul.

AS THEY NEARED THE HIGHWAY, Eddie suddenly perked up. "Stop!" he shouted.

"What?" Wyatt pulled over. "What's wrong?"

"They're near here," Eddie announced. "Quiet."

Eddie's nerves were raw, so he was more alert. He felt the anxiety from Adam and Blake before he zeroed in on who it was. *Adam? Blake?* Eddie thought.

"Eddie?" Adam asked, looking around their van.

"You heard it too?" Blake asked him.

"Yeah. Give me your hand," Adam said, putting his hand out. "Now, close your eyes and focus on my thoughts."

Blake did as Adam instructed, while he and Adam sat in the second seat with Holly. Alex was in the passenger's seat, Colby continued to drive, and the Wyoming children and Justin sat in the last two seats – four in one seat, with five in the other.

Eyes closed, Adam thought, *Eddie? We're here.*

*I know,* Eddie responded. *Freya's gone.*

*We felt something brutal a bit ago. What happened to her?* Adam's thought tone was sharp.

*She was shot by multiple men of The Professor's. We buried her about a half-hour from where we are here in Idaho.*

*We're in Idaho!* Adam thought, excitement, dread, and anxiety churning within him until he felt Blake push peace through the entire vehicle.

"Not too much of that, brother," Colby cautioned. "We can't sleep. If we're too relaxed, it won't end well."

"Sorry," Blake said and toned it down.

*Where are you?* Adam thought.

*Near Hayburn,* Eddie sent.

"Stop!" Adam ordered. When Colby pulled over, Adam thought to Eddie, *We're just entering that area. We pulled over.*

*Good. Stay there.* Eddie thought and then said to Wyatt, "Go ahead, but keep an eye on the other side of the road."

This went on for the next fifteen minutes until they saw the other van pulled over. Wyatt pulled over to the side of the road while Colby took off, turned around, and pulled in behind him.

"You may want to stay here," Adam warned Alex. "Colby, you and Holly stay here with everyone. Holly, keep the peace."

"You got it," Holly agreed. "See if they have space to give these younger ones some room to move."

"No problem," he said, and he and Blake got out of the van.

They met Wyatt and Deanna outside the vans. After hugging each other, Adam asked, "What happened?"

"They knew we were coming," Deanna explained.

"Yeah. We were on our way to help you guys," Blake said. "Alex told us it was a trap."

Deanna furrowed her brow. "Alex? Is she here?"

"She is," Adam said cautiously. When Deanna went to go toward the other vehicle, Adam put his hands on her shoulders to stop her. "Listen first."

Deanna crossed her arms, her face red. "You don't have a lot of time to talk before I blow! Her father is the reason Freya was shot to death!"

"Explain!" Blake demanded.

"You first!" Deanna ordered.

"Okay," Adam said. He explained what happened in Wyoming. When he finished, Deanna explained what happened in Oregon – and afterward. "So, we have Justin, and you have Mitch?" Adam asked.

"Yes," Deanna said. "Do you honestly trust Alex?"

"Yes," Adam said. "I read her mind. She's telling the truth."

"So, the second and third groups are our clones?" Deanna asked, making sure she heard correctly.

"Yes. That's why they look just like us," Blake said.

Deanna nodded. "I see."

"And we can't sleep?" Wyatt asked. "At all?"

"No. Neither can the Pennsylvania group. Yes, they already know," Blake said. "Holly called them."

"Then, we had better get there sooner than later," Deanna said. Looking at her watch, she explained, "They've been awake for fifty-three hours. Now, I know teens have amazing stamina when pushed, but we still have about thirty-four or thirty-five hours to go. That will be 88 hours! That will be three and a half days they have to stay awake! That's insane!"

"Then, we'd better shift some of those kids around and get out of here," Wyatt said. "Enough wasting time. We can catch up later. On the way, we need to think of a trap for that animal Professor Roth!"

"Can we go nuclear when we find The Professor now?" Deanna asked.

"Not yet," Wyatt said. "Let's shift the kids, and then we can work on a plan. We have to get to the east coast crew. The longer we stay here, the longer they have to wait."

"Can we stop by Wyoming and blow that facility too?" Deanna pushed. When they gave her questioning looks, she explained, "We blew the Oregon facility in case there was some research. We wanted to stop any further experiments."

"Now that sounds like a good plan," Wyatt agreed. "What do you guys think?"

"Just so you know, Alex destroyed the main research stuff already. I think she can send everyone away so the facility will be empty. If Eddie needs to blow steam, he can blow it there," Adam suggested. "If he doesn't want to, I'm sure Holly would do it."

"I agree," Wyatt said. "Let's go."

Justin, along with a few of the youngest group, moved over to Wyatt's van. Holly's clone, Zoey, wanted to stay with her. Vince was Adam's clone, so he stayed in the van with them, along with the little boy, William, who was Blake's clone. The others moved over to the other van to stretch out.

Once they reached the Wyoming facility, Eddie got out of the van. Alex called about an hour earlier to clear the facility.

"Anyone in there?" Holly asked as she stood beside Eddie. They were the only two outside.

"Nope."

"You sure?"

"Absolutely," Eddie said. "Ready?"

"Yes."

They joined hands. Eddie used Holly's knowledge of the facility to locate what he needed. "Push," Eddie said.

Both Eddie and Holly reached their hands forward. With their combined power, they thrust their power toward the facility, creating a lot of pressure in various parts of the facility until explosions were heard. Because of their power, they kept the debris in an enclosed area. Then Eddie shoved it down, creating another explosion, sending all the debris high into the air, so there was nothing left but rubble raining down.

"Well done," Holly encouraged.

"Can I ride with you guys?" Eddie asked. "The kids are pretty loud in our vehicle."

"Sure," Holly said. She let Wyatt know as Eddie got into the van. Once she was in, she shut the door, as she said, "Let's go rescue the Pennsylvania crew."

# EASTERN TIME

**"Strive not to be a success, but rather to be of value." Albert Einstein**

"That's everything," Mac said, filling Tanya, Lindsey, Gemma, and Megan in on everything Shawn told him. "So, we need to figure out a way to stay awake until they get back here."

"You do realize we'll be awake for over eighty-some hours before they get back here. Right?" Megan asked. Gemma was no longer sobbing. As she lay her head on Megan's lap, Megan ran her fingers through Gemma's hair to calm her. "Do you understand what that will do to us?"

"We'd better make a lot of coffee," Tanya said, getting up to make coffee. "I don't want him creeping in my dreams or nightmares. If we fall asleep, we'll sleep hard. Once they find us, it won't be difficult to find Hope. We can't let him get a hold of Hope."

"Agreed," Lindsey said. Looking toward Gemma, she asked, "Can you focus enough to protect Hope?"

Gemma only nodded in response.

"I'll ride back with you," Mac volunteered. "That way, I'll know you got there safely."

"Thank you," Gemma said, getting off the bed. "I appreciate you all."

"You're part of the family," Megan said, giving her a hug. "You're stuck with us."

"I don't feel a part of a family anymore," Gemma admitted as she hugged Tanya and then Lindsey.

"Gemma," Tanya rested her hands on Gemma's shoulders, "your family is bigger than you know. There were twenty-six siblings. At this point, we're not sure how many made it out. Worst case scenario, you still have fifteen to twenty. We pray it's more, but we don't know. My point is –"

"I get it," Gemma cut her off. "I'm just struggling. My chest has hurt since Freya died."

"You lost your twin," Megan said. "That's going to take a while to work through. Maybe some time with Bells will help."

"I think Bells should come back here for a bit," Gemma said. "She could use some normalcy. These few hours meant more to me than you know."

"What if I go sit with you?" Lindsey offered. "That way, Mac can stay here, and Shawn and Bells can come back here together."

Gemma looped her arm through Lindsey's. "I would like that. It'll be a refreshing change. Bells is great company, but she can be a little too insightful at times."

"Understood. Lindsey, get into costume," Mac said.

"Give me a few." Lindsey ran to the bathroom. Looking in the mirror, she debated on what to do. Over the last several days, wearing no makeup allowed her to see how pretty she actually was on the outside. While the auburn color in her hair was stunning, she missed her blond hair. She put her hair in a ponytail and then fed it through the loop in the back of the baseball cap. She pulled a few loose strands down for effect before putting her glasses on. "Not bad," she said in approval. "Not bad at all."

When she walked out, Tanya commented, "Looking good, Linds!"

"Thanks!" She smiled. "Let's go."

◁▷◁▷

IT WAS a quiet ride on the trolly back to the hospital. When they got there, Shawn and Bells met them downstairs. Bells gave Gemma a hug and said, "I'm so sorry. We're here for you, sis."

"Thank you," Gemma said appreciatively. "Unfortunately, even with all our gifts, no one can bring her back to me."

"She and Charlie are together," Bells encouraged.

"This is true," Gemma said, knowing Bells knew how she felt. Losing Charlie so young made Bells pull back from getting close to anyone else.

"We'll stick together," Bells said. "We share a bond no other sibling of ours has faced yet."

"Agreed," Gemma said, giving her another hug.

"We're going to stay here," Lindsey explained. "You guys are going back to the hotel."

"Are you sure?" Bells asked.

"Yes. Go have some normalcy," Gemma encouraged Bells. "Enjoy a movie and being a real teen for a bit. Just don't fall asleep."

"Agreed." Bells gave Gemma another hug. "Be careful, and don't fall asleep either. If any of us falls asleep, it won't take him long to connect the dots."

◁▷◁▷

MEGAN GROWLED in frustration after several hours of watching television, alternating with teaching Bells how to play Texas Hold 'em. "I'm so tired," she complained. "And, if I have another coffee, it will be too soon!"

"What if we go to the store on the corner and get some energy drinks?" Shawn offered.

Megan shook her head. "Too many cameras."

Tanya went over to the table with the binder on it for the room. "Let's see what room service has for food."

"It's four o'clock in the morning," Mac pointed out. "I don't think they even have room service right now. Normal people are sleeping."

"Guys," Megan said, her face draining color, "did you see that?"

"See what?" Bells asked.

Megan gulped. "I saw a shadow go into the other room."

"Meg, you're seeing things. It's from not sleeping," Tanya explained. "This is going to get worse as time goes by."

"H-how do you know? It looked real."

"I got it." Mac got off the bed and went into the other room. "Nothing," he said when he returned. "We're going to see things. The longer time passes, the worse it's going to get. If you see something, or think you see something take a moment. Close your eyes and take two deep breaths and look again."

"Agreed," Tanya said. "We're all in this together. We're going to have to fight sleep *and* the visions and hallucinations."

⬤⬤⬤⬤

"WHERE IS EVERYONE?" The Professor growled. He slammed his fists on the desk of the hotel suite in Boston, Massachusetts. Figuring Boston was the first big city they would stop at to get Hope to the hospital, he headed there.

The two-bedroom penthouse suite was on the top floor of a luxury hotel near the Charles River. He had them bring an extra bed in each room to accommodate the teens. The Professor also made sure there were three guards in each room and two more in the main room with him. With three girls and four boys, it was an easy split.

Before leaving Oregon, The Professor drugged the dinner the teens ate that night. After they were unconscious, they were easier to transport in his private plane. When they arrived at the hotel, while The Professor checked in, the guards took the kids up to the pent-house via the maintenance elevator to his level. The Professor was a regular there, so they did not bat an eye in accommodating his requests. He also requested no housekeeping while he was there. Housekeeping would simply leave the towels at the door, and he would leave the dirty ones along with the trash outside the door.

Once in the hotel room, The Professor hooked up each of the seven teens to an IV with saline, along with a sedative to periodically release in order to keep them under until he needed them. In the meantime, they would sleep.

"Sir?" one of the guards interrupted his thoughts.

The Professor turned toward him. With strained politeness, he asked, "Yes?"

"I messaged Alex like you asked, but there's no response."

The Professor narrowed his eyes. "What do you mean?"

"Alex hasn't responded. I let her know where we were and asked her the status of the Wyoming site. I got nothing."

"For how long?"

"I gave her a few hours," he said. "I thought maybe she was busy."

The Professor sighed as he got up to pace. Running his hands through his hair, he said, "She's not busy. At least, she shouldn't be busy anymore. Why don't you guys go stand outside while I try to find them again…in peace?"

"Yes, sir," he acknowledged. He grabbed the other guard by the arm, and they left the suite, standing outside the door.

"Finally! Solace! Blessed silence!" The Professor growled. He laid down on the couch. Taking a few deep breaths, he closed his eyes. "Where are you?"

⬥⬥⬥⬥

"Do you think he knows yet?" Holly asked.

"That we leveled two of his facilities?" Alex raised an eyebrow. "It wouldn't surprise me. If nothing else, he would get frustrated by not being able to connect with anyone…especially me."

"What will he do?" Blake asked.

"It'll fuel his rage," Adam said. "He may go into a search frenzy."

"With six kids in tow?" Holly asked. "Wouldn't that put them in danger?"

"He may not. What are the chances he'll leave them somewhere and search?" Colby asked.

"About 50/50," Adam said. "If he does, he'll likely start in Boston."

"He does have a favorite hotel there," Alex said. "That would be a good place to start."

"What other places would he search?" Blake asked.

"The bigger cities," Adam said. "He would think we got Hope to a hospital as soon as possible."

"So, we're talking which cities?" Holly asked.

"Places like Portland, Manchester, Boston, Worcester, Springfield, Providence, Hartford, New Haven, New York City… They could be anywhere," Alex said. "Where are the others?"

"Won't answer that." Holly shook her head. "The less you know, the better."

"Agreed." Alex nodded. "While I understand the restraint, it does sting a little."

"Would you do differently?" Holly challenged.

"No."

"Glad we have an understanding," Holly said. "You did love our dad, Ben. However, through all those years, you also spied for *your* dad. You provided a time for them to come and take the others. I'm not okay with that. It'll take me a long time to trust you again."

"I understand."

"Good. Until then, you have a lot to prove."

"I understand. Thank you for the opportunity to earn your forgiveness."

"I forgive you," Holly said. "That's not in question. I did that more for me than you. However, it doesn't mean I trust you right now."

"I get it. Thank you."

"It's what Jesus would want me to do."

"There's that Jesus again. Why is He so important?" Alex asked. "Ben never mentioned Jesus much, but He said he knew Jesus too. Hope and Wyatt are close to Jesus. I know there are a few of you kids who are as well."

"This could take a while," Colby said, "but I would be happy to share with you who He is. This is something I can answer."

"I'm pretty sure we have time," Alex gestured for him to continue.

Eddie rolled his eyes in his seat. He hoped to avoid Jesus by switching vans. Obviously, this Jesus had a sense of humor. While Eddie appreciated His sense of humor, it still irritated him to no end!

DURING THE MOVIE, Bells kept glancing at Shawn as he continuously glanced at her. Finally, Mac stopped the movie for a bathroom break. While he was gone, Shawn asked Bells, "Hey, Bells. I know you've had a rough night. Want to go talk about it in the other room?"

"I would like that," Bells said, getting off the bed.

Once they left the room and closed the door between the rooms, Tanya turned to Megan, and asked, "Is that a good thing?"

"Not sure." Megan shrugged. "That depends if he has honorable intentions."

"If who has honorable inten – where are Shawn and Bells?" Mac asked, coming out of the bathroom.

Megan nodded toward the closed door.

"Oh," Mac said. He pursed his lips as he headed back to his spot on his bed. "Looks like we're going to have to trust some of the stuff we talked about lately sunk in, and he won't revert back to his standard."

⟐⟐⟐⟐

"SHE HAD SOME BEAUTIFUL MEMORIES," Bells said, remembering her time with Hope as she sat on one bed and Shawn sat on the other. "She seems like a sweet lady."

"Hope is," Shawn agreed. "I grew up in the same church she attended. She was too busy to teach or go to outings, but I saw her every Sunday. Everyone in youth group knows who she is and who her kids are."

"What were Blake and Holly like growing up?" Bells asked.

"They were close. Hope kept them away from all of us. Of course, now we know why."

"Their gifts." Bells nodded in understanding. "They had to have their gifts under control before they could go out in public."

"Oh, they were out in public, just not close to anyone but

their family and a few other adults in town," Shawn explained. "They always went out on Sunday afternoon. Sometimes we ran across them. Sometimes we didn't."

"Let me guess," Bells said, tucking a portion of her hair behind her ear, "you liked Holly?"

"Not really. Mac and Colby did. Don't get me wrong. She's pretty and all, just a bit out of my league as far as I'm concerned."

"Lindsey?"

"No. Well, I did, but then she got a little too rude. Honestly, I wouldn't let myself fall head over heels with any girl. I just did what I thought they wanted and let them go on their way."

"So, you chose quantity over quality," Bells observed.

Shawn chuckled. "You have such a way with words."

"Am I wrong?" Bells asked.

"No. I'm not sure if I like this friendship or not."

"Why not?"

"Because you can literally read my mind. I can't have any secrets with you."

"Oh, I haven't read your mind yet. Not while we've been talking anyway," Bells said. "These are just observations I picked up while you talked. Being a mind reader, I have good insight into the human psyche."

"You're going to be trouble. Aren't you?"

"No. I'll be only what you need me to be."

"What if I need you to be more than a friend?"

"That's something we'll have to talk about when you reach that point." She smiled. "Until then, I'll continue to be me and make sure to call you out when needed."

"I would appreciate that."

"What do you think your friends are thinking with us coming in here?" Bells asked.

"I would hope they would think I would be nothing but a gentleman."

"What if I don't want you to be a gentleman…fully?"

Shawn narrowed his eyes. "What do you mean?"

"You and I have feelings for each other."

"We do," Shawn said cautiously.

"Well, I've never kissed a boy," Bells admitted.

"Do you-you want me to kiss you?"

"Do you want to kiss me?"

"Very much so! But I also want to respect you."

"What are you not respecting by kissing me?" Bells asked. "I don't want to do anything else."

"Fair enough. C'mere," he said, tapping the side of the bed.

Bells got off her bed and sat beside Shawn. He took her hands into his and looked into her eyes. Bells' heart rate skyrocketed when they touched. "I've never held hands either."

"Well, then this will be a first of many new experiences," he said, resting one of his hands on the side of her face, with his other on her waist. He never took his eyes off hers. "Are you sure?"

"Yes," Bells said. She got her hands free and then pulled him closer with her hands until their lips touched. Electricity shot through her body when they kissed. She took a deep breath and enjoyed the kiss as he rested both hands on her waist.

After a few tense moments, Bells pulled away. "Wow," she said with her eyes still closed. "That was incredible!"

"That's what happens when two people who care deeply for each other show their true feelings."

"I can see how this could escalate quickly."

"I agree. Let's head back over to the other room. Would you mind if I held your hand?" he asked, putting his hand out.

She grasped his hand and they walked over to the other room.

"Good talk?" Mac asked, stretched out on the sofa bed.

"Yep," Shawn said. "Can I get you to move over to the bed with Megan or Tanya? We'd like to be able to be together."

"Sure," Mac said, getting up. Looking at Tanya and Megan, he asked, "Which of you lovely ladies would like to share with me?"

"Let's not get too comfortable," Tanya said, getting off her bed. She moved to the bed Megan was on. "I don't want anyone to feel like a fifth wheel."

"Good point," Mac said, lying on the now-empty bed. "Ahhh," he sighed, stretching out. "This is way more comfortable than the sofa bed."

Shawn laid down and put his arm out. Bells laid down, resting her head on his chest, listening to his heartbeat while they watched the movie.

◌◌◌◌◌

"How do you think the others are holding up?" Gemma asked Lindsey.

"Not sure. It's an interesting mix over there," Lindsey pointed out.

"Do you like any of them?" Gemma asked.

"Actually, not right now. I think I may need to take a sabbatical from dating for a bit."

"Bells and Shawn like each other," Gemma said.

"What do you mean?"

"I mean, I felt it when they were here at the hospital before they left. They like each other."

"Well, I guess talking for hours will create a bond."

"That's more than a bond I felt," Gemma pointed out. "They really like each other. Remember, we've only had our siblings all of our lives. We never ran across other teens."

"True." Lindsey nodded in understanding. "I guess we'll have to let nature take its course."

"Can I talk to you about some things?"

"Of course!"

"And will it stay a secret?"

"Um," Lindsey tightened her lips. "Don't know about that. I'm not known for keeping secrets."

"Okay, then I won't tell you the deep, dark secrets."

"Probably a safer plan."

"H–how do you know if you like someone?"

"Well, it's more of an instinct." Placing her hand on her stomach, Lindsey said, "You feel it here first. Anytime they're close, you can't seem to breathe."

"That doesn't sound pleasant."

"Oh! But it is! You get this feeling of butterflies in your stomach when you hear their voice," Lindsey explained. "You want to look your best whenever they're around. You want them to notice you without you having to say hi, but you can't help yourself."

"That sounds embarrassing."

"Oh! It can be!" Lindsey giggled. "I have done more than my share of embarrassing things to get the attention of a guy."

"Such as?"

"Wearing clothes too tight. When I first started using makeup, putting on too much. Walking in an outfit I knew I looked good in, and tripped."

"Oh!" Gemma covered her mouth, giggling.

"You can laugh. It was super embarrassing. I mean, I can laugh now, but at the time, it was mortifying." She shrugged. "It happens."

"What about the guys?"

"They can be worse than girls some days. We girls tend to hit our hormones earlier than guys, so when we're trying to get their attention, they don't care. Once they do care, they can strut like the best of us. They try to act cool at the school gym, but I've seen them overdo it to impress us. I've even seen them run track and completely trip over their own feet trying to make sure the girls are watching."

"Oh, dear!" Gemma laughed.

"Oh yeah! They think they're all that. They act cool and laid back, but they're just as antsy about us as we are about them. They want girls to throw themselves at them. Well, that's not true. Some do, and some don't."

"How do you know which ones are which?"

"You don't. That's part of the game."

"Why does it have to be a game? Why can't people just be honest with each other?"

"That would be too easy. Plus, hormones play a massive part in that. We're not always in control."

"That sounds unnerving."

"It is. It's like you try to figure out if they like you. You don't want to embarrass yourself if they don't like you the same. It gets interesting, to say the least."

"Not sure if I'm going to like this avenue of real life." Gemma groaned. "Let's talk about something good. What's Texas like? I keep hearing you guys are taking us back there."

"Hot and humid!" Lindsey exclaimed. "Especially when you're used to Maine weather."

"Yes...and no. We saw a lot of cold and snow up there, but the summers were beautiful. We weren't outside a lot. The Professor kept us busy."

"What did you do for Vitamin D?"

Gemma furrowed her brow. "What do you mean?"

"Sunlight is a natural Vitamin D. Your skin and body need it."

"I'm not sure what you're talking about. I know he gave us vitamins all the time. Sometimes he had us go to a room and lay under the lights with our eyes closed."

Lindsey nodded. "Bet they were UV lights."

"Not sure what that means."

"Don't worry about it." Lindsey waved her off. "Now, let's

see. Texas. Well, the summers reach temperatures easily between ninety to one hundred and ten degrees."

"That's hot!" Gemma exclaimed, wide-eyed.

"Yep. Our winters are normally mild. There are some rare winters where we get freak snow or ice storms. However, we're normally between forty to sixty degrees in the winter."

"That's it?" Gemma asked, amazed.

"Yep. Our winters are our reward for surviving the summers."

"I see."

"Spring and fall are my favorite seasons."

"Why?"

"Well, in the spring, everything is green, gardens and trees get planted, flowers grow, and everything just seems fresh and new. Of course, spring in Texas is also the most dangerous part of the year."

"Why?"

"It's tornado season."

"As in…?"

"Yes. They're usually F0s through F3s in East Texas, but every once and a while, there is a freaky one that is stronger, or there are multiple at a time. It's enough to wreak havoc on your property if you're in the path of one of those monsters. However," Lindsey looked at her over her glasses, "you could probably push it away from your property."

"What do you mean?"

"With your gift. Can't you push it with your telekinesis? Are you strong enough for that?"

Gemma considered it for a moment. "I probably could."

"The wildflowers are gorgeous in the spring," Lindsey continued. "Especially if you find bluebells."

"What are bluebells?"

"They're the state flower. They're really pretty. You can't pick them in Texas. It's illegal."

"Seriously?"

"Seriously. I'll show you a picture when we have the benefit of finally being online again."

"I'm really curious."

"It's a Texas pride thing," Lindsey explained. "Anyway, there's also the fall. In the fall, there is a lot of rain, but the cooler weather allows for bonfires."

"What are those?"

"Bonfires?"

"Yes."

"Oh! That's right," Lindsey said, face-palming herself. "There's a lot you don't know. Okay." She took a deep breath. "A bonfire is a huge pile of wood that's lit on fire. Usually, people talk, sing, and have fun relaxing as the fire burns. Then, as it goes down, we roast these fluffy things called marshmallows."

"What do they taste like?"

"Marshmallows?"

"Yes."

"They have this creamy, sugar-vanilla taste. They are simply delightful! When we roast them, it turns the marshmallows into a gooey mess. Then, we place them in between two graham crackers with a chocolate bar."

Gemma's eyes widened. "That sounds amazing!"

"You have no idea! Stick with me, and I'll introduce you to some of the most amazing things ever!"

"You got it!"

As Megan watched the movie, she would periodically see things. For example, she thought she saw a spider on the wall out of the corner of her eye. She jumped and looked closer. Shaking her head, she let out a slow breath of air and returned to the movie.

Tanya would feel Megan periodically jump. She understood why as she battled visions on her own. She would see shadows or things cross in front of their window, even though they were several stories up. The sounds were worse. She would hear things that sounded as if someone was in the bathroom or out in the hallway. Sometimes she heard voices. As she fought sleep, she also fought the hallucinations.

Mac laid on the bed with his arms crossed above his head. He would yawn and stretch once and a while. He heard periodic gasps from the girls in the bed next to him. He would glance at them out of the corner of his eye to make sure they were okay, but not to cause attention. He did not want to embarrass them. As it was, he was fighting the same things. Sometimes it felt like a bug was crawling on his skin. He would jump and rub the area, only to find absolutely nothing there. *It was going to be a long few days!*

As they watched the movie, and Bells rested her head on Shawn's chest, her eyes got heavy. She thought if she closed them for just a few minutes, it should not be a problem. They almost burned when she closed them after being awake for so long, so she rested them for a bit longer, listening to the sound of Shawn's heartbeat.

# TIME'S UP

**Time flies over us, but leaves its shadow behind." Nathaniel
Hawthorne**

"We really need to hurry up," Deanna said as they neared Omaha, Nebraska.

"Hold your horses. We still have almost nineteen hours to keep those little ones awake," Wyatt reminded her. "I'm going as fast as I can. If I go any faster, we could get pulled over, and it'll take longer. And I don't even think my badge would get me out of the pack of trouble this van looks to be carrying. There's blood on the floor, bullet holes in the van, a window shot out, multiple children of various ages, and one adult. It doesn't look good."

"I'm tired!" Yvette whined.

"Me too! Why can't we sleep?" Ulyssa asked.

"I'm sorry, darlin'." Wyatt shook his head. "No one can sleep until we get to the others."

"Why not?" Xander demanded.

"Honestly, it would be an easier trip if you could, but we can't," Wyatt said. "If we do, some people really close to us, including two more of your sisters, could be in serious trouble."

"Why?" Sydney asked.

"Because The Professor will find them and do bad things," Deanna explained.

"Daddy will hurt them?" Sydney asked.

"Yes. You don't want that, do you?" she asked.

"No."

"Then, we need to stay awake."

"I know a way. Hang on, folks, it's about to get loud in here," Wyatt said, flipping through the radio stations until he found a fun song.

Together, while Wyatt sang, the kids laughed and danced across the rest of the state. Periodically, the two vans would stop for bathroom breaks and to pick up energy drinks. Wyatt was not sure if he would survive this trip sane with all the children. They were either crying, whining, laughing, or fighting. Deanna did her best to play referee, but even she was getting pushed to her limits.

⊕⊕⊕⊕

"CAN YOU TELL ME A STORY?" Zoey asked Holly when they were back on the road again.

"I can if you promise not to go to sleep," Holly warned.

"Here, kids, have another energy drink," Blake said, passing them to everyone in the van. "Especially you, Colby."

"No doubt!" Colby said. "All this driving is not helping."

While Holly and Adam told the kids in the van a story from one of Holly's many stories she made up through the years, Colby, Alex, and Blake talked, and Eddie paid attention to both conversations.

"What happens if one of the others goes to sleep?" Colby

asked.

"No one should," Alex said. "We warned them."

"Shouldn't and won't are two different things. I can honestly say that I could crash somewhere right now if given the opportunity," Colby confessed. "It wouldn't take but a moment."

"We warned them," Alex said, worry creasing her face.

"Accidents happen," Blake said. "And, quite honestly, if it does, I won't fault anyone…especially if it's Bells or Gemma. Those two have been up this entire time. Wyatt's van has too."

"True, but the other van has screaming kids to keep them up. Those in Pennsylvania don't," Colby pointed out. "Seriously, telling them to stay awake this long without sleep is a huge task."

"And, if Bells or Gemma used their gifts, it would drain them, making them even more exhausted," Adam pointed out. "That's not even adding in the emotional toll it has taken on them from losing Freya."

"I didn't think about that," Blake admitted. "I wish there was a way for us to somehow connect with them to keep them awake."

"There's not. We're going to have to rely on them to keep each other awake," Colby said. "Lord willing, they'll stay awake."

"They've already been awake for sixty-eight hours," Alex reminded them. "I don't know how much longer they can stay awake at this point."

"As long as they have to," Eddie said. "Everyone's counting on them."

BELLS FELL DEEPER and deeper into sleep. Soon, she was dreaming of her and Shawn at a school dance. She saw dances on television and in movies and wanted to experience one for herself. The kiss earlier was her first experience with a boy. She was glad it was with Shawn. He was handsome, funny, smart, and seemed to be a gentleman around her. She hoped her assessment was correct.

"Would you care to dance with me?" he asked in his suit, with his hand outstretched toward her.

Bells was dressed in a navy-blue beaded bodice dress, with a sweetheart neckline and strap back. Her skirt was navy-blue chiffon that went to the floor. Her brown hair was in a French twist with a few loose strands. The colors set off her chocolate-brown eyes.

To her, Shawn was beyond handsome. He was wearing a navy-blue tuxedo, with a black bow tie and black lapels. The pair looked like they were created to be together. Exact opposites in their coloring, they still seemed to fit.

"Of course, fine, sir," Bells said as she curtsied in front of him.

He chuckled. "You're cute."

"Thank you." She smiled and blushed.

He rested one hand on her waist while he took her other hand into his, and they twirled onto the dance floor. All of the students were there, dancing, laughing, and having a good time. Bells soaked in the idea of being his date. She rested her head on his shoulder for the slow song as they swayed with the music.

◑◑◑◑

THE PROFESSOR LAID down on the couch with his hands resting on his chest. Knowing the six were still sedated, he could relax and try to find the others.

He did his best to bounce from mind to mind, hoping one of them would be asleep. His frustration grew, so he had to fight it to stay focused.

Suddenly, he made a connection. His eyes flew open.

122

"Gotcha."

⟨⟩⟨⟩

"BELLS?" Shawn jostled her after she did not answer him if she wanted something to eat. "Bells!" he said, getting louder.

"Is she asleep?" Megan asked as the others abruptly sat up.

Climbing over Megan and Tanya's bed to get to her, Mac jostled her when he got to her. "Bells! Wake up!"

⟨⟩⟨⟩

"THE KING and Queen for this year's prom are Isabelle and Shawn!" the announcer said. "And to present her crown is Isabelle's dad!"

The Professor made his way to the stage. Bells gasped at seeing him. "No, no, no, no, no!" She shook her head. "No! He can't!"

"Bells!" she heard people shouting at her. "Wake up!"

"Come to me, sweet Isabelle," The Professor said with an evil grin. She obediently went to the stage. He reached down to help her on stage. With her hand in his, he winked as he said, "Gotcha."

Bells gasped…and suddenly sat up in bed, heart racing. "I'm sorry!" she said, tears streaming down her face. "I'm so sorry!"

Shawn grabbed her and held her close. "It's understandable. You've been awake longer than any of us."

"No! He knows where we are!" she said, body shaking. "He saw me! I'm so sorry! What are we going to do?"

"Does he know our exact location when he does this?" Megan asked, as she and Tanya were sitting on their bed to give her space. Mac sat down on the bed with them since Bells was now awake.

"He knows what state," she said. "That's why it took Alex a

year to find Hope and Ben. He knew they were in Texas, but she had to figure out where."

"So, he knows we're in Pennsylvania," Megan said, thinking through the different cities.

"What's going through that genius brain of yours?" Mac asked.

"There are multiple cities he'll check. There's Scranton, Allentown, here in Philadelphia, then there's Harrisburg, Lancaster, Pittsburgh…it could still take him a while to find us," she explained. "Unfortunately, we don't have the luxury of him having to look through several other states first."

"We just have to hold out for eighteen more hours," Tanya said, looking at her watch. "C'mon, guys!" she said, looking up at the ceiling as if they could hear her. "Hurry up!"

"We need to call the hospital and make sure Gemma doesn't go to sleep," Bells said, worried. "If-if I fell asleep, she could just as easily do the same. I had a nap after I worked with Hope for several hours."

"That may be the difference," Shawn said. "You used your gift. She didn't. She may still be okay."

"Making someone stay awake for almost ninety hours is a huge task," Megan pointed out. "Using your gift or not. We're pushing the seventy-two-hour mark ourselves."

"I'll call and tell them what happened," Tanya said, picking up the phone.

"They're going to be mad," Bells said, still shaking. "They're going to hate me."

"Bells, you know what everyone here is feeling. Is there even an ounce of hate in this room toward you?" Shawn asked.

Bells shook her head.

"Trust me," Shawn continued. "Gemma probably wishes she could go to sleep too. I wouldn't be surprised if it's starting to make her sick."

"I know my head feels woozy," Bells admitted.

"Between using your gift for so long and not feeling good, I'm not surprised you fell asleep," Shawn said.

"Probably more like passed out," Tanya added. "No one blames you. We're just going to have to be careful not to get so comfortable."

Bells nodded while Tanya dialed the hospital to put them on alert.

"It'll be okay," Shawn said. "Just relax."

"Not too much," Mac reminded her. "Just calm down, so you're not shaking anymore."

"I know we don't want it, but we have to have more caffeine," Megan said. "I know I don't feel good right now either. I feel like I have vertigo."

"I'll go get some soda out of the vending machine," Mac offered.

"I'll go with you," Megan said, and they left the room.

"Think she'll be okay?" Mac asked as they headed down the hallway.

"She will in time. We all just have to survive the next twenty-four hours."

"Why twenty-four?"

"Hope's not awake yet. They'll get here in about eighteen or nineteen hours. Wyatt's going to have to figure out a way to get her transported to Texas. After that, we need to load up and get out of Pennsylvania. New Jersey's the closest way to get out of the state."

"That's going the wrong way," Mac pointed out.

"But it will get us out of Pennsylvania."

"Even if we make it all the way to Texas, he'll find us," Mac said. Standing in front of the machine, he started buying sodas for everyone. "He knows where our families live. We can't bring this back with us. Those kids will be our only way to get rid of him for good."

"What are you saying?"

He stood and looked her in the eyes as he adamantly stated, "The only way for all of us to be free is for him to die."

"Mac! You can't be serious!"

"Do you honestly think he'll get arrested? If he does, can you, without a doubt, imagine he will stay in jail long enough to stand trial? The only way for everyone to be able to breathe is for him to die."

Megan went pale "Who's going to do it?"

"That's an excellent question," Mac said, handing her a few of the cans while he carried the others. "That's going to be up to God."

❊❊❊❊

"I'M GOING to be leaving for a few days," The Professor explained to all eight guards in the suite. "You four will be in charge of keeping them under sedation. Do you understand?"

"Yes, sir," the four said in unison.

"That means you four will come with me. We have a few subjects to find."

"Yes, sir," the other four said without wavering.

"Sir?" the head guard, Felix, asked.

"Yes, Felix?" The Professor asked.

"Where are we going?"

"On a hunt," he said with a sinister grin.

"Right. But to where?"

"Pennsylvania."

"That's a big state, sir," one of the other guards, Pacey, stated.

"Well then, Pacey, looks like we have to act quickly," The Professor said, "before we lose them."

"Yes, sir."

"Don't worry. I'm sure you'll be able to have some fun, gentleman," he said to all his guards. "Their time is up."

# TIME'S RUNNING OUT

**"The future is something which everyone reaches at the rate of sixty minutes an hour, whatever he does, whoever he is."**
**C.S. Lewis**

"Where are we?" Adam asked.

The kids in their van were telling their own stories, thanks to Holly teaching them how to make up stories. They were outlandish, but it was keeping them awake and entertained. They were so tired. The stories they created did not make sense, but they would break out in fits of laughter over them, so the older ones let them go.

"Close to Chicago, Illinois," Colby said. "Wyatt's moving."

"Isn't he afraid of us getting pulled over?" Adam asked.

Holly and Blake laughed. "I don't think he cares anymore," Holly explained when Adam gave her a questioning look.

"I see," Adam said. "If we get pulled over, how are we going to explain all the kids?"

Alex furrowed her brow. "I have to admit, this won't look good,"

"He just has to keep us clear for the next twelve to thirteen hours," Colby said. "I have a feeling he'll be able to get us out of any tickets with his badge."

"Good point," Blake said. "How do you think the others are doing?"

"Others as in the other van?" Eddie asked. "Or others, pertaining to the other crew?"

"The other crew. I'm sure poor Deanna's probably pulling her hair out about now." Blake chuckled. "I know Justin and Mitch will help. We probably should have separated a little more balanced."

"So we can all lose sanity?" Eddie asked, and everyone laughed. "That won't help anyone."

"True," Holly agreed. "At least they're cute."

Eddie rolled his eyes. "As tired as they are, that's their only redeeming quality at this point."

"Ease up," Colby reprimanded them. "They've had it just as bad as the rest of you. The ones we should be seriously concerned for are those kids still in The Professor's custody."

"How are we going to get them away from him?" Alex asked.

"I would highly recommend a little sleep before we do anything," Colby said. "I don't think any of us are alert enough to help anyone."

"We have to be," Eddie said. "When we come against him, we'll have no choice."

⬤⬤⬤⬤

"THANK YOU. I'll make sure she stays awake," Lindsey said and hung up.

"What happened?" Gemma asked.

"Bells accidentally fell asleep."

"Oh no." Gemma groaned, dropping her head in her hand, shaking it. "How much does he know."

"He knows what state, but that's it. We don't know what city he's hitting first," Lindsey said. "Honestly, I'm not upset at her. It could have happened to any of us. The two of you have been up this entire time. At least our group had one good night of sleep. You two haven't had one since this started."

"True. I don't really feel good. It's a combination of woozy, dizzy, and nauseous."

"Probably overtired, along with heavy doses of caffeine. You've been eating, right?"

"We had dinner in the hotel," Gemma said.

"Okay. Anything else since?"

"No."

"What if I go get us sandwiches from the vending machine?" Lindsey offered.

"I think that would be good. Maybe some crackers while you're at it?" Gemma suggested.

"Great. I'll be right back. We need to be on our toes. We don't know when or if he'll find us. If he does, we need to be strong."

When Lindsey left, Gemma took Hope's hand into hers and quietly said, "Hope, we could be in trouble here soon. The Professor knows we're in Pennsylvania. Don't fault Bells. Sitting with you took a lot out of her. So, we really need you to wake up. The sooner you wake, the sooner we can get out of here."

"Sir, how are we going to narrow down where they are if we're only hitting big cities?" Liam, one of the guards with The Professor asked. The Professor's private plane was descending into Scranton, Pennsylvania, at the Wilkes-Barre Scranton International Airport.

"Hope should be in a hospital," The Professor explained. "We go to the hospitals and see if she's in there. You, gentlemen, are handsome and charismatic. I'm sure between the five of us, we can find out if they have a Jane Doe, Hope Hunt, or Grace Matthews in their hospital."

"That shouldn't be too difficult," Craig, another guard, said. "Just find a couple nice nurses and do our magic."

"That's why you're with me, gentlemen," The Professor said with a smile. "It won't take us long in each city. We'll hit the big cities and then move to the smaller."

Felix raised his hand.

"Yes, Felix?" The Professor asked.

"I don't mean to be a pain. And I'm not questioning your brilliance. I'm just curious. How do you know they're not in a smaller town?"

"Because it's easier to hide in a big city. Trust me on this."

❦❦❦❦

"TOLEDO," Colby said aloud as they passed a sign. "Welcome to Ohio, folks."

"What's in Toledo?" Adam asked.

"It's a decent-sized city," Colby explained. "It's got quite a bit, but the bigger stuff is in the Cleveland area."

"Like what?" Eddie asked, interested.

"Well," Colby thought through what he knew, "there's the Rock n' Roll Hall of Fame. There are malls and markets."

"What's a mall?" Adam asked.

Colby raised his eyebrows in surprise. "A mall? Well, um, it's this place where there are a lot of stores in one building or area. There are various kinds, like outlet malls, where you can get name brand stuff at great prices."

"Some of the outlet malls are still pretty high priced, though," Alex pointed out.

"Sometimes there are outside malls, and sometimes there are inside malls," Colby continued.

"Usually, teenagers like to walk around them," Holly added.

"Why?" Adam asked.

"Well, man, it's like this," Blake said, resting his hand on Adam's shoulder, "the girls love going to the mall. That allows us guys to notice them."

"Not all girls," Holly groaned. "Not all of us are mall rats."

"Actually, most of us aren't that way anymore," Alex pointed out. "Malls have lost their attraction lately. They used to be a great place to hang out…especially around the holidays. That would be an easy way to go shopping because you wouldn't have to get in and out of your vehicle to change stores. You could also be pickier because if you liked what you found several stores back, you could just walk back and get it."

"I can see the attraction," Adam said. "On all counts."

"There are also markets. Those are different than malls," Colby continued. "Markets are smaller vendors or shops. You can find some really unique things there."

"I can only imagine," Adam said.

"You'll see," Blake encouraged. "There are multiple markets in Texas. There's a huge one we go to called First Mondays of Canton. It's only open one weekend a month in Canton, Texas. You could seriously walk the whole thing for a few days and still not see it all."

Adam's jaw dropped. "Wow!"

"There's a lot we can do down in Texas," Blake said. "And once the rodeos start, Shawn, Mac, and Colby ride in those."

"I don't ride in them anymore," Colby said.

"Shawn and Mac do," Holly added. "Colby's there more for support."

"They're really cool," Blake went on. "I think everyone will like them."

"One of these days, we'll have to take them to a Ranger game," Colby said.

"We went to a couple of those, too," Blake said. "They're fun!"

"Ranger?" Adam asked.

"Baseball," Colby explained.

"Baseball?" Adam asked.

"Sports," Colby translated.

Adam shrugged. "Okay."

"We'll introduce you to all sorts of fun things," Blake said. "We just have to get there."

"First, we have to get to Philly," Colby corrected. "There are people counting on us."

"I think maybe we should find out what gifts we have in this van, and then I'll get ahold of the other van," Eddie suggested. "We can figure out a plan that way."

"We really didn't plan this well," Adam said, looking at who was in their van. "Blake, can you go to the other van when we stop next?"

"That won't be too long." Colby pointed to the gas gauge sitting on the line above empty. "Our gas is pretty low."

"If he goes, I would like to go too," William spoke up.

"What if we bring some of the other kids over here too?" Colby suggested. "That way, the vans are more balanced. Wyatt and Deanna really shouldn't lose complete sanity. We need them."

"Agreed," Blake said. "Let's figure out how to divide better."

◑◑◑◑

THEY DROVE for the next ten hours, trading out vehicles to give the kids variety. That also allowed everyone to get to know everyone else.

Throughout that time, The Professor and his men visited multiple cities. Starting with Scranton, they then went to Williamsport, Erie, Pittsburgh, Altoona, State College, Harrisburg, and then Lancaster. Hopping between the various airports, they had a plan, which sometimes meant separating to hit all the hospitals.

Systematically, they searched the bigger cities and hospitals until there was only one big city left...Philadelphia. The race was on!

# DUE TIME

"TIME IS WHAT WE WANT THE MOST, BUT
WHAT WE USE THE WORST." WILLIAM
PENN

Finally pulling into the hotel parking deck, everyone was beyond exhausted. For the past several hours, those in the vans fought to keep each other alert and focused.

"Finally!" Colby said, putting the van in park and turning it off. "Hallelujah!"

"My body feels like we're still driving," Holly said, opening the sliding door so Eddie could get out first.

As everyone else slowly left the vans, they all felt a little tipsy. "This is so not cool!" Deanna remarked, toppling into one of the concrete pillars in the parking deck, catching herself.

"Give it time," Wyatt encouraged.

The younger kids held the hands of the older kids on the way up. They separated into three elevators to get to the floor. "Not sure how we're all going to sleep, but we'll figure it out," Wyatt said to Colby, Alex, and Adam in the elevator.

"Not sure how much sleep we're really going to get until Hope's released and we're out of Pennsylvania," Colby pointed out.

"At this point, we're not really fit to drive," Wyatt added.

"I agree. However, we have more drivers now," Colby countered.

⬦⬦⬦⬦

EDDIE, Justin, and Mitch were the first to reach the floor. "Gentlemen," Eddie gestured for them to get out of the elevator.

"That's okay. You first," Justin said. "You know where you're going."

"True," Eddie said. He wheeled out of the elevator and down the hall with the other two behind him. Resting his hand on the doorknob, the hairs on his neck stood on end. He slowly removed his hand.

"What's wrong?" Justin asked. "Are we are the wrong room?"

"I –" Eddie stopped short. He did not hear a sound on the other side of the door. He felt a huge amount of terror, though. "They're in trouble," he whispered.

Wyatt's elevator made it next, closely followed by the girls and Blake in the third elevator. When they walked out, Eddie put his hand out to stop them in their tracks.

"Just a sec," Adam said. He closed his eyes, and thought to Eddie, *What's wrong?*

*Terror. Sheer terror.*

*Where?*

*On the other side of the door.*

*Just a sec.* Adam grumbled before looking toward Wyatt and Alex. He whispered, "Something's wrong in the room."

"What does that mean?" Wyatt hissed. "We're finally here. How could something be wrong already?"

"Terror."

Eddie waved Holly and Deanna over and sent Justin and Mitch back to the others down the hall. Wyatt and Alex ran

136

down the hall behind Holly and Deanna, leaving Colby with the kids. When the four of them reached the room, Eddie pointed toward the door and mouthed, *Count of three?*

When they nodded, Eddie held up one finger. Then, two. Finally, three. On the third, he opened the door. They were not expecting what they saw! Momentarily stunned, they stood there frozen.

Megan and Tanya were duct-taped to chairs, with their feet in water. There were tanks slowly heating the water. Both of their faces were red, and they were sweating profusely. Mac was soaked, as were his clothes, as he sat on the floor. His hands were duct-taped around the bottom of the bed frame while his head rested on the bed. He looked exhausted. Shawn was drug out of the bathroom, soaked to the skin. Bells walked out behind him, with The Professor's hand firmly on her shoulder. Tears streaked her face. There were also three rather large men in the room with the teens, and the fourth walked out of the bathroom behind The Professor.

"Daddy!" Alex said, horrified.

"What in blazes is going on here?" Wyatt boomed.

"Wyatt, I know I promised you, but I also had a stipulation," Eddie said, with his knuckles white, gripping the armrest of his wheelchair. "Can I go nuclear now?" he asked through clenched teeth.

"Absolutely!" Deanna gave him permission. "If you don't, I will!"

Eddie lifted The Professor into the air. Before anyone had a chance to react, he snapped his neck. He was gone in a split second. His body dropped to the floor in a heap. Alex gasped.

"Who's next?" Eddie demanded.

Holly and Deanna rushed past Eddie into the room. Deanna lifted two of the guys into the air by levitation and slammed them together. When it did not knock them out, Eddie snapped both of their necks at the same time. Deanna let their bodies fall to the floor in a heap.

Holly had the other two in the air by their throats. "Where are the others?" she demanded.

"Never!" one shouted. The other one just shook his head.

Wyatt and Alex rushed past Eddie into the room. Wyatt used the switchblade in his pocket to release Mac while Alex stopped the tanks from heating the water. Together, they released Megan and Tanya from the tape. Meanwhile, Shawn dropped to the ground on his hands and knees before falling to his side, exhausted and waterlogged. Bells ran over to him and put his head on her lap.

Eddie wheeled into the room. He glanced into the bathroom to see the tub filled with water. He knew The Professor must have been holding both Mac's and Shawn's heads under the water to get Bells to give up Hope's location. Anger pulsed through him once again. He narrowed his eyes at the guards in the air. "What did you do?" he demanded.

The guards laughed.

Eddie lost it. Despite Holly's hold on them, Eddie snapped the first guy's leg. The guy shouted at the top of his lungs in pain. "What did you do?" Eddie growled.

Tears streaked down his face, but the guard still did not say anything.

"Enough!" Eddie said and threw his body through the window. Then he turned toward the other one. "Want to join him?"

"N-n-no," the guard stammered.

"Count of three! What did you do?"

The guard tightened his lips.

"One?" Eddie said. *Nothing.* "Two," Eddie said with a warning tone. *Still nothing.* "Three! What did you do?" When the guard shook his head, Eddie broke both of his legs, and the man let out an ear-shattering scream.

"Let's try something else," Eddie said. "Where are the other kids?"

"You'll never find them," the guard growled, tears streaking down his bright red, almost purple, sweaty face.

"Last time!" Eddie warned. "This is your last chance to save your life!"

The man swore at Eddie, so Eddie threw him out the window to his death as well.

Wyatt ran to the window and looked down to see a pool of blood coming out from under both guards. "How do I clean up this mess?"

"And how do we find the others?" Deanna asked.

"They-he said." Megan was shaking but tried to form a complete thought. "B-Boston."

"I know where they are," Alex said confidently as she helped Megan off the chair. "He has a favorite hotel there."

"Great. However, there are five dead bodies, and two of them are outside," Wyatt said sternly. "And we still haven't checked on Hope. How am I supposed to explain this? This room looks like a torture chamber!"

"Not sure, but you'd better call the police before the hotel does," Holly said, gesturing out the window toward the hotel desk clerk, who was looking at the bodies with a phone in his hand.

Wyatt grumbled under his breath. "Take these five to one of the other rooms down the hall with the other kids, and get everyone calmed down," he ordered Deanna, Holly, and Eddie. "Lock the door behind you. Only answer if it's me. Keep everyone quiet. I know you're scared, but you're going to have to be strong for the younger kids."

"Yes, sir," Holly said.

As the teens left, Alex and Wyatt looked around the room, shaking their heads.

"What do we do?" Alex asked.

Wyatt picked up the hotel room phone. "We call the police. Holly's right. It'll be better coming from me than for them to find us here. Can you go down the hall with the others to keep the younger kids calm? Here's the keycard."

"I can do that," she agreed. Taking one last look at the heap that was her father, Alex shook her head and left the room. Once the door closed behind her, she whispered, "Checkmate."

⊕⊕⊕⊕

HOLLY, Deanna, and Eddie herded everyone toward the rooms down the hall, so they could separate into both of the boy's rooms. They divided the younger siblings into two beds in one room. Then showed Justin and Mitch how to work the remote. Eddie stayed in the room with them while the others went to the other room. They left the door open.

"It won't matter," Holly said, coming into the older teen's room once she got everyone settled. The teens were separated onto the beds, the chair, and they pulled out the sofa bed. "There are kids with super hearing and mind-reading over there. If they want to know what's going on in here, they will."

"True," Colby said. He got off the chair he was sitting in and wrapped his arms around her. "I'm sorry. This has been a nightmare."

"The nightmare is over," Deanna said firmly.

Alex walked into the room. When everyone looked up in surprise, she held up the keycard and explained, "Wyatt's got that end of things covered. I'm going in there to keep the younger ones calm."

"That would be appreciated," Eddie said, hanging in the doorway between the rooms. "I would rather be in here."

"We would rather you stayed in here and helped us figure this out," Holly said to Alex.

Alex smiled. "Really? You want my help?"

"Alex, there is no winner in any of this," Holly explained. "We need to work together to navigate everyone through this. I would appreciate your assistance. You have more experience in this sort of thing."

"I do," she agreed. "If you're looking for my opinion, I think we should empty the Maine facility and blow it up," Alex said. "That's where a lot of the information is stored. It was backed up to the other facilities, which you already took out. I feel the Maine one needs to go, too, in order to keep everyone safe."

"Don't we need to get some sleep first?" Colby asked. "Frankly, with everything we've been through, I have no idea how we're all standing."

"I can't sleep right now." Tanya shuddered. Blake pulled her close to him. She laid her head on his shoulder as she admitted, "It was like something out of a horror movie. They drowned Mac at least three times into unconsciousness while they continued to heat up the water at our feet. We couldn't get free."

"They did it to me at least five times," Shawn said, dropping his head into his hands.

"That's because he knew we were close," Bells admitted. "I'm sorry. This is all my fault."

Tanya shook her head. "He would have found us eventually."

"Not anywhere near as quickly," Bells said. "I fell asleep. He found us that way."

"That saved us from having to search him out," Eddie said, staying at his position in the doorway so he could keep an eye on both rooms. "He would have found us down in Texas."

"If he did, he could have tortured our families," Megan added. "Now, once y'all take down the Maine facility and find the other kids still missing, then we're all free to go to Texas without looking over our shoulders."

There was a knock on the door. When Alex answered it,

Wyatt walked into the room. "Hey, guys," he said, rubbing the back of his neck, "I need to ask you a favor."

"What?" Shawn asked.

"I told the cops I was searching for you because of the AMBER Alert. I told them I finally found you guys in the room, and you were being tortured. I lied. I told them I killed everyone. They still want to see you guys and talk to you. Also, Lindsey's still MIA. We need to account for her. This will help cancel out the AMBER Alert on you guys."

"If this will help clear everything, we're all for it. What do you need from us?" Tanya asked.

"Get Lindsey here. Her DNA and fingerprints are all over those rooms," Wyatt explained. "She's also included in the AMBER Alert. She needs to be here when y'all talk to them."

"Got it," Shawn said, getting on the phone.

"Also," he rubbed the back of his neck again, "I may need y'all to get together and come up with a story before I take you to them."

"Wyatt, it's okay," Mac encouraged. "We know we have to lie."

"Just make it convincing. Holly? Maybe you can coach them?"

"I can," she agreed.

"Great. Thank you."

"She'll be here shortly." Shawn hung up the phone. "She has to get a ride on the trolley. It will be about seven to ten minutes, depending on how close the trolley is to the hospital. She'll get here as soon as possible."

"Then, you all come up with a believable story while I delay the police and crime scene people. In the meantime, keep it quiet down here, please?" Wyatt asked. "I'll be back." With that, he left.

"What kind of story are we going to come up with?" Megan asked. "I'm not good at lying."

"Need to stay as close to the truth as possible." Holly started pacing as she worked out the story in her mind. Everyone silently watched while she paced back and forth, lost in her thoughts.

Finally, just as Lindsey was let in the room by Mac, Holly said, "Got it!"

"Got what?" Lindsey asked. Then she got a look at everyone in the room. "What happened? Shawn said to get over here as soon as possible. There are cops everywhere, and you all look horrible!"

"Lindsey, go take your hat and glasses off, and get into the shower…fully clothed," Holly instructed.

"I–what?" She furrowed her brow. "Why would I do that?"

"Please?" Holly asked. "Just enough so your clothing and hair are soaked. Go ahead and take your shoes and socks off, so it looks like you were already here. When you get out, just wrap yourself in a towel, but keep your clothes on."

"Random, but okay." Lindsey shrugged. With that, she went into the bathroom. It did not take her long to come back out in a towel and her clothes. "Now," she asked, sitting on the bed, "what's going on?"

Megan, Tanya, Bells, Eddie, and Holly filled her in on everything that happened. By the time they finished, Lindsey sat there for a moment, stunned. "So, if I'm following you correctly, it's over?"

"Almost," Holly corrected her. "There are some loose ends that need to be tied. Once the police talk to y'all, we'll have to get Hope sorted. Then, we head to Boston to find the other kids and deal with the guards we're sure are there as well."

"Then, we make sure to get to Maine and blow up that facility, too, before heading back to Texas," Alex finished.

"Wow. Okay. I missed quite a lot. Makes me want to head back to the hospital. It's calmer there," Lindsey said. "I'm really sorry y'all had to go through that."

"*You* did too." Shawn emphasized the word *you* to make a point.

"Is that why I'm wet?" she asked.

"Yes. You got drowned a couple times as well."

"What information were they trying to get from us?" Lindsey asked.

"That's what Holly's about to tell us," Shawn said, looking toward Holly. "What's it going to be, Coach?"

"Okay," Holly started. "While you were in Texas, you knew something happened to Hope and Ben. You guys tried to figure it out. The chase was on the news, so that's public knowledge."

"Right," Mac said. "I'm following you."

"So, while searching, it seems you tripped some kind of red flag, and you were followed. In fear of your lives and the lives of your families, you ran."

"This is all mostly true," Colby said. "I like it. Keep going."

"This is where it gets creative," Holly warned. "So pay attention."

Wyatt walked into the room. "Ready?"

"Just a minute." Megan nodded toward Holly. "We're getting our story."

"Then…" Wyatt gestured for her to go on as he leaned against the wall, crossing his arms.

"Okay, so Wyatt was on vacation when he found out y'all were missing," Holly continued. "He left his vacation in a search for you teens."

"Sounds plausible," Wyatt said. "Go on."

"He knew you from church, so when he found out it was you all who were missing, he made it a priority to find you. So, Wyatt tracked you guys through the states. He lost the trail near Pennsylvania. That's where he focused his search until he finally found you," Holly said, satisfied. "Now for the details. They found you guys," she said, pointing toward the Willow Bend teens, "just outside of Texas, where you lost your phones, but y'all got away."

"Good!" Megan said, encouraged. "This is keeping really close to our story."

"Right. Now, they wanted to know what you knew, but you guys got away. You guys said you did a lot of research in town, so that will track. And you were researching The Professor, so that will track as well."

"Right!" Tanya said, smiling. "Like it. Keep going."

"So, they finally caught up to you in Kentucky," Holly continued. "To keep you in between where they found you in Kentucky and where The Professor was in Maine, they brought you here."

Wyatt nodded in approval. "That makes sense."

"Then, *you* finally tracked them here," Holly said to Wyatt. Walking over to Colby, she took some duct tape from the bag Wyatt brought up from the van, from when they buried Freya's body. She picked up Colby's hands and put them together. "When you found them," she continued as she wrapped Colby's wrists with the duct tape. "Colby was secured to the base of the bed. He would have been next," she said, tearing the tape. She patted it to secure it. "Mac and Lindsey were already tortured and were soaked, as they were secured to a bed frame with their heads on the bed. Megan and Tanya were in the same position they were when you found them. Shawn was in the bathroom getting drowned. Since Colby wasn't tortured yet," she said, as she ripped the tape off Colby's arms. Colby groaned in pain. "He won't have water on him." Then she went over to Lindsey to do the same thing, so they both had tape residue on their wrists. As she worked the tape on Lindsey's wrists, she continued, "You were furious when you found them in their tortured state," she said to Wyatt. "You killed The Professor first, knowing he was the one in charge because of your research." Ripping the tape off Lindsey's wrists, Lindsey squeaked in pain before she groaned.

"You then tossed Mac and Colby your knife as you fought the guys who went out the window. Shawn released Mac and Colby, and they held the other guys until Wyatt could get to them. A struggle ensued throughout the room, causing the damage until both guys Wyatt was fighting ended up going through the window. Then other two guys, who were being held by Colby, Shawn, and Mac, were killed by Wyatt breaking their necks as well."

"Brilliant!" Wyatt said, pleased. "Looks like we have all bases covered."

"Yes, and no. You," she said to Wyatt, "found Hope in the Maine facility. That's what took you so long to find the Willow Bend teens. That's why Hope is here in Philadelphia. So, Blake and I need to get over to the hospital, and Gemma needs to get back here. The gifted kids should not be anywhere near this. That includes *you*," she said to Alex.

"Fair enough," Wyatt agreed.

"I'll go with you," Bells said to Blake and Holly. "That way, Gemma doesn't have to come back alone. I already know which room to come to as well."

"Or we can call and have her just come while we head that direction," Holly countered.

"I want to go with you," Eddie said.

"Wait until they leave," Holly suggested. "We need you, Adam, Alex, and Deanna to watch the younger ones."

"Fair enough. Once they're released," he pointed toward the Willow Bend teens, "I'll head over to the hospital."

"Once they're released, *we'll* head over to the hospital," Wyatt corrected him.

"Agreed," Eddie said, heading back into the room with the other kids.

"Shawn, please call Gemma and tell her we're on our way and that she needs to get back here as soon as possible," Holly said. He nodded, so she turned to Blake and said, "Let's go."

"This is going to be fun." Wyatt stood. He turned to the others and explained, "Make sure there are variations in your stories where one shares more than another. It can't be exact. Imagine her story from your perspective. Also, remember you're in shock. If you're too exact or detailed, it will be suspicious."

"It'll be a fine balance," Megan agreed.

# TIME HEALS ALL WOUNDS

**"In the book of life, the answers aren't in the back." Charles M. Schulz**

he police finally left a few hours later. The hotel moved the two rooms for the girls. The new rooms were closer to the other two rooms, so the Willow Bend teens would feel more comfortable. Since it happened in their hotel, the hotel owners gave them the two rooms for free overnight, with a free room service meal for each of the Willow Bend teens and Wyatt. That way, they would be able to get good rest after the events of the day.

After the police left, Wyatt and Alex got everyone settled with some older and some younger kids in each room so they could sleep. Alex stayed awake to keep an eye on the rooms. If the kids woke, one of the teens in the room was to get ahold of Alex to help them. Meanwhile, Wyatt and Eddie headed toward the hospital in one of the vans.

"Thank you for letting me come," Eddie said from his seat in the second row. "The younger kids were starting to get to me."

"They're going to be asleep. This is the time you *want* to be around them," Wyatt pointed out.

"No." Eddie shook his head. "They're going to have nightmares. What everyone has gone through over the last several days will trigger them. It won't be a solid sleep."

"I follow you. Are you okay?"

"I am now," Eddie said. "At least I think I am. I protected my family."

"While I don't condone what you did, I understand it."

"I appreciate that."

"Eddie, I'm going to need that wonder-brain of yours."

"For what?"

"We need to figure out how to divide and conquer."

"I've actually been thinking about that."

"And?"

"We will need to divide and conquer, but we need to do it wisely. Hope will probably need to stay here for a bit more from what the others told me."

"I agree."

"I want to try something when we get there."

"What's that?"

"I want to see if I can find her," Eddie explained.

"I thought Bells and Adam said not to because she's in a coma. You could get locked in if she stays unconscious, or worse, stuck if she dies."

"I'm stronger than everyone else," Eddie reminded him.

"Is that why you wanted to come? You wanted to see if you could do it?"

"Yes. Also, the kid thing. Love them, but I can only handle them for so long."

"I get it. Trust me! Deanna and I had the two thirteen-year-olds and the rest were ten for most of the trip home," Wyatt said in a chuckle.

"I don't even want to know what that was like. Those in our van were slap-happy."

"I think we all were. It was almost like we were intoxicated. Okay. So, let's focus. How should we divide?" Wyatt asked.

"Let's see if I can reach Hope first."

"What if you do and don't want to leave because you actually found her?"

"Okay," Eddie said as they pulled into the hospital parking lot. When Wyatt turned off the van, he turned to Eddie and gestured for Eddie to continue. "This is what I'm thinking," Eddie started. "Leave me with one other person here in the hospital. You can bounce between the hotel and the hospital to take care of the younger kids. The one left here could be Bells or one of the Willow Bend teens. There's no more danger for us here. In the meantime, there needs to be two separate moves going on at the same time so everyone can get back here faster."

"Which are?"

"Deanna, Adam, and Mitch go with one of the Willow Bend teens to Boston and rescue the kids. In the meantime, Holly, Blake, and Alex go to Maine with one of the Willow Bend teens to take out the Maine facility."

"Okay. Why would you separate them that way?" Wyatt asked, fascinated by his mind.

"Number one, you're out of the equation. So, if they leave a mess, you're not connected. You'll be here in the hospital on camera. Just make sure you're here most of the day. Number two, Deanna is the strongest telekinetic outside of Holly and me. Adam can help her figure out where everyone is with his mind gift and the best way to get to them with the least number of injuries. However, they only need to lure the big guys out into the open, where Mitch can use his gift of persuasion to stop the men. That will free them to rescue the younger ones."

"Okay. And Holly, Blake, and Alex?"

"Alex will help them into the Maine facility. She'll also clear the facility. While she's clearing the facility, Blake and Holly can figure out what they did with Ben's body. That will give them closure. Once the facility is clear, Alex, Blake and Holly can go back to the van, and Holly will blow up the facility. She was with me at the Wyoming facility when I blew it, so she knows how to do it. She also knows how to do it with the least amount of debris damage outside of the safety parameters. And the Willow Bend teens are drivers."

"Very well thought out. I approve. Glad you're on our side."

Eddie chuckled.

"No. Really. You could use that mind for evil, but you're choosing to use it for good."

"Thank you. Now, the remainder of the Willow Bend teens, and those older ones left here, will help the little ones navigate this mess we have right now."

"One little issue with your plan."

"What's that?"

"We only have two vans. If they take both of them, we'll be here without a vehicle," Wyatt pointed out.

Eddie looked over at him and cleared his throat.

"What?"

"You know what you need to do," Eddie said.

"Seriously?" Wyatt rolled his eyes. "Do y'all think I'm made of money?"

"Do you not have it?"

"Well, I do, but..." his voice trailed. He shook his head. "I guess we'll need it to get back anyway. We're running out of space in the vans."

"Running out?" Eddie challenged.

"Okay," Wyatt said in a chuckle. "I concede. I'll get another van."

"Good. Now, let's go see if I'm as strong as I think I am,"

Eddie said, opening the sliding door with his mind as he levitated into his chair.

⌖

"OKAY, so that's the plan we need to explain to everyone?" Holly asked after Eddie reiterated the plan to her and Blake in Hope's hospital room.

"Yes," Eddie said. He wheeled to the other side of the bed. "Now to see if I can find Hope."

"Bells said she was hiding in the black room when she talked to her," Holly said.

Eddie groaned. "Perfect."

"I haven't worked with that yet," Blake said. "Why is that a problem?"

"What happens in the dark?" Eddie asked.

"Scary things?" Holly offered.

"And it's difficult to find your way out. Also, when we go in, we bring our own darkness into that room as well," Eddie explained.

"Wait," Wyatt said. "That means –"

"Yes," Eddie cut him off. "I have to face my demons too."

"Well, son, we'll be praying for you."

"While I don't believe in prayers, I have a feeling I'm going to need them," Eddie said. He took Hope's hand into his and closed his eyes. Taking a deep breath, he dove in.

⌖

EDDIE OPENED HIS EYES, surrounded by blackness. He squinted, hearing whimpering in the distance. "Hope?" he whispered loudly.

"Who-who's there?" she asked nervously.

153

In his normal voice, as he rolled toward her, he explained, "My name is Eddie. I'm one of the siblings from Maine."

"It's dark in here," she said, as he moved closer to the white and tan, gingham pattern, wingback chair in the center of the darkness. Hope was curled up in the chair with her arms wrapped around her legs.

"I know," he said calmly. "I'm here to help you. You've been in here a long time."

"Do you know how to get out?"

"You're going to have to be strong," Eddie warned, pulling up beside her, locking his chair in place. "You're going to have to fight your way through the darkness to find the light."

"Am I strong enough to do that?"

"I'm sure you are. Any woman who can handle Wyatt, The Professor, and raise two children with very strong gifts is stronger than she thinks she is."

She looked over at him and studied him for a moment before she asked, "What happened to you? Why are you in a wheelchair?"

"An accident when I was younger. My sisters were in a fight, and we got in the way," Eddie explained. "They didn't hurt us on purpose. They just wanted us out of the way. I landed near the steps and fell down them, breaking my back. It was not fixable, no matter how many surgeries that man put me through. He finally stopped trying when I was thirteen."

"How horrible! I can't imagine the pain you went through."

"It wasn't fun. I begged him to stop. Around ten years old, whenever he scheduled more surgeries, he would drug my food, so I wouldn't know until I woke up. My body was on fire every time."

"I'm so sorry that happened."

"It is what it is," Eddie said on a sigh. "However, I'm more concerned with you. You have some very concerned individuals out there who are scared for you."

"What's going on?"

"You flatlined and have been unconscious for several days."

"What?" Hope asked, wide-eyed.

"They obviously brought you back, but Bells was afraid to come back in."

"Why?"

"Because she could get stuck in here with you. Or if you pass, she would be lost too."

"Then…why are you in here?" Hope asked, sitting up in her chair, her body tense.

"Well, first off, I'm stronger than Bells. Secondly, Wyatt and your kids need you. And when I say your kids, I want to point out that there are now over twenty."

Her jaw dropped. "What?"

"Deanna, Adam, and Mitch left to get the final six. There were twenty-six of us, but we lost Charlie when he was younger. Then, during these recent missions to Wyoming and Oregon, we lost Freya. So, we're down to twenty-four."

Hope let out a low whistle. "How did y'all get out alive?"

"Well, like I said, we lost Freya in Oregon. There are still six to rescue and the Maine facility to level. We're almost done. We already leveled the Oregon and Wyoming facilities."

"Goodness! Y'all have been busy."

"And you have been sleeping. You need to wake up."

"I'm scared."

"Trust me. It's pretty scary out there!" Eddie said in a chuckle.

Suddenly, there were screams heard throughout the room.

"What was that?" Hope asked, grasping the arms of the chair. Trembling, she looked around. "I have never heard that before!"

Eddie groaned, dropping his head into his hand. "I'm sorry. That's me."

"What's that from?"

"As I said, you've missed a lot," Eddie said on a sigh.

He took the time to explain what all happened since they left Philadelphia. As he explained it, the more dramatic and graphic scenes played out in front of them. Everything from hearing the men shoot each other in the Oregon facility to finding Freya's bloody body after rescuing Mitch. They watched as they buried Freya's body. And then they watched moment-by-moment of what happened when they got to the hotel room where the Willow Bend teens and Bells were being held. The events froze when the second guard went flying through the window. He was frozen mid-air.

Hope sat there in shock. "I-I don't –" she shook her head, wiping the tears from her eyes. "I don't know what to say."

"Neither do I," Eddie admitted. "Now that I see it, I looked like a monster. Maybe I'm just like him. Like father, like son."

"No. Not true. You did what you did in defense of others. I cannot imagine what you went through all these years at the hands of that man. And to see what he did to those innocent teens is beyond reprehensible! I don't know what I would have done in the same position if I had your gifts."

"I didn't think," Eddie confessed. "I just acted. Wyatt tried to stop me."

"But you made a deal with Wyatt. You promised not to hurt anyone unless it was in the defense of others. You stopped him from hurting those teens anymore. If you didn't rid this world of that evil, none of us would have been safe. You're concerned you'll turn out like The Professor. Yes. Sometimes the sins of the father can be passed down to the next generation. However, if you make wise choices and lead with your heart, you can over-come and defeat that curse, creating your own legacy."

"Is it weird that I feel a little bad? Just a little. And, I don't feel bad for killing him. I feel bad for the teens who were tortured before we could get there to help."

"Eddie," Hope said, resting her hand on his shoulder, "you did what you did for a reason."

"But Wyatt said it wasn't good. How am I supposed to fight something that's literally in my DNA?"

"Wyatt meant it's not good under normal circumstances. These were not normal circumstances. The Professor and these circumstances were anything but normal. He was a ruthless killer who was bulletproof. He tortured for pleasure. He killed all *twenty-six* of your mothers. He thought he was a god and could get away with anything. You showed him differently. The irony is you, one of his children, was the one who finally got justice for those lives taken."

"Just say it," Eddie grumbled. "I murdered him. Not just him, but the other four, too."

"Those other men were not innocent either!" Hope declared. "Those were the ones who took me! They brought me to him to be tortured."

"They also helped as muscle when the others didn't obey in the Maine facility. They always traveled with him." Eddie sighed. "Wyatt said God wouldn't like it if I killed someone. While I don't know if I believe in God, He doesn't sound like Someone I want to make angry."

"He's not. However, in the Old Testament, God used others to do His will…including killing. Now, I'm not saying I condone it. Just like in the Bible times, you were not in normal circumstances. You guys were in a state of war. That's a completely different scenario from the average everyday situation."

"I don't understand."

"You're not God. You're not in control of who lives or who dies."

"No, but I do have the ability to take a life," he said, gesturing toward the frozen scene in front of them. The Professor was dead on the floor in a heap, two of his men were crumbled on the floor right next to each other with broken necks, and one man was mid-way through the window on his way out, while the other was already through the window. The Willow

Bend teens and Bells were in their spots from where he found them.

"You do have the ability. You could have also done a lot more damage than you actually did. There is a lot you could have done, but you chose not to."

"I didn't make wise decisions."

"I disagree. You didn't kill The Professor or the others in the Maine facility before you left."

"I almost wish I did. Then Freya would still be alive, and Gemma would still have her twin sister."

"Eddie, once again, you are not God. You are not all-powerful or all-knowing. You had no idea what would happen after you left Maine. You tried to give The Professor the opportunity to make the right choice."

"I did have an idea of what he was going to do. One of my gifts allows me to predict how someone will act within 99.9 percent accuracy."

"Really? I don't know if I would want that gift."

"That one, along with the one to retain literally everything I read, hear, and see. It's not always fun. I have seen, read, and heard some pretty horrific stuff. Adam, Blake, Bells, and the others with mind gifts can take away a memory, but I don't know if I want them to."

"I wouldn't."

"Why not?"

"Our thoughts, memories, and the events in our lives make us who we are today. That includes events like this," Hope said, gesturing toward the frozen scene in front of them. "When we go through things or run across people, they are either a lesson or a blessing. It's up to us to determine which one. If it's a lesson, we also need to determine what that lesson is."

"And what did you learn from your ordeal with The Professor, because I'm pretty sure that was not a blessing?"

"A couple things, actually," Hope said, praying for the right words. "First off, the blessings. Had I not worked at the facility, I wouldn't have had the honor of knowing Ben, nor of raising Holly and Blake. I would also not have Wyatt either because I would still be in Maine."

"Those all sound like good that came out of bad."

"They are."

"Did you know The Professor had a gift too?" Eddie asked. "He could track you to your state when you sleep? That's how he found you in the first place."

"Are you serious?"

"Yep. That was his gift. He had the gene."

"So, those nightmares I had –"

"Were him invading your dreams, turning them into nightmares."

"That man *was* a nightmare," Hope said, processing the new information. She shuddered. "What if we look at the lesson portion to take my mind off the idea of him actually being in my nightmares…literally?" She shuddered again. "That's just wrong." She took a few deep, cleansing breaths. "Okay. Let's go back to what we were talking about earlier. In Romans 12:19 through 21, it says, *'Do not take revenge, my dear friends, but leave room for God's wrath, for it is written, "It is mine to avenge; I will repay," says the Lord. On the contrary: "If your enemy is hungry, feed him; if he is thirsty, give him something to drink. In doing this, you will heap burning coals on his head." Do not be overcome by evil, but overcome evil with good.'* God wants to be the One to avenge His children. He doesn't want you to have to live with things like what you're dealing with right now. You have to live with those memories of killing those people. He created us to love one another. He wants us to live life to the fullest. He wants us to bring others to Him and show them Who He is. The main lesson I learned from The Professor is what happens when evil goes unhindered. He's what happens when good people know about his kind of evil and do nothing to stop him. We've seen the pictures of the murders. You saw what happened to Freya and Charlie."

"Makes me wonder what life would be like if that man didn't start his experiments."

"Eddie, you don't really want that."

"Why not?"

"Despite all that happened since his experiments began, you wouldn't be here if he didn't do what he did. This by no means condones what he did before, during, or since that time. It does, however, show what that man intended for evil, God used for good. You have a gift...obviously multiple. It's how you use those gifts that makes the difference between the two of you. You are not like your father. It's kind of like guns. A gun can be used as a weapon or a form of protection. A gun is an instrument...a tool. A knife is the same thing. A knife can be used to take a life. It can be used to cut meat. It can be used to clean meat after a hunting trip. It can also be used to defend when necessary. When used for evil, evil will reign. When used in defense of self or others, good comes from the use of both of those tools. Each of your gifts are a tool. In the hands of the right person, a lot of good could come of it."

"A lot of bad can as well."

"That's my point. It's not the gift, the gun, or the knife that kills. They are just tools. It's what you choose to do with them that make the difference."

"What happens when people like The Professor are around, and the law can't or won't touch them?"

"Those situations need to be assessed individually. The Professor is a perfect example of using his gifts – both in his intelligence and his dream invasion gifts – for bad. He could have chosen to do good with them. Instead, he used his intelligence to manipulate the genes of babies in the womb. When the gene was formed and the children were born, he murdered your mothers. When we chose to help two of you, he used his gift to

spy on us and send Alex after us. When the time was to his spec-
ifications, he then chose to do worse. He was given some unique
and powerful tools, but he chose to use all of them for evil. Yes,
killing is bad. It's against one of the ten commandments.
However, good can still come out of it. You are all now safe, and
you have these amazing gifts you can use to help others, and that
man is no longer in this world. I have to admit I'm not sorry
about that."

"I don't have any remorse about it either," Eddie admitted.
"He tortured and tormented all of us our entire lives, starting way
back when he killed our mothers. Did you know he cloned all of
us? That's who the younger ones are. They're our clones."

"Are you serious?"

"Yes. Did you also know he killed the women who carried
the clones too? They weren't the Beta and Gamma group's mothers. They were their carriers. He had sterile titles for all of us. He
called us, his children, subjects. He even gave us designations –
Alpha, Beta, and Gamma groups. He called our mothers…resi-
dents. He called the surrogate mothers…carriers. He did this so
people wouldn't have compassion or a connection with us. That
man severely abused all of us. He was untouchable. He left an
insane trail of bodies in his wake. His reach was unimaginable."

"These gifts…do they vary from kid to kid?

"I'm not sure. I think it's in our genes. For the most part, the
clones who look like us have some of or all the gifts we do.
Some have more. The gifts are woven into our DNA. When he
activated them, certain gifts ignited. Speaking of which, do you
feel any different?" Eddie asked.

"What do you mean?"

"He did something to your DNA. It was in those shots he
gave you in Maine. Between the poison and what he added,
we're pretty sure that's why it took Ben out so quickly. His body
may have rejected the additive. The poison would have killed
him anyway, but I think the additive sped up the process."

Hope let out a slow breath of air. "I'm pretty sure there's a special place in Hell for that man right now."

"I'm glad I was the one who sent him there."

"That's not really a good way to live," Hope pointed out.

"I know. I really don't know another way to live, though."

"I'll tell you what. What if I show you a better way?"

"How are you going to do that?"

"We've seen your darkness. What if we see my light?"

"In order to do that, we have to come out of this black room." Eddie gestured around them.

"I'm ready. How do I do that?" Hope asked, knowing Eddie needed to see the good in the world.

"If I help you to the white room, you're going to have to stay there until you wake up," Eddie warned. "I don't want you hiding again. It's not easy to get out of this room, especially if there is darkness within you like what you saw of mine."

"Deal!" she said, shaking Eddie's hand.

"Okay. This is going to take a lot of energy. Take both of my hands, close your eyes, and concentrate on the good. The memories will swirl around us, trying to tear us apart. You need to hold my hands as tightly as possible and push through the bad to get to the good."

Hope grasped Eddie's hands into hers, closed her eyes, and took a deep breath. She focused on the good memories. As painful as it was to think of Ben, she pushed through to the good thoughts.

"Stay focused," Eddie grunted, as the entire room spun around them, slowly at first, before the speed picked up, threatening to split the pair. "Hold on! Focus!" Eddie shouted.

Hope shut her eyes tighter, remembering the day she and Ben took the kids from the Maine facility. There was fear and terror surrounding the escape, so she focused on when she would feed Blake and Holly their bottles. Their tiny hands would wrap around the bottle. Sometimes, they would clasp around her finger. As their bottles emptied and their bellies were full, they would slowly drift into a peaceful sleep.

Then she remembered when her ex-boyfriend walked into Willow's Bend Diner.

"The good, Hope!" Eddie shouted as he strained against the pressure. "Focus on the good!"

The force tested their strength as Hope pushed through the guilt she felt about taking the Holly and Blake in the first place, until she found out what the other kids went through. Then, she tightened her grip on Eddie's hands while she dealt with remorse for not taking all of the children, even though she knew there was no possible way at that time.

"Almost there! Keep going! Push through the bad to find the good. All of it! Keep it up, Hope!" Eddie yelled over the sound of the memories swirling around them. The sounds came from the sounds in the memories. When they blended together, it sounded like a running freight train.

Hope remembered the day they bought the house… in all its glorious disaster. She remembered the hours, days, months, and years of work she and Ben put into the house. She remembered the little joys of when each room was finished. They would have a party to celebrate the completion of each space.

"Go! Focus, Hope!" Eddie encouraged.

"Ahhh-eeeee!" Hope screamed. She pushed through the feeling of fear when Wyatt first told her about what he found during his investigation of her and Ben. She remembered the feeling of love that grew from that day forward between the two. That's when she flashed forward to when they were in the car in front of Ben's house, with guns pointed toward the vehicle. Holly and Blake were talking to Deanna and Adam in the yard. Hope's heart felt like it would beat out of her chest as she looked from the men to the group and back again before making a choice to go with the men to save her kids.

"Focus, Hope! The good! Focus!"

Hope desperately searched her memories for the good times. She thought of the first time Blake and Holly each showed signs of their gifts that day in the living room when they were about a year old, and Holly's bottle floated through the air. She then thought about when Holly would make the stuffed animals dance for Blake and how Blake would shove thoughts and feelings into their minds. She remembered how scary yet exciting it was to watch them grow into their gifts.

Hope's hands started to slip. "Almost there!" Eddie cheered, squeezing her hands with all his might so her hands would not slip out of his. "Hold on!"

Hope's memories spun around them in a continuous circle. She remembered their Sunday afternoon family outings. She remembered the pumpkin patches and the hay mazes. She remembered the rodeos, the markets, professional sports events, the high school football games, and the county fairs. She remembered going to some of the comic cons, so the kids could see the superheroes and other fandoms. She remembered the picnics and camping.

"Don't let go!" Eddie growled.

Hope held tighter as the last memory played out. It was the Sunday she was taken. She remembered watching Holly listen to the message Pastor spoke on that day. She saw Holly's heart break when the hymnals rose from the pews. Blake calmed her, but the words sunk into Holly's soul, forever changing her view of the world and Jesus Christ.

"Yes!" Eddie said as the memory froze, showing Holly's tears pouring down her cheeks while she sat on the pew.

The scene shrunk to one of the walls of the room. As it did, a wave of white caused the black to fade to gray and then to solid white. "Finally," Eddie said in relief as their hands released.

Hope gripped the arms of the chair while she shook her head to clear it. "Whoa."

Focusing on the scene in front of him while he recovered,

Eddie cocked his head to the side and asked, "Why was Holly so affected that day?"

"Because on that day, she discovered Who Jesus is and what He did for her," Hope explained, sitting in the same chair in the white room.

"Why is this Jesus so important? I keep hearing about Him, but I already had one man in control of my life." He sat back in his wheelchair, trying to catch his breath from the experience. "I'm not sure if I want another."

"Oh, honey," Hope said, setting her hand on his, which was resting on the armrest of his chair. "When it comes to Jesus, The Spirit, and the Lord God Almighty, you want to give Them control. They have a plan for you. They created you."

"I don't understand."

Hope sat back in her seat and started from the beginning... back to Genesis.

❖❖❖

ADAM, Deanna, and Mitch rode with Mac to Boston. Mac focused as best he could, while he continued to drink energy drinks. He was tired, but he understood how important it was to get those six kids back from the big guys with guns, so they could all get back to Texas – to safety. He let the others sleep the entire five-hour drive. Colby volunteered to drive, but Mac did not want Colby to drive anymore. He did his stint and looked beyond exhausted.

"We're here," Mac said, jostling Adam, who was asleep in the passenger's seat. "Adam?"

Adam sat up, alert. "What? Huh?"

"Breathe," Mac said, turning the engine off. "We're here. The last of your brothers and sisters are upstairs. One last battle, and you are all free."

"Got it," Adam said, unbuckling his seatbelt. He woke Mitch

and Deanna, who were in the second seat before they headed inside.

"Can I help you?" the concierge at the desk asked when the trio walked into the lobby.

"No. We're going up to our friend's room. They told us how to find them," Deanna said, and they continued walking all the way to the elevator.

Once in the elevator, Mitch let out the breath of air he was holding. "I don't know how you guys have been doing this. This is scary. We're in the middle of a big city. They could call security or the police on us at any time."

"You, my man, have the gift of persuasion," Adam reminded him. "You can tell them to let us go."

"True. I never thought of that."

"Just nothing violent," Deanna added. "By the way, you may want to direct Mac to the back entrance," Deanna said to Adam. "We're not going to get out of here easily with six kids in tow."

"Good point," Adam said, closing his eyes. *Mac?*

*Yes?* Mac thought. He understood it was weird to talk to someone in his mind, but he knew it would be something he would have to get used to around this crowd.

*Can you see if there's a back entrance? We need to get these kids out another way.*

*What about a laundry cart?*

*Brilliant idea! Find the back entrance, and we'll meet you back there.*

*Sounds good.* Mac started the van and headed around to the back to wait.

"Mac had a good idea," Adam said, pushing the button for the lobby.

"What are you doing?" Deanna asked. "We're trying to avoid the front desk. Why are you sending us back down there?"

"Mac had the idea to get a laundry cart to hide all the kids. We could also get a couple uniforms as cleaners."

"Me too?" Mitch asked.

"Well, you can be our lookout or our help to get what we need," Adam said. "You're a little too short and young to have a job."

Mitch grinned. "I can do that."

The elevator reached the level they needed to get the siblings, but they stayed against the wall inside the elevator so no one could see them on the camera just outside the elevator and in the hallway. Once the doors closed, the elevator headed back down.

When they reached the bottom floor, they read the signs showing the direction to the laundry room. They had to pass an open area near the desk, so Deanna distracted the concierge by having something fall in the room behind the desk. As soon as he stepped back to look, they ran across the area toward the laundry room.

"Whew!" Mitch said, breathing heavily. "This is exhausting."

"But easier with gifts." Deanna smiled. "This way," she said, grabbing his hand so he would not lag behind.

Thankfully, there was no one in the laundry room, so they got what they needed, which included an empty cart and two uniforms. They put Mitch into the cart and covered him with a king-size sheet. They decided a king-sized sheet would be a good size to cover all the kids once they freed them from the men upstairs.

Adam poked his head around the corner to see the man back at the desk. He pointed to Deanna. She closed her eyes and made it so a stack of paperwork tumbled in the back room all over the floor. They heard the man swear before leaving to clean it up.

Adam and Deanna pushed the cart across the area to the service elevator. Once there, they headed up to the penthouse level once again. Adam dove into the minds of the guards and gave Deanna the layout of the room, so they had a good idea of what they were walking into.

Adam rested his hand on the door of the suite and closed his eyes. He searched the rooms until he found a couple minds in each. Using their minds, he saw what they did to the siblings and shook his head. "There are three kids in one room and four in the other, with two guards in each room. The kids are sedated. I can't get fully into their minds."

"How are we going to get the guards out of the way?" Mitch asked.

"You tell them to go to sleep," Deanna whispered as she pushed him down the hall in the cart. "There's been enough killing. Once they return to Maine and see it leveled and then find out the other two facilities are leveled, I'm pretty sure they'll disappear on their own."

Mitch just nodded.

Adam knocked on the door.

"Just leave it at the door," a bass voice yelled out.

Adam knocked again.

"I said to leave it at the door!" the man shouted.

Adam knocked again a little louder.

"You really are not listening!" the man yelled before the door swung open. "Which part of *leave it at the door* did you not understand?"

Mitch stood up in the cart and forcefully said, "You are beyond exhausted. Go to sleep!"

The man stumbled back, grabbing onto the couch. He shook his head. Making his way around the couch, he went to lay down, already snoring before he went down. He bounced off the couch, landing on the floor.

"Ouch!" Deanna cringed. "That'll leave a mark," she said, referring to where he hit his cheek on the table.

"Beautiful!" Adam grinned. "I love this gift!"

"Your gifts are all pretty cool, too!" Mitch pointed out. "Everyone's gifts are cool."

"Just be careful how you use them – especially that persuasion gift," Adam cautioned. "It could get you into a lot of trouble. There's also a moral dilemma regarding their use. I've seen when people use their talents badly."

"I'll do my best."

"That's all I ask," Adam said, patting Mitch's arm.

"Let's go in," Deanna said, resting her hand on Mitch's shoulder to guide him to sit back down in the cart. "Tuck down until someone else comes in. There are three more." When he was seated, Adam pushed the cart inside.

Deanna and Adam pretended to pick up things like they were dusting, listening to every sound around them.

"Hank! Where are you?" a big man demanded, flinging the bedroom door open.

Mitch stood in the cart and sternly said, "You are beyond exhausted! Pass out now!"

The man slid down the doorframe before dropping to the ground with a thud.

Deanna went over to the other room and knocked on the door.

"What's going on?" another man asked, opening the door.

Deanna stepped in and immediately lifted both men off the ground. They flailed in the air while she levitated them out into the living room. "Your turn, short stuff!" Deanna winked at Mitch.

He stood below both men. Looking up at them, he said, "You are sick. Your heads are swimming and spinning. Pass out now, and don't wake up until Hank wakes you!"

Both men suddenly went limp. Deanna set them on the ground next to the other guard. "Let's get the kids," she said, running into one room while Adam ran into the other. In each room, Deanna and Adam pulled the IVs out of their arms, securing the site where there was a bit of blood by wrapping their arms with a hand towel. That way, if they bled, they would not bleed all over the cart or beds.

After Deanna finished, she lifted all three unconscious girls with her gift and floated them out to the living room. Mitch climbed out of the laundry cart. Deanna then lowered the girls, one at a time, into a seated position in the cart.

"Care to lend a hand?" Adam asked after he finished pulling the IV's and wrapping the arms of all four boys.

"Sure," Deanna said, going after the other four.

After she finished, she lifted and lowered Mitch to the center of the group of kids so she and Adam could cover them. If the kids fell over, Mitch set them back up so they would not hurt themselves or another. Having him in there would also keep him out of sight.

They went down the service elevator to the bottom floor. Once free from the elevator, they followed the signs to the loading dock in the back of the hotel where Mac waited. He backed up the van, so anyone watching would not be able to see them load the kids. He also made sure to avoid the camera angled toward the loading docks.

He stayed in the driver's seat with the engine running, while Mitch climbed into the passenger's seat. With all seven of the children still asleep, Deanna gently lifted each young child until they were all either lying on the floor or on a seat. She then lifted the sheet that was over the kids and wrapped up the towels inside. She put them inside the van, taking any and all DNA and blood evidence with them. Afterward, Deanna and Adam both climbed in, navigating the four kids on the floor. They took whichever kid was on the seat and lifted their heads to lay their heads on their laps. Deanna was in the second seat, while Adam was in the third.

"Let's get back to Philly," Adam said, exhausted.

"Go ahead and go to sleep," Mac said. "If they wake, I'll wake you."

"No," Adam said. "They all have gifts. Considering who their clone was, at least four are most likely telekinetics."

One of the boys looked like Charlie, and another looked like Eddie. One of the girls looked like Deanna, and one looked like Freya and Gemma. Meanwhile, one of the girls looked like Bells, while there was one boy who looked like Adam and one who looked like Blake.

"Are they going to be that much trouble?" Mac asked. "They're kind of small."

"It's not their size. It's their gift. You're going to need me awake. They could trick you," Adam warned, "but not me."

"True. Thank you," Mac said and headed toward Philadelphia, thankful it went off without incident. He prayed it would stay that way.

⊙⊲⊳⊲⊳⊙

By the time the Boston team was almost back, the Maine team was just nearing the Maine facility.

"Alex!" The guard at the gate smiled when he saw her. "Been awhile. I thought The Professor had you staying in Wyoming indefinitely."

"Thankfully, that situation has been neutralized, Carl," Alex said, leaning forward in the passenger's seat while Tanya drove, and Blake and Holly were in the second seat. "I'm under new orders you won't like."

"What's that?"

"We have to run a drill, evacuating the facility. Daddy," she said and felt bile come up from addressing him as such. She quickly swallowed. "He wants to clear the facility of any and all personnel."

"Just to stay in the parking lot?" the guard asked.

"No. He wants everyone to go home. He wants the campus completely emptied."

"Why?"

"Because someone blew up the Wyoming and Oregon facilities, and he doesn't want any casualties here. He said to send everyone home until they hear from their supervisor."

"Really?" the guard looked at her, surprised. "I didn't hear that. Let me verify –"

"Excuse me?" Alex said, highly offended. "You're questioning Daddy's orders? For real? Do you have a death wish?"

"I-I, no," the guard stammered.

"Then you'd better execute his orders immediately!" Alex said sternly.

"I'll note this is under your order," the guard pointed out.

"Go ahead. Just do it. You're included in that order. I'll lock it up when I'm sure the campus is completely empty."

"Understood," he said, standing at attention.

"Now, Carl!" Alex growled.

"Y-yes. I-I'll do it right now," he stammered, stumbling over his own feet to get back to the guard house.

When Alex heard the alarms, which signified an evacuation, only then did she tell Tanya to drive forward. "Stay here," Alex said as Tanya pulled into a parking spot. "Blake, stay in contact with my mind. I'll let you know when to come in."

"Got it," Blake agreed.

As people were rushing out, Alex confidently walked into the building. Grabbing one of the walkie-talkies from Security Officer Rick Miller, she said into it, "This entire campus needs to be emptied. Everyone. No exceptions! If someone resists, let me know, and I will have a word with them myself. This is a direct order from Professor Roth himself. Evacuate the entire compound, houses included," she said sternly. Handing back the radio, she glared at the security officer as she asked, "Understood, Miller?"

"Y-yes, ma'am," he said.

She ran up to her office and got on her computer, fighting the stream of people leaving the building. Clicking away, she first searched the files to find out what they did with Ben's body.

Seeing that they cremated him, she cringed. "They can't say goodbye." She shook her head.

She printed out the report showing his cremation and then sent a virus through the computer so it would infiltrate the servers, destroying anything in its path. She wanted to clear any and all information so it would not fall into the wrong hands. Seeing her own computer start to pixelate, she left her office.

*Blake?* she thought.

*Yes?*

*Ben's body isn't here. They cremated it. Stay in the van out of sight. Once it's clear, I'll have Holly blow it up.*

*Fair enough. Thank you.*

"What's going on?" Holly asked, knowing what Blake looked like when he talked to someone in his mind.

"They cremated Dad's body. It's not here," Blake explained.

"So, what do we do?"

"She said to stay here while the facility empties out. Once it's clear, you can blow it."

"Got it. I'm going to need you to help me search and direct," Holly said.

"How do I do that?"

"We'll use Alex's knowledge of the facility," Holly explained. "I need your ability to search her mind. We're going to have to all three join hands to find what I need."

"Got it." He peeked out the window to see people leaving the building. Cars pulled away left and right. "They're leaving."

"How long is this going to take?" Tanya asked, keeping her baseball cap down to shield her face from any cameras.

"I know you're tired," Blake said. "That's why I stayed up with you during the drive."

"I don't think y'all understand what this looks like," Tanya said. "People are being told to leave without a date or time of return. Meanwhile, we're just sitting here in this van." When Blake went to peek again, Tanya scolded him, "Seriously! Stop it! This is stressful enough. I don't want someone to see you. Just stay down."

Blake snickered from his seat on the floor with Holly.

"You're bad!" Holly laughed, lightly slapping his arm.

"Ornery," Tanya corrected.

"I'll tell you what," Blake said to Tanya.

"What?" Tanya asked.

"When this is over, I'll sit in the passenger's seat on the way home. You can talk to me about Jesus the whole way home, and we can pray."

"Wait! What? Really?" Tanya asked, excited. "Why are you waiting? Just do it now!"

"Well, actually," he rethought his proposal, "maybe I'll wait until Mom wakes up."

"If she'll wake up," Holly corrected. "Eddie's trying his best."

"Let's just hope Eddie's best is good enough," Blake said, irritated. "We already lost dad. I don't think I can handle – you know what? I change my mind. I'm going to make a deal," he said, pointing toward Heaven. "When Mom wakes, I'll know You care enough about Your children to save her."

"You can't do that!" Holly said, appalled. "You're putting contingencies on the Lord God! What is wrong with you? Jesus gave His life for you! He didn't say, 'Well, maybe. You have to do this list first.' He willingly and knowingly gave His life for you!"

"Holly, I'm tired of losing people. I'm not gonna lie," Blake said, "I don't know if I can handle losing Mom so close after losing Dad. And the worst part? I can't get justice because that man is already dead."

"That *is* justice," Holly said. "When he died, he had to stand before God and answer for his multitude of sins."

A smile slowly formed on Blake's face imagining the scene.

"Don't get smug," Holly snapped. "What you don't seem to understand is you're just as guilty."

"What are you talking about? Have *you* lost your mind?" Blake snapped back. "I never killed anyone."

"Blake, sin, is sin, is sin," Tanya explained. "It's all the same in the eyes of the Lord. Jesus died for every single sin, no matter the size. He paid the penalty for all of them. Holly's right."

"Why are you taking her side?" Blake looked cross at her. "You're supposed to support me."

"I will only support a righteous and true decision. The choice you're making is not godly."

"Nice." Blake snorted. "At least I know where I stand with you."

"If you wanted to rob a bank, would you seriously want me to support you?" Tanya asked.

"No, but let's get real. We're literally about to blow up a building."

"That's to save your family from any further scrutiny or being lab rats for the rest of your lives," Tanya said, rolling her eyes. "There will be no one in there when you do it either."

"It's still destruction of property."

"The property of a dead man!" Tanya said, shaking her head. "And technically, it all falls to Alex. She's the one helping to blow it up, so you have permission."

Blake sighed. "Gray area."

"Seriously. Do whatever you're going to do." Tanya threw her hands in the air in surrender. "I want no part of it."

Blake furrowed his brow. "What are you saying?"

"I'm saying you're playing games with the Creator of the Universe. You have some nerve!"

"Tanya!"

"Yes. I'm serious!" she said before he had a chance to ask. "If you want to play games, go ahead. I don't want any part of it. I have more respect for the Lord than this."

"I'm mad."

Tanya clicked her tongue. "Now you're acting like a two-year-old."

"So not helping the situation," Blake shot.

"Neither are you."

"Children!" Holly snapped. "Do I need to separate you two?"

"No need. If he feels he can play games with the Lord God, the One who spoke the world into existence, then more power to him. I'm not playing." Tanya crossed her arms.

"Are you saying you'll break up with me if I don't accept Christ?" Blake asked.

"I'm saying I don't appreciate your line of thinking. Breaking up with you or staying with you is a separate matter. However, this is non-negotiable: do not play around with God! He created you, this entire planet, and everything in it. Have respect and awe when you refer to Him. If you choose to accept Christ, then do it. If you don't, then don't. Don't put any more contingencies on Him. That's not right!"

"Well, at least I know how you feel."

"How I feel is that I love you. I know you know that. However, I don't love what you're doing to God. I don't like the pain you're causing Jesus."

"What do you mean by the pain I'm causing Jesus?" Blake asked.

"He already died for your sins. He allowed Himself to be tortured, whipped, betrayed, and literally nailed to a cross until He died for you. He then fought the gates of Hell to get back to you, so you could spend eternity with Him in Heaven. Yet, you feel He needs to suffer more? Your arrogance in this matter is appalling," Tanya said sternly. "You already said you would accept Christ once everyone was rescued. To my knowledge, everyone has been rescued. There were only two children lost out of twenty-six that started this, along with Ben. By rights, we should have lost many more."

"We could still lose Mom," Blake pointed out.

"We could get in a car accident on the way home, too," Tanya argued. "There are many things that could happen in this world. You're playing Russian Roulette with your eternal security. You want to go to Hell when you die?"

"No one wants to go to Hell."

"By not accepting Christ's gift, you are choosing to go to Hell. You know the truth. By continuing to put contingencies on Jesus, you're playing with the literal fires of Hell. Why are you willing to take the risk?"

"I don't know," Blake admitted.

"Do you know the truth?" Tanya asked.

"Yes."

"Do you believe the truth?"

"Yes."

"Then what is holding you back?"

"I'm mad."

Tanya crossed her arms in a huff. "Two-year-old!"

"Just set it aside and let me think about it," Blake finally said. "I need to think."

"You need to make a choice and stick with it," Tanya growled.

"Enough," Blake cautioned.

"Will you please calm the area?" Holly asked. "You feel everyone's emotions. Everyone is afraid and anxious right now. They went from leaving in an orderly fashion to total chaos. Please send a wave of calmness so people will quit freaking out? They'll get into accidents, and it will take longer."

"Fine," Blake said. He took a few deep breaths to calm himself before he sent a wave of calmness out from the van. Those who were panicked slowed down and relaxed. The vehicles drove a little slower, and everyone left in an organized fashion.

WHILE THE MAINE FACILITY EMPTIED, the Boston crew got back to the hotel. With all the sofa beds open, there was room for six people in each of the four rooms. Wyatt rented two more rooms to hold everyone while Megan sat with Hope and Eddie.

*We're here,* Adam thought to Wyatt when they pulled up to the entrance of the hotel.

*Coming,* Wyatt thought back.

It took a few moments before Wyatt appeared at the front entrance to see the van sitting under the awning.

"We're back, Daddy," Mac teased. "We brought more kids, but they're asleep."

"We're going to have to separate them with those of like gifts," Adam pointed out. "When they wake, they're going to be afraid. There needs to be a telekinetic and a mind-gift person with each group."

"Good idea," Wyatt agreed. "Question is, how do we get them upstairs?"

"Go to the back, and we'll get them up how we got them down from the other hotel," Mitch suggested.

"You, my man, are brilliant!" Adam said, resting his hand on Mitch's shoulder. "I think that's a great idea."

Mitch grinned.

With that, Mitch left with Deanna and Adam to get another cart. If they ran into anyone, Mitch would help them out of trouble. In the meantime, Wyatt jumped into the passenger's seat, and Mac headed toward the loading docks in the back of the hotel.

Once back there, Deanna carefully placed the children into the laundry cart, out of sight of anyone else. Then, they all headed up the service elevator to the rooms. When they got to the rooms, they adjusted the kids into the six rooms rented, making sure there was at least one person in each who had the gift of telekinesis and one with a mind gift.

"Now we wait," Wyatt said. "If y'all have it handled here, I'll go back to Eddie and Hope and send Megan back."

"That'll work. That'll help in having older kids with younger, and those with compassion and heart to work with those who have nightmares," Adam agreed.

Wyatt took off for the hospital, while Adam and Deanna shifted everyone around.

<br>

ALEX RESTED her crossed arms on the window next to Tanya while she stood outside of the van. "The compound: buildings, homes…everything, are supposed to be empty now."

The officers left Alex the keys to the facility and headed home.

"Give me a moment," Blake said. "I'll check. Let me borrow your mind?"

"Of course," Alex said, reaching into the vehicle for Blake's hand. He sat next the driver's seat but out of sight on the floor.

Clasping hands, Blake and Alex both closed their eyes. Blake used Alex's knowledge of the facility to float through the levels, searching for any minds. He then followed her train of thought to all of the other buildings, along with the homes on the campus. It took him a good twenty minutes before he was satisfied. "Empty."

"Good. Time to blow it up," Alex said to Holly. "Can we blow it from outside the gate?"

"As long as your mind is connected to me, I can get what I need," Holly explained.

Alex jumped back into the passenger's seat, and Tanya drove out the gates of the facility. On camera, Alex could be seen locking it down from the guard station. She then closed the gates and put a giant padlock on the gate before getting back into the van. "Go out of sight of the camera."

"But not too far," Holly warned. "I need to be close enough to be effective."

Tanya drove just out of the line of sight of the camera and pulled over. "Okay."

Holly, Blake, and Alex got out of the van. Standing at the back of the van, the trio joined hands. "Concentrate on the various spots in the facility containing explosive material, as well as something to ignite it all," Holly explained.

Alex nodded. "Got it."

Blake used his mind gift to help guide Holly through the facility with Alex's help. She found the lab, the storage buildings with more chemicals, along with an old-fashioned boiler. "Bingo!" Holly said with a smile.

Holly built up pressure within the boiler until it finally burst, exploding the boiler room, which in turn created the chain reaction she needed. Holly released Alex and Blake's hands as the facility continued to blow, one building after another. She brought her hands together, creating a funnel around the area. Keeping all the debris within a funnel, the buildings continued to explode as they came into contact with other combustible materials and homes nearby.

Holly strained to keep it all together. The size of the campus and explosions made it difficult for her to control the debris field, but she pushed through it. Finally, when she was not sure how much more she could take, she let out a scream as she shoved her hands together and down. When she did, the debris thrust into the ground before it shot up into the air and rained down around the area. Despite the weight of all the materials, Holly was able to control its descent, so there was not much damage outside of the main building areas.

"Whoooo!" Alex cheered and gave her a hug. "You did it! Great job!"

When Alex let go, Holly whispered, "Yeah." Out of sheer exhaustion, she passed out. Blake caught her before she hit the ground.

"Gotcha, little sister," he said, scooping her up. He carried her around to the side of the van and laid her on the middle seat. He set his jacket under her head as she fell asleep. "She's beyond exhausted," Blake commented when Tanya gave him a questioning look.

"Let's get out of here before the authorities come," Alex said, getting into the seat with Holly, resting Holly's head on her lap so she would not fall off the seat in her sleep. "Head that way." Alex pointed toward a street to the right. "We'll go that way. The authorities will be coming from the other direction."

"Good idea," Tanya said, starting the van. She headed in the direction Alex told her. "Is Holly okay?"

"She's wiped out. She fell asleep almost immediately," Blake said, buckling his seatbelt while sitting in the passenger's seat.

"Don't worry about it," Tanya said. "Just get some sleep. I'll refuel and get some energy drinks at the next gas station."

⌖

"AND THEN, after his resurrection and gifting the apostles the Holy Spirit, Jesus went back to Heaven, leaving His apostles to carry on His ministry," Hope finished.

"Why did He do it?" Eddie asked. "Why did He voluntarily give up His life for mankind? He had to know that not everyone would believe in Him."

"He did it for those who would believe. He came to offer an alternative to all the sacrifices and us living by the law set out in the Bible," Hope explained. "He did it because no matter what choice we make, He still loves us."

"So, if I'm following you correctly, He knew what was going

to happen to Him before and during the crucifixion and did it anyway?"

"Oh yes! There are multiple times while He was here, where Jesus told his apostles what was going to happen. Now, did He want to go through all that pain and agony? No. In the Garden of Gethsemane, He prayed so hard blood came from His forehead. He prayed, asking God if there was any other way to do this, to please let Him know. There was no other option, so He willingly let them take Him, knowing what they would do to Him."

"Why, though?"

"Because He loves you. John 15:13 says, *'Greater love has no one than this: to lay down one's life for one's friends.'* When Jesus voluntarily died on the cross, letting them torture and crucify Him while He took the sins of the world onto Himself, He could have gotten down, but He didn't. That is the greatest example there is in this world of pure love. No one can top that example. He wants you to enjoy Heaven with Him when you leave this earth. If I were to die today, I know beyond a shadow of a doubt that I would wake up in Heaven. Jesus would welcome me with open arms. He would do the same to every one of those who accept the gift of His sacrifice. Eddie, this life has not been easy for you by any stretch of the imagination. If you were to die tomorrow, would you not want to literally rest in the peace and glory of being in Heaven with God, Jesus, and The Spirit?"

"Well, yeah, but I know that's not all there is to it."

"It's not," Hope agreed. "If you don't die tomorrow, but you choose to accept His gift, you have a responsibility. Your responsibility is to tell others of His life, along with the crucifixion and resurrection. There are others waiting to hear exactly what I just told you."

"I don't know if I could tell them all that."

Hope snickered. "You don't have to tell them everything I told you. Most people have a basic understanding. Having said that, your responsibility is to listen to The Spirit. He'll tell you what that person needs to hear. It's not your responsibility to change the hearts of others. That's God's responsibility. Your job is to tell them."

"I feel like there's more to it."

"Oh! There is!"

He rolled his eyes. "I knew there was a catch."

Hope smiled. "The catch is to listen to the voice of The Spirit to guide you in finding your purpose in this life. God has a plan for you. Jesus will walk the path with you. The Spirit will guide you. All you have to do is listen. It may be something as simple as giving someone food. It may not mean much to you, but it may be the only food they have for that day. It may be stopping wherever you are and praying for someone He put on your mind. Again, that's just as important as anything. You also need to understand what His voice sounds like. Your responsibility is to have a relationship with Him by reading His word, applying what you read to your life, learning to live like Christ through His example and be in prayer with Him. When you are in a close relationship with Him, you'll hear His still small voice and recognize Him when He wants you to do something."

"How will I know what His plan is for me?"

"You don't." Hope shrugged. "You don't need to either. As you know, knowing the future isn't all it's cracked up to be. You'll make mistakes. He expects that. Your job is to stay focused on the steps He puts in front of you. You need to have faith to take those steps, not knowing what's in your future."

"That's unnerving."

"That's faith and trust in Him. When bad things happen, and they will, find the good. Find the lesson He wants you to learn. Satan will attack you, but you'll never be alone. Even in the middle of that cell The Professor had me in, I knew I wasn't alone."

"Of course not. Ben was just a few cells over."

"It didn't matter if Ben was there or not. I still wasn't alone. Jesus was with me. He kept me calm. When that concoction was injected into me, He gave Ben the presence of mind to teach me how to fight it. He helped me focus. As Ben was dying, Jesus gave me the clarity to help Ben find his way back to Jesus. What Satan intended to use for bad, God turned it around and used it for good."

"How do you figure?"

"Ben was the prodigal son. He found His way back to Jesus before he died. I lived with Ben for years, and he never once let on he was a Christian. It took something this drastic to bring Ben back to Christ. Life is full of ups and downs. It's full of joys and disappointments. It's full of excitement and disaster. It's how you deal and process it that makes the difference. If you are not one of His, this world may chew you up and swallow you whole. Without Jesus, I would have lost my mind a long time ago."

"I can see that," Eddie agreed. "So, you keep saying accept Jesus' gift. How do I do that?"

"In Romans 10:9 through 11, it says, *'If you declare with your mouth, "Jesus is Lord," and believe in your heart that God raised Him from the dead, you will be saved. For it is with your heart that you believe and are justified, and it is with your mouth that you profess your faith and are saved. As Scripture says, "Anyone who believes in Him will never be put to shame."* All you have to do is pray. I would be happy to help you do that."

"I would be happy to let you help me do that," Eddie said with a smile.

# TIME TO COME HOME

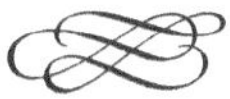



After the prayer, Eddie continued to hold Hope's hand. "Hope, you need to wake up now. I don't know what effect The Professor's concoction will have on you. You may wake up as yourself. You may wake up with a gift. I honestly don't know. I can't even hazard a guess. There is no precedence for this."

"The fact that you cannot hazard a guess terrifies me beyond words," Hope admitted.

"While I will admit I'm nervous too, I'm pretty sure God would not have brought you all this way to leave you now."

"True. So, how do I wake up?"

"That's something you have to figure out. You have to find your own way back. I would suggest a very serious conversation with God."

"Good idea," she said with a smile.

"Okay, we've been at this an extremely long time. I need to go."

"Will you be back?"

"I will say no. Let it serve as motivation for you to make your way out of here," he said with a wink and a smile.

"I can appreciate that. I'm curious to see what living with all of you will be like."

"Wyatt said he would find homes for us."

"Except Blake, Holly, and you," Hope pointed out. "You already have a home."

"True. Thank you!"

"All right. Get out of here. I have to chat with Jesus about getting out of here."

"See you in a bit."

"Just a second!" Hope said, getting off the chair. She wrapped her arms around him from behind, and he froze.

"I-I've never been hugged before," he admitted.

"Never?" she asked, appalled.

"Never. When I said we were raised in a sterile environment, I meant it. He wouldn't let the nurses get close to us. As for us, The Professor used us against each other. We did our best not to show any affection for each other, especially for the one we were closest to in the group. Having said that, I really wasn't close to any of them. As far as they knew, I was The Professor's pet and didn't have gifts. I was treated differently from the beginning."

"Well, you'll still be treated differently. You'll be showered in love and affection," she said and kissed his cheek.

His face flushed bright red. "I like it. Just not used to it."

"Well, get used to it," she said, going back to the chair. "You're in our world now."

He waggled his finger. "Not yet. You have to get out of here first."

"Fair enough. See you as soon as I can." When Eddie went to wheel away, she added, "And Eddie?"

He stopped and turned toward her. "Yes?"

"I love you."

"I honestly do love you as well, Hope. Hurry up," he said and wheeled away. He went to the other side of the room and closed his eyes. The room and memories of the last almost twenty-four hours swirled all around him at a dizzying pace.

Just at the point where he thought he would vomit, his eyes flew open, and he found himself sitting in the hospital room next to Hope's bed. Wyatt was asleep on the couch.

Eddie rested his hand on Hope's as he said, "Time's Up. It's time to come home, Hope."

Hope's fingers moved.

"Wy-Wyatt!" Eddie said, heart racing, excited she was already fighting to get back. "Wyatt!"

"Wha–what? Huh?" Wyatt sat up suddenly from a deep sleep. He groaned as he laid back down to let the rest of his body catch up with his brain. "What?" he grumbled.

"Hope's hand moved."

His head spun toward Eddie. "What?"

"Hope's hand moved. Come here."

Wyatt went over to the chair beside the bed and reached for Hope's other hand. "Hope? Darlin'? Can you wiggle your fingers for me?"

Hope's fingers moved. Her eyes fluttered open. She groggily looked around the room trying to process where she was. She looked toward Wyatt. "Wyatt?"

"Yes!" Wyatt said, a few tears escaping down his cheeks. "I'm so glad to hear your voice and see those beautiful eyes looking up at me!"

She turned toward Eddie. "Eddie?"

"Yep. Long time no see," Eddie said in a chuckle.

"I know. Right?" she said weakly.

"I'll go get the nurse," Wyatt said and left the room.

While he was gone, Eddie leaned forward. "How did you get out?"

"I prayed and asked Jesus what to do. I promise I'm not lying when I tell you that He stood before me. He held His hand out, and I took it. Of course, once I realized it was Him, I bowed my head and closed my eyes, but He lifted my chin and told me He wanted to see my beautiful face. He said I was a precious child of the Lord's and to always hold my head high. Then, He had me close my eyes and take a deep breath. The last thing I heard was when He said for me to open my eyes. I felt His hand leave mine as I opened them. Then I found myself in this room."

"Well done!" Eddie encouraged.

"I didn't do it."

"You took the steps."

"True."

"Sometimes it's just a matter of taking the steps, even if you don't know what's going to happen," Eddie said. "For me, that's a rare issue. However, I may seem confident, but I promise you I'm just a good actor. While I know the odds, I don't know everything one-hundred percent."

"I can see that. Thank you for taking the leap out of the darkness with me."

"Anytime."

The nurse came in and checked out Hope. Afterward, Wyatt sat down, and Hope told him everything that happened from the point she was taken.

⦿⦿⦿⦿

THE GROUP from Maine returned about seventeen hours after taking off from the hotel. It was a long drive, and they were completely exhausted. The four of them immediately went to sleep as soon as their heads hit the pillow.

In the meantime, the other kids progressively woke up over the next twenty-four hours from when they were rescued from the hotel in Boston. When the others woke from sleeping so hard, the older kids with gifts talked to them. Once they were calm, the Willow Bend teens took over so they could move to another child. The older teens were stressed, but keeping all the kids calm and explaining what happened was their priority.

"When are Wyatt and Eddie coming back?" Deanna asked, lying on the floor of one of the rooms where Adam and Megan were attending to the kids.

Adam shrugged. "That depends on when Hope wakes up."

"Doesn't doing what you do exhaust you?" Megan asked.

"Using my gift and talking these kids out of panic mode? Yes," Deanna admitted.

"Eddie's been with Hope for literally hours, if not a day or so. How is he doing that?" Megan asked.

Adam stroked his chin. "That's a good question."

"I know he's supposed to be stronger than you, but this is next level," Megan pointed out. "That's a marathon. What if he's stuck?"

"I think Wyatt would have called if he thought that," Adam said.

"Would he, though?" Megan asked. "How does he know if too much is too much?"

"Good question." Deanna sat up. She got off the floor and paced the room. The younger kids who were in there were eating while watching the three talking. "Adam, can you reach Wyatt?"

"I don't know." Adam shook his head. "That's pretty far. Eddie was the one who got to him last time."

"You don't know if you don't try," Deanna pointed out. "How are you supposed to get stronger if you don't push yourself beyond what you know?"

"Agreed," Adam conceded. He closed his eyes and searched for Wyatt. *Wyatt?* When he did not hear anything, he pushed harder. *Wyatt!*

*Adam?*

*Yes! I did it!*

Wyatt chuckled. *Good job!*

*Is Eddie still with Hope?*

*In a manner of speaking. Hope's finally awake.*

*Really? How is she?*

*Doc will be here in an hour or so to check her out. She asked for food, though.*

*Great! I'll tell the others. When are you coming back? This is exhausting with all of these kids, despite how many teens there are.*

*I understand. I really want to stay with Hope, though.*

*I get it. Let me know what the doctor says.*

*Fair enough. Reach out again in a couple of hours.*

*Will do. Is Eddie okay?*

*Yes. Tired, but good.*

*Thank you,* Adam said and cut the link. He reiterated the conversation to those in the room. Megan went to the rooms to tell the others while Adam and Deanna looked after those in their room.

❧❧❧❧

WITH HOPE IMPROVING, the doctor agreed to send her to a hospital closer to home via ambulance so she could be near everyone else. He would make arrangements the following day. With that information, she sent Wyatt and Eddie back to the hotel so they could get some sleep for the long drive starting the next morning.

❧❧❧❧

THE NEXT MORNING, they finally checked out. They split between the three vans, Wyatt drove one, Colby drove one, and Alex drove the other, along with thirty-one teens and kids total. There were the six Willow Bend teens, eight Maine teens, nine thirteen-year-olds, and eight ten-year-olds. With Ben's death, no one had the heart to drive his car, so they left it in Pennsylvania.

The drive would be a solid twenty-one hours with breaks. However, with all of the kids, it stretched to twenty-three hours. Anyone who saw them at the rest areas or at the drive-thru restaurants, Wyatt would mention they were a church group. No one bothered them.

Finally, they pulled into Wyatt's twenty-acre property. His two-story home only had four bedrooms, so they would have to share for a bit until Wyatt could get the house added onto. After seeing everything that happened, he did not want to separate the kids.

Blake took one of the vans to drop off the Willow Bend teens at their homes. He left Tanya for last. "Well, I guess this is it," Blake said as they sat on the side of the road in front of Tanya's home in the van.

"I guess it is," she said on a sigh. "Blake, this is the one and only time I'm going to ask this question."

"Sounds ominous."

"No. Not really. What was your choice regarding Jesus Christ?"

"Well, we talked a lot on the way home from Maine."

"We did, but no real closure on the conversation."

"I know. I'm not normally this flaky when it comes to making decisions. I'm having a tough time reconciling losing Dad and Freya during this. Why would God take them home? Freya never even made it to adult age, and we just missed Dad by thirty minutes. Had we been there earlier, could we have saved him?"

"No."

"No. What do you mean? How do you know?"

"Because I researched Belladonna after the police left and we were allowed back online. If he was that far, then there was no turning back for him. Him going sooner than later was a godsend."

"Why didn't God stop The Professor from giving him that stuff?"

"Blake, it wasn't just the Belladonna. He also tried to initiate that gene in him, too. So, he was battling the poison and The Professor messing with his DNA. He was dead the moment they took him. The only reason your mom's still here is she had less than he did."

"Dad was stronger than Mom. Yes, she had less, but she still had the poison and that DNA scrambler stuff. How is she still here?"

"Thank God for that blessing, and don't question it. She shouldn't be here either. She flatlined while y'all were gone," Tanya pointed out. "That doesn't answer my question to you about Jesus, though."

"I can't figure out how He picks and chooses who lives."

"Blake," Tanya said, shaking her head. "You are not in control. God is. He makes this world spin every day. While it probably breaks His heart when one of His dies, it doesn't surprise Him. He knows it's going to happen long before we do. Also, if you remember, God gave us free will. That free will allots us the opportunity to make choices – whether good or bad. In this case, the choices The Professor made hurt ohhh so many people. However," she held up her hand for him not to talk when he went to open his mouth. "However, that free will also allow us to be human. It allows us to experience the joys and celebrations, as well as work through the tragedies and disappointments life throws at us. We're not puppets. God didn't want that. He wants us to choose Him. He wants us to make that choice, not force us to make it. So, what do you choose?"

"I still don't know."

"Why not? You found your parents. That was your first contingency. The second was that your mom lived. He answered that one with a yes. You challenged Him. He not only met that challenge but He also granted it. What's your next one? World peace?"

Blake sighed, shaking his head. "That was uncalled for."

"I think challenging God is uncalled for, but you did it anyway. Look, I have to go. You make the choice. It's yours. I want to go see my family. I love you, Blake Hunt. No matter what happens, I do love you."

"Thank you for giving me the choice."

"Of course! God is, too."

"I know." He leaned over and lightly kissed her lips before she got out of the van and ran to her house. Blake sat in the van for a moment, watching as her mom opened the door. She threw her arms around her daughter with tears in her eyes as she yelled to the others that Tanya was there. Her entire family came out of nowhere and sucked her into the house amongst the warm embraces and cheering, mixed with happy tears. "I wish that was what I had," Blake said aloud before starting back home.

For the entire ride home, he thought about what Tanya said, along with looking around his hometown. Then, his mind wandered toward his siblings who grew up with The Professor as their father in the lab, and he shuddered. A feeling of guilt started to surround him, almost suffocating him. Hope and Ben gave up everything to raise both him and Holly in a small town with a loving family. Meanwhile, his siblings were abused and pushed beyond their limits every day.

"What is wrong with me?" he asked aloud. Then, looking toward Heaven, he said, "I'm sorry. I don't deserve this. You gave me the best of the two worlds, and here I am complaining. Holly and I had Hope and Ben all of our lives. We even had Wyatt to help. The others are just now getting the benefit of living with the love we had all our lives. I'm sorry for being a brat. Tanya's right. I was acting like a two-year-old. Please forgive me?" he asked, tears in his eyes. The more he thought about the memories he saw in the mind of the others, the more his heart broke. "I'm so sorry. Jesus," he said, remembering the conversations with Tanya and the messages he heard at church and the youth outing, "You gave everything for me…literally. And here I sit judging You. I'm not worthy. You did put up with my selfishness. You also had the grace to not only keep my mom alive but also the benefit of knowing Dad came back to You in the end. You also gave us Wyatt and protected him throughout this ordeal. You had everything in place – Alex, her guards, the kids – everything. Nothing surprised You. Actually, nothing surprises You. Jesus, thank You for your sacrifice. Thank You for taking my sin on Your body and paying the ultimate penalty for my actions. Please take my life in return? Please allow me to be one of Your children? I'm Yours, Lord. Take my life and let it be for You."

◍◍◍◍

FOR SLEEPING in Wyatt's four-bedroom home, Wyatt got cots and sleeping bags. That was the least expensive solution he could figure out. The kids were separated in the rooms available, as well as the living room and kitchen. Sleeping this way, the kids got close really fast. He also took them, five at a time, to the discount store for at least five outfits and seven sets of under-clothes. With all the new clothing and extra kids, he purchased two industrial-sized washers and dryers. He put the appliances out in his workshop, which already had running water and elec-tricity. With the older kids helping the younger kids with chores and staying on track, the entire crew got into a decent schedule… or at least one that was functional.

On his way to see Hope at the hospital, Wyatt came up with a viable plan to explain the new situation to Hope and see if she was up for raising twenty-four children. He knew it was a big task, but he felt strongly about it. While praying, the Lord impressed on him the reasoning.

"Morning, Darlin'!" Wyatt said, walking into Hope's room with a bouquet of twenty-five roses.

"Wow! That's a lot of roses! I didn't die." Hope grinned. She reached her hands up to hug Wyatt. While he was down near her, she kissed his lips. "I missed you."

"Missed you too."

"Saw him coming in with the huge bouquet," Hope's nurse, Sarah, said, coming in with a vase of water. "Such a gentleman."

"Always, Nurse Sarah," Wyatt said. Wyatt knew her from the years of being the county sheriff. Nurse Sarah was also on the ambulance company for Willow Bend. The town had a volunteer fire station and ambulance company.

"I wouldn't expect anything less," she acknowledged, arranging the flowers in the vase. "Okay. I'll leave you two alone for a while. The doctor should be here soon."

"Sounds good. Thank you," he said, sitting on the side of the bed. After the nurse closed the door behind her, Wyatt took Hope's hand into his.

"You're making me nervous," Hope admitted. "I feel like you're going to tell me something bad."

"No." Wyatt chuckled. "Well, at least I hope not."

Hope took a deep breath. After she let it out, she said, "Okay. Spill it!"

"I love you."

"I love you too."

"Good. Then please listen to everything I have to say before you respond?"

"Agreed."

"Those children have been through it all."

"Eddie told me a lot. No need to go into it again. My heart breaks for them."

"Good. Then, you'll understand my desire not to separate them." When he said that, her eyes widened and her heart monitor sped up. Wyatt glanced at it before looking back to

Hope. "You see, I was praying about it," he explained. "I prayed, wondering how I was going to separate them, especially with all their gifts."

Hope only nodded in response, following along.

Wyatt looked toward the ceiling, asking God for guidance in his head before he looked back down at Hope. "I want to adopt them all."

Hope's jaw dropped.

Wyatt chuckled as he slowly closed her mouth. "Yes. All of them. Think about it. They have never been together until the hotel. They have the shared trauma that only another sibling who lived through it would understand. We also have the older teens, who can teach the younger ones how to use their gift, especially in public."

"We're going to need three vans everywhere we go!"

"Not necessarily. There are twenty-four of them. We have two fifteen-passenger vans. If we separate into two groups, with each of us or an older sibling driving, we can do it. Now," he said, putting his finger on her mouth to quiet her when she went to object, "I have a plan. I'm going to add to the house. I have a friend who is an architect. He'll figure it all out, and then I'll hire a construction company to do the work. I have plenty of money saved. Being a bachelor all this time is finally paying off. Now, before you say anything, thinking I planned our future without consulting you, we're not married yet. I love you with all my heart. However, I know this is a big task." Glancing at the monitor when her heart rate sped up again, he rested his hand on hers to calm her. "If you choose to leave me and take some of them with you, I understand. However, I do not want to separate them if we can."

"Are you sure?"

"Yes."

"Do you not want to marry me?"

"I do!" he said, taken aback. "Why would you think otherwise?"

"Because it sounds like you're telling me you don't want to be with me."

"No. No! No, not at all. Quite the opposite. I love you with all my heart, and it would make me a very happy man to finally be able to call you my wife. However, I know this is huge, so I'm giving you an out. I understand raising twenty-four children sounds insane."

"Oh! It does. However," she said, putting her finger on his lips when he went to object. "However, I love you with all my heart. I did not wait for fifteen years for you to back out now. I don't run. I wish we could have rescued all of them when this whole mess first started. I would be the happiest woman alive if you were by my side as we raised all twenty-four of them."

Wyatt grinned. "Really?"

"Absolutely! I'm just sorry Ben isn't here to see this. This whole thing was originally his idea."

"Oh! I'm sure he's watching from Heaven. He's probably going to get a kick out of this!"

Wyatt and Hope both burst out in laughter at what Ben's reaction would be.

"He's probably shaking his head," Hope said.

"Or he would go off on one of his comedic sets about raising children, let alone raising twenty-four!"

"Oh!" Hope laughed. "He would go off on this tangent about this or that and have us laughing for hours!"

"He did. He was a good man. I wish he could be at our wedding," Wyatt said. "Speaking of which, when do you want to marry me?"

"As soon as possible!"

"Would you want to wait until you're home?"

"I think so. That way, all the kids can be there."

"Perfect! I'll work with Tom to get the plans going for the

house. Then I'll get ahold of Zane to do the construction work with his company."

"I think that's a great idea!"

"Do you like gazebos?"

Hope furrowed her brow. "Why would you ask that?"

"Well," he blushed, "I was thinking we could get married on the property in a gazebo."

"I like it!"

"What about a honeymoon?"

"Honey, we're about to be responsible for raising twenty-four children. I don't think we'll have time to have a honeymoon. Besides, we had our time for fifteen years. I'm good."

"Are you sure?"

"Yes."

"Great!" He grinned. "I'll get ahold of my social worker friend, Delilah, to start the process for the adoptions."

"We have all the death certificates of the mothers. We just need The Professor's."

"Pretty sure Alex will help with that."

"Alex?" Hope raised an eyebrow. "You do understand that she's been spying on us all these years."

"Yes. And you also know because Eddie told me everything you two talked about on the way home, that the only reason Holly, Blake, Adam, Colby, and the Wyoming teens are still here is because of her. Also, that's how they were able to level the Maine facility with no casualties. She cleared the building first. Through this whole thing, she finally figured out who and what The Professor was. She understands each of these kids are not a subject, but her brother or sister. She knows she is just as much an experiment as they were. She's a clone of her mother."

"This is a lot to process. I mean, I saw it while Eddie explained it all. It's just after her betraying me, I don't know how I feel. Ben's dead because of her. Is she really here in Texas?"

"Yes. She had nowhere else to go. Plus, they are all her

siblings. They're all orphans now…Alex included. She's a different girl than what you saw in Maine."

"I'm sure. I'm just struggling."

"Think about how Peter felt after betraying Jesus," Wyatt said. "He knew he was doing wrong but did it anyway. And when Jesus's prophecy proved correct about the betrayal, Peter fell into a state of depression. Jesus had every right to be angry with Peter. However, when He came back, He chose to forgive Peter instead. Do you think you can find it within yourself to forgive Alex?"

"I have to pray about it."

Wyatt chuckled. "If you have to pray about it, then you already know the answer."

"What does that mean?"

"You know what Jesus' thoughts are on forgiveness. Matthew 18:21 through 22 says, *'Then came Peter to Him, and said, Lord, how oft shall my brother sin against me, and I forgive him? till seven times? Jesus saith unto him, "I say not unto thee, Until seven times: but, Until seventy times seven.'* Do you really think He's going to tell you not to forgive her?"

"No," Hope said on a sigh. "I need to do it for the both of us. It needs to be done for me just as much as it needs to be done for her."

"Agreed. Do you want me to send her here when she's available? She's settling back into Willow Bend right now. I got her job back for her as my secretary at the station."

"Are you sure?"

"Who is she going to tell? Roth is dead. She's free. This also gives her an opportunity to help us raise all those children we're about to adopt."

"And to show her what a real family, and what real love is supposed to look like," Hope said in understanding.

"Your heart is one of the many reasons why I love you. You know that?"

"Right back at ya. And yes, please send her when she's available."

"Thank you," he said and leaned down, giving her a kiss. "She's got a guy. One of her former guards, Kendrick, met us down here a few days ago."

"That's a good thing, right?"

"Actually, yes. I talked to him and have a good feeling about him."

"If you trust him, so do I."

"Good. Well, I have a lot of work I need to do. Are you going to be okay here by yourself?"

"Yep!" She grinned. "I've been catching up on television, and the nurses are taking very good care of me."

"Good. I love you," he said and kissed her again before he left.

Once he closed the door, Hope laid back on her bed. She listened intently for a moment. Not hearing anything, she concentrated on the tub of toiletries the nurses left for her on the nightstand. Slowly and shakily, the tub rose into the air and floated over toward Hope until she caught it mid-air.

Resting it on her stomach, she laid back on her pillow out of breath. "Whew! This is not easy," she said aloud to herself.

She glanced around the room, straining to listen again… that's when she heard it. The nurses at the nurse's station were talking about another case a few doors down from her, and she heard every word. Suddenly, it was like her ears popped, and there was an explosion of sound. She covered her ears as the noises slowly bubbled around her until it became like a symphony orchestra tuning all of their instruments. Grabbing the remote, she shut off the television and then quickly replaced her hands on her ears. Breathing rapidly, she struggled to sort through all of the noise. The monitors. The phones. The voices. The people tapping on the computers. People talking, yelling, crying, or laughing. The machines. It was almost deafening!

"Breathe, Hope!" she coaxed herself. "Breathe! Focus. You can do this!"

Slowly, she took her hands off her ears. Her acute hearing would take some getting used to, but she knew the kids did it, so she would learn as well.

She knew she would have to tell Wyatt when the moment was right what happened to her. Right now, they needed to focus on the kids and getting them settled. She wondered what their world was about to look like.

"Hello, Hope!" her doctor said, coming into the room.

"Shh!" Hope shushed him. To her, it sounded like he shouted at the top of his lungs.

"I'm sorry. Do you have a headache?"

"Yes." She grabbed her head. "Make it stop!"

"I'll be right back."

⬥⬥⬥⬥⬥

It took Alex a few days before she could get to Hope's hospital room. When she walked in, she was pleasantly surprised to see Hope sitting up, eating her lunch. "You look great!" she said with a smile.

"Thank you," Hope said, setting down her fork. She pushed the tray away as she said, "I'm not hungry anymore."

"Well, it's hospital food. I can go get you something decent from the cafeteria if you want?"

"I appreciate it, but I'm good. I'm glad you came today, but I will also admit that seeing you makes me want to vomit."

"I know." Alex looked down, shoving her hands into her pockets. "I've beat myself up pretty good over the part I played in this. I'm so sorry." Looking up at Hope, she said, "I'm not even going to ask for your forgiveness. If it were me, I wouldn't give it. And I definitely don't deserve it."

"Then, it's a good thing you're not me."

"What do you mean?"

"I forgive you, Alex."

"You don't have to."

"I know I don't. I want to. I forgive you."

Alex's face lit up. "Really?"

"Yes. I forgive you. Come, have a seat. We need to talk," Hope said, gesturing toward the chair next to her bed. When Alex sat down, Hope said, "I know you've had a few pretty good shocks yourself through this."

Alex groaned. "Seriously. The Professor created a disaster that sent a tsunami wave through everyone's lives who are connected to this mess. However, I am sincerely sorry for the part I played in this."

"You were just a child yourself when this was happening. And as an adult, you didn't know any different or any better. It was all you knew."

"I understand that in my head."

"You have to come to terms with it in your heart as well."

"Growing up, I never thought of them as my brothers and sisters. They were his research projects. I was his child. He also trained me to be an assassin – and a good one at that!"

"I don't doubt it."

"It wasn't until I was in Wyoming that I found out who he truly was."

"I don't think that's accurate. I think you knew who he was when you were in Texas. I think you realized the extent once in Wyoming."

"I think that's accurate," Alex agreed. She shuddered. "I can't believe he was my dad."

"Technically, he wasn't," Hope said.

"What do you mean?"

"You're a clone, right?"

"Right. A clone of my mom."

"Well, last time I checked, he can't be your dad. You're no

blood relation to him," Hope pointed out. "If you're a clone, then you are the product of *her* parents."

Taken aback for a moment, Alex said, "You're right! That's actually a bit of a relief! At least his DNA isn't clawing its way through my veins."

"It's not. It is, however, going through your brothers' and sisters' DNA. So, Wyatt and I will need your help in keeping everyone on track and away from the dark side of their DNA."

"If they're going to have you as parents, I'm pretty sure that won't be a problem. You guys are sweet and loving. Look at the great job you all did with Blake and Holly." When she nodded, Alex continued, "There is a portion of our lives, such as intelligence, that is dictated by our DNA. However, in the balance of nature versus nurture, the nurture aspect does play a massive role in their personality."

"The ten-year-olds will have a better shot than the thirteen or sixteen-year-olds," Hope pointed out.

"Then, you'll need the extra back-up of Kendrick and me."

"Speaking of Kendrick?" Hope raised an eyebrow. "Please fill me in on this gentleman?"

"He was one of my guards from the Maine facility."

"Have the kids met him yet?"

"They probably have seen him around the facility."

"That may be a struggle for them for a little while."

"I know. I talked to Wyatt about having a welcome home party for the kids and for you when you came home and having him come there."

"All twenty-four at once? That could be bad," Hope warned.

"Not for him. He wasn't one of the cruel ones."

"You sure?"

"Yes. He was protective of me and would watch out for me, but he wouldn't harm the kids. He didn't like The Professor at all."

"I already like him," Hope said. "Can I interest y'all in coming to church with us some Sunday?"

"I'm sure that can be arranged, with the understanding of no pressure."

"Agreed." Hope shook Alex's hand. "Now, sit back and tell me everything from your side, starting with when you first got sent to Texas."

"That's going to be a long story."

"Good thing we have nothing but time!"

# MOMENTS IN TIME

**"The only reason for time is so that everything doesn't
happen at once."
Albert Einstein**

By the time the hospital discharged Hope, construction on the additions were already underway. The gazebo was completed – Wyatt made sure that was first. Wyatt and Hope planned to get married in their yard, surrounded by all of their children and most of the church family about a week after she got home. This would be a dual occasion. It would enable them to introduce the church to the children and to celebrate their marriage.

On the day Hope got home, the kids were told to stay back in order not to overwhelm her. As she walked into the house with her arm looped through Wyatt's, Blake and Holly ran and hugged her.

"I'm sorry! I know we're supposed to give you space, but I just couldn't!" Holly mumbled, as she held onto Hope.

"I know, honey. It's okay," Hope said.

Blake kissed her head as he said, "I couldn't wait either."

"I know. I understand. Um, I need to talk to the two of you, if you have a few minutes?"

"We do," Holly said.

"Yep," Blake agreed.

"Great! Then, afterward, I want to meet y'all up close and personal, starting with Eddie and Bells," Hope said to the other kids. Both Eddie and Bells blushed at Hope mentioning them. "Then, once I meet everyone, I think we need to bond by making chocolate chip cookies for everyone!"

"Really?" Deanna grinned.

As everyone laughed, Wyatt quietly explained, "Deanna's now addicted to chocolate. She's been looking forward to chocolate chip cookies since Blake showed her what they tasted like."

"I see," Hope said. Then she looked at Deanna with a smile and a wink as she said, "A girl after my own heart."

Deanna's grin widened.

"Okay. Let's get you settled," Wyatt said, ushering her into his room, with Holly and Blake behind him. Afterward, Wyatt started with, "We know you two were with us all through growing up. We wanted you two to be the first to understand the full dynastic plan here."

Blake chuckled as he asked, "What is it, King Wyatt?"

Wyatt could not help but burst out in laughter. "Not really a king, just head of this crew." He nervously cleared his throat as he said, "I know you've noticed over the last few weeks that the construction guys don't seem to be stopping at just the gazebo but adding onto the house."

"Yeah. How many rooms are you adding?" Holly asked.

"At least ten," Wyatt said. Blake and Holly gasped.

"Are you saying…" Holly's voice faded as the realization of what they were telling her set in. "You're adopting all of them? What does Delilah say?"

"She says it will be a trick, but it can be done. She would rather we raise them, knowing they grew up in extremely abusive situations. It would make her job easier. We just have to prove that we can do it."

"And we'll need you guys to pull it off for a bit," Hope added. "You guys know what life outside of the campuses looks and functions like. You exposed Deanna and Adam to some of it, but in reality, all twenty-two of them need a slow infusion into the social stream. We're going to have to homeschool them, at least for a little while."

"Delilah's aware of the lack of social influence, so she's behind this idea," Wyatt continued. "She'll be making frequent visits, so we'll have to get a schedule and stick with it. If we go off-schedule, that could prove disastrous."

Holly giggled at the thought. "I could see that. It would be a mess."

"And then some!" Blake chuckled.

"Now, I truly hope you are both okay with this invasion?" Hope asked.

"Of course!" Holly said. "They're our brothers and sisters, too. It'll just take a few adjustments on our part. How will we sort the rooms?"

"Two-by-two," Wyatt said. "We'll sort it out as they finish each room."

"I'm good with it, too," Blake said. "Pretty sure William wants to room with me if he can. He hasn't left my side."

"William?" Hope asked.

"One of my clones."

"I see. This whole clone thing is going to take some time getting used to as well," she pointed out. "That's not even adding in the gifts."

Wyatt chuckled. "It's been interesting. However, there is still one more big thing we need to talk to you about."

"What's that?" Holly asked.

"The wedding," Blake said.

"Blake! Were you reading our minds?" Hope asked.

"Strangely, no. It's like I don't even have to push to read minds anymore if the feeling is strong enough. It's just there. Like second nature."

"Your gifts are getting stronger," Hope said in understanding. "Okay," she took a deep breath, "I know we asked you to be part of the wedding. However, with the added kids, we really don't want to seem like we're playing favorites."

"I get it," Blake said. "We can still help in the planning and set up, right?"

"Definitely!" Hope agreed.

"I would appreciate it," Wyatt added.

"Holly?" Hope asked her.

"I understand. It hurts, but I get it."

"Honey, we're not even going to have any groomsmen or bridesmaids. I'll ask Alex to be my maid of honor. If nothing else, it will help solidify her position as your oldest sibling and help me to get everything done as I continue to recover."

"I-I get it," Holly stammered. Tucking a portion of her hair behind her ear as she looked down, she cleared her throat. "I do." Looking up, she said, "I understand where you're coming from. Not going to lie…it hurts."

"I know. I'm sorry. We have a lot of changes going on in our lives right now. Please just do me a favor?" Hope asked.

"What?"

"Please don't just swallow your feelings? If something is bothering you, please tell me? I don't want you two in particular to become resentful. I want to keep communication between all of us open. This is going to take a lot of cooperation to achieve this. Do you think you both can do that?"

They both nodded.

"Okay. Now, Holly, while you may not be part of the

wedding, I do love your taste in décor. Please come up with a design for the gazebo?"

Holly perked up. "What colors?"

"We were thinking blue, tan, and white," Hope said.

"What shade of blue?" Holly asked. "And do you have a theme?"

"Ocean blue," Wyatt said. "And we were thinking of keeping a natural theme. We both love the outdoors."

"Can you do that?" Hope asked Holly.

"Definitely! I'll have Deanna, Bells, and Gemma help me. I'll probably call-in Lindsey, Tanya, and Megan, too."

"I think that's a great idea!"

"And, Blake, would you please hold the rings and walk me down the aisle?" Hope asked Blake.

"I can do that," he agreed.

"Good," Hope said. "We're going to have Kendrick and Alex witness since they're legal adults."

"Fair enough," Blake said. "A suggestion?"

"Yes?" Wyatt asked.

"Maybe break the kids up into smaller groups, like at least one older with a middle and a younger. That way, they can all keep track of each other, especially the youngest ones," Blake suggested.

"I think that's a great idea," Wyatt agreed.

"Well, I know there are many young ones who want to see y'all, so we'll scoot," Holly said.

"Please send in Eddie and Bells?" Hope asked. "We'll take the kids two-by-two."

"Good idea," Holly said, giving Hope a hug. "I'm glad you're home."

"Me too," Blake said, hugging her after Holly.

EDDIE AND BELLS came into the room. "Feeling like we're in a bit of trouble," Eddie commented, locking his chair in place.

"No. Quite the opposite," Hope said. "Actually, I'm here because of both of you. I wanted to say thank you."

"You did it," Bells said. "We were just along for the ride."

"You helped me remember what I was fighting for," she said to Bells. "And, you," she said to Eddie. He looked at her, wide-eyed. "You literally fought for me. Only you and I know what went on, and I cannot thank you enough for risking what you did to pull me out."

"My pleasure."

"And, making good on my promise," Wyatt said. "You two are the first to know that we will be doing our best to adopt all of you."

Eddie gasped. "All twenty-two of us?"

"All twenty-four for me, and all twenty-two for Hope…yes," Wyatt confirmed.

"Are you serious?" Bells asked. "That's *a lot* of kids!"

"I know. We're going to need to enlist the older kids to help us," Hope said. "We want to keep y'all's gifts a secret. In order to do that, we need to have all y'all in one place. We're going to need you older kids to pull it off."

Bells looked over at Eddie, who was rubbing his chin in thought.

"It'll work, if everyone cooperates. If everyone is aware of the stakes, I'm pretty sure they'll cooperate," Eddie said. "The odds are very high."

"I'm willing to help where needed. I want to get to know the others," Bells said.

"We're hoping that'll be everyone's mindset," Hope said. "This is more for everyone's safety, not out of convenience by any stretch of the imagination. There'll be a lot of work on everyone's behalf…including the younger ones. They'll work just as hard."

"As long as it's balanced, I don't have a problem," Bells said.

"Do me a favor?" Wyatt asked Bells.

"Yes?"

"As one of the kids with mind gifts, please keep a temperature on the general mindset. If someone starts to tilt toward resentment or anger, please let me know. I want to try to head off any emotional issues. I'm also going to get in touch with a friend of mine who is a psychologist. I'm going to see if she'll protect our secret and take all y'all on," Wyatt explained.

"That's huge!" Hope pointed out.

"I know. She's one of the few I trust with this secret."

"Fair enough," Hope agreed.

Hope and Wyatt spoke with each of the kids, two-by-two. In doing so, it allowed them to get to know each other in a small circle. This enabled them all to connect and for no one to get lost in the large number of children. They also promised to meet with each set of two at least once a week together. This alleviated many concerns, knowing they would still have a voice.

⬥⬥⬥⬥⬥

To SAY it was not easy adjusting to twenty-four kids would be an understatement. Everything that happened was next level. Fights took on a new meaning when dealing with children with gifts. Getting twenty-four children fed was a chore. Going to the store was a nightmare! They finally decided that Hope would do the grocery shopping with two older teens, alternating which teens she took each time. This gave her some time with each of the teens. When the older ones left for college, she would take the next group on the shopping trips.

⬥⬥⬥⬥⬥

IT TOOK a good six months before they completed the additions on the house. It was chaotic at best as they shuffled kids around as the rooms opened up.

The additions to the home included an industrial kitchen, a game room, an extra-large living room area, and ten more bedrooms. The thirteen rooms allowed for two kids per room, leaving Hope and Wyatt a master suite to themselves.

It was not easy with all the children. The older kids helped immensely! This allowed things to flow smoothly when it came to things as simple as laundry or cooking. Some of the older teens helped with the additions to the house to keep the price down. The younger kids did not escape the work. They were all assigned chores to do. They assigned them with partners. If a child refused to do the chore, there were various levels of punishment ranging from running laps, to yard work, to extra homework, to other creative ways of guidance. They still ended up doing what they were refusing to do, but they did it by themselves, along with the punishment that fit the scenario. Eventually, the kids decided on their own it was not worth it, and a relative amount of peace reigned throughout the home.

School was a feat! They tried homeschooling for a bit, if nothing else, to catch the kids up to their grade level. Once they reached their grade level, they were allowed to attend school, under strict instructions not to use their gifts. If they found out a child used their gift, they would be punished at home, using one of the creative punishments concocted by Wyatt, Hope, and their psychologist friend, Savannah.

Once all the kids started public school, they kept an eye on their siblings. The ages allowed for each group to be in a different level in school. This gave all the kids a break from each other. Most did very well in school. There were a few who struggled in different areas. That's where the other kids stepped up to help, especially if it was their roommate.

NEXT ON THE list were the adoptions. The judge just about fell out of his seat when he realized they were all going to the same home. However, the social worker, Delilah, stood up for them. She made sure the judge knew how they ran their house. She would stop by unannounced to check on them over the year at least once a week, and it was never at the same time. While the regular growing pains and adjustments occurred, the fact that Hope could stay home and be there for them helped, along with the other siblings.

The judge knew what a nightmare it would be to find homes for twenty-two children if they all went into foster care. Delilah also did her homework. She made sure all t's were crossed, and i's were dotted before she pushed it through. She also committed to continue making unannounced visits to ensure the safety of the children. With that condition in place, the judge signed off. As his gavel dropped, cheers erupted throughout the courtroom. He wanted to object, but let it play out, enjoying the celebration for a bit.

After the hearing, the entire group went home to celebrate, along with Alex, Kendrick, Delilah, and Savannah. Delilah and Savannah also brought along their husbands. Hope and Wyatt had Willow's Bend Diner cater, and of course, invited the Willow Bend youth group teens and their families. It was an amazing time, which included a feast no one would soon forget. Afterward, they had a massive bonfire, sang songs, and roasted marshmallows. The stories would have to wait for another time when guests who did not know about the kids' gifts were not there.

While they sat around the fire, there were multiple conversations going on.

"Here's your soda," Colby said, handing it to Holly as he sat on the log next to her. "How are you feeling?"

"It's a lot," Holly admitted. "I now legally have twenty-three brothers and sisters and a new last name. I mean, I knew it, and for the last year, understood it, but it sunk in as he dropped the gavel. Not to mention that it's actually over. I mean, all the questions are answered. We were nervous about whether we could all be adopted, but Delilah assured us that she was doing everything in her power to make it happen. To see it all come to fruition is insane!"

"I can see that. I'm just glad it all got sorted before you graduated, so you can have *Reynolds* as your last name on your diploma," Colby said. "That means you won't have to explain it every time you present your diploma. Saves a bit of a headache."

"Well, the beauty of the way it was done, all but Blake and I get their college tuition paid for," Holly explained. "Technically, the other twenty-two went through the foster system, so they get their tuition covered if they go to a state-supported college or university. Wyatt and Mom only have to figure out mine and Blake's tuition."

"Books are pretty expensive, too," Colby pointed out. "Plus, y'all just got connected about a year ago, and in less than a year, you're separating into different colleges."

"Not necessarily," Holly said. "We have all agreed to do community college for the first year to knock out our general courses. That gives us all another year together, as well as helping the others navigate the college social life."

"That's going to be interesting. So, what is your major going to be?"

"I was thinking graphic arts and English major. I like writing, so I thought that would help with either writing or being a teacher if I wanted to do that later. Additionally, I love doing graphic arts. I thought that would come in handy in creating my own covers and ads for writing."

"Smart! I like it!"

"What about you?" Holly asked.

"I like weather, so I'm going to do meteorology. I kind of like the idea of being a storm chaser."

Holly laughed. "I can see that. So, have you gotten your letters yet?"

"I did," he said. "I haven't decided which school I am going to go to yet. I have scholarships to some of the bigger schools thanks to my sports."

"Oh! You have to go, then!" Holly encouraged. "Maybe, if we're still together, I can join you if my major is at your school choice for sophomore year?"

"I would love that. And I don't think that'll be a problem," he said, taking her hand into his. "I'm not looking at anyone else but you. Pretty sure I won the lottery there!"

"What if you get to college and those hot, young, sexy freshmen girls start throwing themselves at you?"

"Are you serious? Nope. I'm done with that life. I have who I want in you. You're smart, wise, funny, sweet, and super sexy yourself! And the best part is that you have a Christ-centered life. You're the complete package!"

Holly blushed. "Thank you."

"Seriously! Don't sell yourself short! You're everything I'm looking for. Now, I know most couples break up when it comes to college, but I plan on staying focused on you and my studies, even if we're not in the same college."

"That's my plan as well," Holly said. "Thank you."

"Thank *you*! Do you want me to get some s'mores?"

"Please…and thank you!"

BELLS AND SHAWN were talking while they sat on a couple lawn chairs on the other side of the fire.

"So, we're heading toward the end of our senior year, and I have to say that you have impressed me in fitting in," Shawn said. "There are many kids who never get close to reaching your level, who have been in school all their life."

"Well, it helps when you can read the mind of the kids and teachers," Bells admitted. "Don't tell anyone. Some of the others in my group know, but that's only because I helped them too. I didn't do it for any tests or quizzes, just emotions."

"Which means you are as brilliant as I thought you were. Not just people smart, but book smart, too."

"It's helped immensely."

"What are you thinking of doing in college?" Shawn asked.

"Psychology. I know I have to get my master's degree, so it will be a bit, but I feel that's where my heart is."

"Appropriate." Shawn nodded in approval. "You really don't need to access your gift very much to do it either. You come by it naturally."

"Thank you!" She smiled. "What about you?"

"Mac and I are going to go to school for firefighting and paramedic."

"That sounds perfect for both of you!"

"Yep! We can also use some of our time off to still ride in rodeos."

"Is that something he wants to continue?" Bells asked. "He's been making a lot of changes over the last several months."

"He will. He still does it now, though not as much. It's not like it'll be his main focus. I'm sure he will for at least a little bit. It helps that when we win, we get money."

"True," Bells acknowledged.

"I need to ask you something," Shawn said and then nervously cleared his throat.

"What is it?" Bells asked.

"Well, normally people make this huge gesture in asking, but since we've been together for over a year, I'm just going to ask. Will you be my date for prom?"

"Of course!" She threw her arms around him in a hug. "Thank you for asking!"

"I'm sorry for not making some grand gesture about it."

"Sweetheart," Bells said, resting her hand on the side of his face, "I know your heart. I know you have made a lot of changes over the last year. I also know you've taken a lot of flack for it. I'm proud of you and proud to be yours."

He hugged her again. "I can't thank you enough for helping me stay on track and for teaching me to be my authentic self."

She rested her forehead on his as she said, "I like your authentic self."

"I do too."

⋄⋈⋄⋈⋄

EDDIE WAS SITTING in his wheelchair when Lindsey walked over and set a chair down beside him and sat in it. "How are you doing, Eddie? How is it to be official?"

He shrugged. "Honestly, I already considered them Mom and Dad. All this was, was a formality."

"But now you're a Reynolds too."

"Now *that* is something to celebrate!" He grinned. "Not having to write that man's last name down as mine anymore will be a relief!"

"What's next for you?"

"I'm going to go to community college for the first year and then go to school for Criminal Investigations and Forensics. I want to work with the FBI."

"Oh! I can see that! You're brilliant!"

"Thank you! What about you? Wait! Let me guess…something with fashion?"

"Actually, yes. I'm doing a dual major – fashion design and interior design. I like both. My true passion is fashion design, but I know that takes a lot to break into, so interior design will supplement my income until I reach the level I need. Plus, who knows? I may like interior design better," she said with a shrug.

"I think you'll do great at whichever one you do."

"Is there a way to tell which one will work better?" she hinted.

Eddie burst out in laughter. "I'm not a fortune teller, Lindsey. I can tell you which one has better odds, but I'm pretty sure you already know the answer to that."

"I do, but you can't blame a girl for trying!"

While they were talking, Deanna and Adam walked up to the pair. "Mind if we sit?" Adam asked.

"Of course! Pull up a chair," Eddie gestured around them.

Deanna and Adam both got chairs and sat down.

"So, feeling anxious?" Eddie asked Deanna.

"I've been holding my own," Deanna said. "I do better in smaller groups."

"What are you going to do in college?" Lindsey asked.

"I'm actually going to the Police Academy," Deanna said. "Much smaller group."

"You're going to be a cop?" Lindsey asked.

"Yep! Helps when your dad is the county sheriff," she said with a wink.

Eddie burst out in laughter. "Does he know yet?"

"Yep. I told him and Mom a few days ago. I wanted them to know before we knew if the adoption went through or not that I wanted to and why," she explained.

"What's the reason?" Lindsey asked.

"Well, if it wasn't for Wyatt, we would still be up in Maine. If he didn't go out on a limb to help us, we wouldn't be here. He could have stopped after we rescued Hope. No one would fault him. He would have broken a promise, but he could have done it. He didn't, though. He went through and rescued all of us. That was not a small feat, but it was also costly. He backed us every way possible. I want to be able to help people like he helped us.

Plus, I figured my, um," she coughed, "gift, could come in handy if I'm careful."

"Agreed," Eddie said. "Helping others seems to be a theme for most of our choices."

"Just be super careful," Lindsey pointed out. "If you get caught, it could end badly."

"Of course," Deanna said. "If I didn't, everything we've done up to this point would have been worthless. Trust me. I can do it."

"I not only know you can, but also that you will be successful," Adam said.

"What are you going to do?" Lindsey asked Adam.

"Criminal Science major to become a profiler."

"You'll be great at that!" Lindsey exclaimed.

"I figured The Professor used my gift for evil, but it taught me a lot, so I'm going to use it for good."

"Making the good out of the bad. Love it!" Lindsey smiled.

"Lindsey, can I talk to you for a minute?" Adam asked her. "Alone?"

"Sure," she said, and they walked away from Eddie and Deanna. "What's up?" she asked once they were out of earshot.

"I'm sure you've had plenty of guys asking, but I wanted to know if you would go with me to prom…as my friend?"

Lindsey grinned. "I would love to!"

"Now, I'm not looking to date you. I just like you as a friend and respect you. I know you don't want any strings, so you can go to college without a boyfriend. You also know I will respect you as a lady."

"I know," she said, giving him a hug. "Thank you. And yes. I would be honored if you would escort me to prom."

"I have to admit that I don't know how to dance."

"It's a good thing we have time for me to teach you."

"Um," he shifted nervously, "I know most of us don't know

how to dance. Would you be willing to come over and teach all of us?"

"I think that'll be fun! If any of the others want to come, they can too."

He gave her a hug. "Thank you."

⊕⊕⊕⊕

"I'm excited we're going to the same college," Mac said as he sat with Megan.

"At least for the first year," Megan said. "Then, I need a bigger school for what I want to do."

"I'm sure your dad already has you applying to his alma mater."

"Yes. Harvard Law is on the top of the list," Megan chuckled. "Being a lawyer will give me the steppingstones I need to get to what I really want to do."

"Have to admit I'm a bit nervous about the idea of you being an FBI agent," Mac said. "You know I care about you. That's not exactly a safe job."

"No, but I'll be helping people and serving my country at the same time. I'm sure they can put my computer skills to good use as well," she said with a wink. "Only they actually give me a gun, too. Being a firefighter isn't exactly safe either," she pointed out.

"I know. It's something I've always wanted to do, though."

"What about the rodeos?"

"I won't be doing those for too much longer. If I hurt myself, it'll affect my future as a firefighter."

"Does Shawn know?"

"I've told him, but you know Shawn. He thinks he can control what I do, no matter what I say."

"That's going to be an interesting conversation."

"I've already had it. It's not my fault he's choosing not to listen. I do worry that he may backslide without me there to keep him in check."

"He's a big boy. He needs to make his choices and stick with them. You're not his conscience, nor are you the Holy Spirit. His choices are not up to you. They're between him and God."

"Good point." Mac nodded. "Have I ever told you how much I appreciate you?"

"You have."

"Have I told you that I'm really going to miss you when you go to Harvard Law?"

"I doubt I'll get in."

"First off, you're a legacy. Secondly, you're a genius. If you don't get in, no one should. If you want to go, you *will* get in."

"What if," she tucked a portion of her hair behind her ear, "would you ever consider moving to Massachusetts?"

"Would I–what?"

She looked up at him, hoping to not have to explain her question.

"You want me to go with you?"

"Would you consider it?" she asked.

"Once I graduate, I would love to! It'll take me two years. Can you handle one year apart?"

"I can," she said. "Would you really do it?"

"Megan," he took her hands into his, "You know I'm in love with you. You've been the reason why we haven't progressed."

"I'm ready."

"Are you sure?"

"Yes."

"Would you be my girlfriend...for real?"

"Yes."

"YES!" he shouted as he jumped up from his chair. When everyone looked over at them, he explained, "She's my girlfriend now!"

Cheers went up throughout the group.

He sat down. "You have made me the happiest man on the planet!"

"And, you have made me the happiest woman!"

"This is just the beginning!"

⟨⟨⟩⟩

AFTER THE GROUP calmed from Mac's announcement, Tanya and Blake were sitting by themselves, chatting.

"Well, that was fun." Blake smirked.

"It's about time," Tanya said. "They've only been skirting that line for the last year. Megan was slow to make a choice. I knew she was going to ask him to go with her to Massachusetts."

"You did? Why didn't you tell me?"

"I didn't want to give you any ideas."

"What does that mean?" Blake asked.

"I mean, you've been pushing a bit more lately. I don't want to cross any lines."

Blake furrowed his brow. "Meaning?"

"Meaning, I don't want to be as free as you regarding our intimate time," she admitted.

"I didn't mean to push you."

"Yes. You do. I keep telling you that I don't want to, but you keep going once we start kissing."

Blake rubbed the back of his neck as he got up and started pacing.

"Blake, let's look at this realistically," Tanya said. "I want to be an elementary teacher, and you want to be a pediatric doctor. There is no way I can help you through college. You're going to be in school and interning forever. And then, your hours will be horrible. I don't know if I'm ready for that yet."

He stopped pacing and stared at her. "What are you saying?"

"I'm saying that I wonder if we should break up?"

"You're serious? After everything we've been through, you

want to stop now?" Blake asked, doing his best to control his own emotions. That was when he felt a wave of peace. He looked over to see Bells watching him. She did a curt nod to let him know she was keeping him calm. He smiled in appreciation. Looking back to Tanya, he asked, "Why would you say that?"

"Because I don't feel respected."

Blake knelt in front of her and rested his hands on her knees. "I'm sorry you feel that way. That's the last thing I want you to feel. You are so important to me – I really can't even begin to tell you."

Tanya looked toward the stars and sighed. "Can we keep going? I feel like we're going in two different directions."

"We can do whatever we want to do, as long as we both want to do it."

"I want you to achieve your dreams."

"That includes being with you," he said.

"Are you sure? You're going to be a doctor. I'm going to be a teacher."

"We can make both of those work."

"Are you sure?"

He got to his knees and rested his hands on the sides of her face. "Tanya, you are my world. You mean more to me than you will ever know. Here, let me show you." He sent a wave to her, letting her feel his feelings for her.

"Really?" she asked, tears in her eyes. "Is that really how you feel?"

He nodded. "Here," he said and then kissed her, letting her feel the feeling even more intense. When he pulled away, he explained, "That's why I sometimes have difficulty controlling how far we go. However, I don't want to lose you. I'll do my best to respect and honor you. Will you give me the opportunity to prove it to you?"

Tanya looked up into his eyes. "You sure you don't want some nurse or another doctor as your partner in this life?"

"No. I want you. These next few years will either make us stronger, or we'll know when we need to part. However it turns out, I do not want you to ever think I don't respect you."

"Thank you. And yes, we can keep going."

"Good." He smiled. "Now, will you please be my date to prom?"

"Of course!" She grinned. "Thank you!"

"Thank *you*!"

⚬⚬⚬⚬

"A NURSE, HUH?" Hope said to Gemma as she, Gemma, and Wyatt were talking.

"Yes."

"I think you would do great at it. You have a good heart," Wyatt said. "Just know it's not an easy profession."

"I know. I figure it can't be any worse than what we've all been through."

Wyatt chuckled. "Keep that sense of humor. It'll serve you well as a nurse."

She smiled. "Thank you. I think Freya would have been good at it, too."

"I agree." Wyatt nodded. "She was ornery, but had a good heart."

"She was feisty too," Gemma said, a smile on her face as memories filled her mind. "I just wish she could have experienced this family."

"Gemma," Wyatt said, resting his hand on hers, "she died free from that man."

"I know," she said, wiping away the few tears that escaped. "That's one of the things I've held onto while Savannah and I worked through it. I'm not all the way through, but I'm getting there."

"You do what you need to do, only when you need to do it," Hope said. "Only when you're ready to take the steps."

"I think I'm doing good."

"She is," Savannah said, walking up to the group. "Sorry, couldn't help overhearing a little of what you were talking about."

Gemma blushed. "You tend to have impeccable timing."

"I've heard that before." She gently squeezed Gemma's shoulder and then crouched beside her. "Gemma, you, Bells, and Eddie were the most challenging of the groups. Eddie for different reasons than you and Bells. Bells had more time to process than you did. She's in a better headspace than you, but you're making strides. Losing a sibling is difficult. Losing a twin is worse. There's a link between twins that cannot be explained. In all of my years, those are the toughest cases for me to work with. Once they reach their emotional processing goals, it's a miracle. It's like working with people who have lost their soul mates. The loss of someone that close is brutal, but you're working through it well. I think your chosen profession of a nurse fits your heart and personality."

"Thank you for working with the kids and us to navigate the next steps in life regarding profession and school," Hope said.

"Oh, honey, we're nowhere near done," Savannah chuckled. "We've still got several more years of this with the other kids. The good news is that we have more time with the other kids to center them. Now, they all also know when they go to college that I'm a phone call away, and they have all asked to come see me on their breaks."

"Wonderful!" Wyatt said, pleased.

"It was actually all of their ideas individually. I didn't prompt it. You have some amazing children," Savannah said.

"Thank you," Hope said. "It hasn't been easy, but it is more than worth it."

"Here's to many more happy and productive years!" Savannah said, raising her soda.

"Here! Here!" Wyatt agreed, and they all touched cans together in a toast.

◁◁▷▷

"I'm so proud of all of them," Alex said, looking around at the groups.

Kendrick rested his arm around her shoulders and gave her a gentle squeeze. "I'm proud of *you* for everything you've done as well. You could have easily followed The Professor's footsteps. You gave up all that money, got rid of the research to protect the kids, and still seem to have landed on top with a great job at the police station."

"That's thanks to Wyatt."

"Nooo, that's all you, sweetheart."

"You're doing well with your security company," Alex pointed out.

"Thank you. I think it's doing really well, too. By the way, we got that contract I gave the estimate for the other day. You wouldn't want to consider coming and being *my* secretary, would you?"

"I really like my job. Plus, I get to see my brothers and sisters around here."

"I'm not asking you to move. I'm asking you to change jobs."

"I don't know." Alex shook her head. "Wyatt trusts me."

"Just think about it?"

"I will."

"Will you think about something else, too?" he asked, moving behind her, wrapping his arms around her waist.

"What's that?"

"Would you marry me?"

Alex gasped as she spun around in his arms. "What did you say?"

He got down on one knee as others hushed those around who saw what was going on. "Alexandra Murphy, would you please do me the honor of being my wife?" he asked, producing a black velvet box from his pocket. When he opened the box, Alex covered her mouth in shock. "Alex, you surprise me every day with your strength and courage. You are one formidable young lady, and I would be honored if you would marry me?"

Alex looked toward Hope. Hope nodded with a smile, giving her silent permission. Alex looked back to Kendrick. With tears in her eyes, she nodded. More cheers erupted as he stood and slid the ring onto her finger.

The couple was mobbed with people hugging and congratulating both of them. The entire day was amazing but exhausting for everyone. There was so much closure, and yet so much to look forward to in the future for everyone.

⟐⟐⟐

THE KIDS WERE THRILLED to replace *Roth* as their last name with *Reynolds*. Even Holly and Blake changed their last name, so the entire family could be one cohesive unit. By the time the first seven graduated, all of them had the last name of *Reynolds*.

The night of graduation, after all the kids went to bed, Hope and Wyatt went to their own suite. "Peace at last," Wyatt said as they lay in bed. "Soon, the first group will be going to college."

Hope nervously cleared her throat. "Um, Wyatt, I need to talk to you."

"Anytime, love," Wyatt said and sat up so they could talk. "What's up?"

"Things are finally to a breathing point. I know it's been a doozie of a year-and-a-half with the additions to the house, our wedding, the adoptions, and finally graduation."

227

"I agree."

"With all of those moments enjoyed as an entire family, I want to enjoy this one moment with you. This one moment will be ours."

Wyatt wrapped his arms around her.

"Wyatt?" she said, glancing up at him.

"Yes?"

"We're going to have a baby."

Wyatt laughed. "We have twenty-four."

"And now…" Hope said. "Twenty-five."

Wyatt let her go so he could look her in the eyes. "Are you serious?"

"Yes. This is our moment. We're going to have a child of our very own!" Hope grinned.

"Great! We need to tell the kids!"

"We do, but not yet. There's something else I need to tell you first."

Wyatt furrowed his brow. "What now?"

"You won't be mad, will you?"

"Hope, why would I be mad at you?"

"Well, we've been so busy, I didn't want to add to the stress," she said quickly. "I figured it all out on my own."

"Figured *what* out all on your own?"

Hope did not answer him. She simply lifted the lamp with her mind.

Wyatt's head spun toward the flickering light balancing precariously mid-air. "Hope, is that you?"

"Yes. I also have that intense hearing. I can literally hear each and every child in their room right now."

"H-how long have you known?" he whispered.

"Since the hospital. It was intense, but I didn't want to burden you with this as well."

"The kids and Alex said he messed with your DNA. Are you okay otherwise?"

"I think so," she said, sitting up. "I haven't felt any different, with the exception of that," she said, setting the lamp down, "and the hearing thing."

"I see. So, you didn't just drop one bomb. You went nuclear on me on probably the second biggest, most stressful day of my life." He got out of bed and started pacing. Running his hand periodically through his hair, he would stop, sigh, and then continue to pace.

Finally, Hope could not take it anymore. "Wyatt?" she asked.

"I just…" He put his hand up to stop her. "Give me a moment."

"Are you mad?"

"More like in shock. Please give me a moment."

Hope nodded, so he continued to pace. He paced for a good ten minutes before he suddenly stopped and looked at her. "My love?"

"Yes?"

"You're carrying our child?"

"Yes."

"Could this child have a gift too?"

"They may, or they may not. I have the gene, but you don't. We won't know until they either show signs or not."

"I see. And you are a telekinetic and have a form of hyperacusis?"

"Not quite. More like Superman's hearing ability."

"I see. So, if someone whispers across the house…"

"There's a reason why no one can get away with anything in this house," Hope said, finishing his thought.

"Okay. So, when are we going to tell the children all the news?"

"I was going to leave that up to you."

"Well, I think the sooner they know about the gifts, the better. It'll help with them in knowing why they can't get away with anything."

"And the baby?"

"Pretty sure those with your hearing gift already know. I've watched several keeping a closer eye on you lately. They either have it figured out or are trying to figure it out. Let's tell them in the morning."

Hope sighed. "Our life will never be boring."

"Honey," Wyatt said, sitting on the edge of the bed beside her, "our life has *never* been boring."

"True."

"We need to enjoy each and every single moment we have with each other and the kids. We know time is like sands flowing through the hour glass. We also know that *'time slips through our hands like grains of sand never to return again. Those who use time wisely are rewarded with rich, productive, and satisfying lives,'*" he explained. "We have a rich and satisfying life. We're teaching these kids to love. We're teaching them to use their gifts for good. While their lives started out rough, they now have a life that is full and happy. We need to cherish those moments, writing them down before they become fleeting thoughts."

"I agree. I started a journal in the hospital," Hope said, nodding toward it on the dresser.

"What if you actually write about it? I mean like write a book. I know there are times when you have downtime while the kids are at school. You could write it as fiction, so people won't know it's true."

"They probably wouldn't believe me if I told them it was true. The problem is when the kids are at school, I am usually doing the cooking, laundry, or cleaning," Hope pointed out.

"This is important. I feel that we need to get ahead of this. We've been living in denial that someday someone from the Maine facility may write a book or talk to someone from the news. If we write it, it will come across as someone trying to copy the book."

"I get it. I have a better idea though," Hope said as a smile formed on her face.

"What's that?"

"I can work with Holly. She's always been a great storyteller. God gave her that talent for a reason. Maybe it was to tell their story."

"I like it!"

"So, family meeting in the morning?" Hope asked.

"Family meeting in the morning," Wyatt agreed.

"I'll talk to Holly as well," Hope said. "This, I feel, is a project only she has the talent to pull off."

"Good idea."

Together, they cuddled in each other's arms, watching a movie on their television until they fell asleep.

# EPILOGUE

*L*ife is a series of tests, trials, decisions, celebrations, joys, successes, failures, loss, and so much more. It's these situations that make us into who we're meant to be. God uses these situations to strengthen us; to teach us lessons; to shape in us the purpose and the reason we're here on this earth. While He may not plaster what direction or plan He has for us on a billboard when we want Him to, He will show you your purpose in life if you continue to trust and follow Him. He makes us this promise in Jeremiah 29:11, *'For I know the plans I have for you," declares the Lord, "plans to prosper you and not to harm you, plans to give you hope and a future.'*

Stay focused on Him, dear children. He will guide and direct you. Just follow Him one step at a time.

\- Holly Reynolds

**"Time slips through our hands like grains of sand never to return again. Those who use time wisely are rewarded with rich, productive and satisfying lives." Robin Sharma**

THEIR STORIES DO NOT STOP HERE. STAY tuned for more in the *Sands of Time Series*, where we dive into the characters you have fallen in love with during this trilogy. Learn more about their pasts and how their futures turned out. These stories will make you laugh, cry, and take you on a journey of the heart as you get to know all of them on a deeper level.

God bless,

C.J. Peterson

cjpetersonwrites.com

"While the stories are fiction, the journey is real."

# BOOKS BY C.J. PETERSON

**Grace Restored Series can be found: https://cjpetersonwrites. com/series-books**

**Holy Flame Trilogy can be found: https://cjpetersonwrites. com/series-books**

**Divine Legacy Series can be found: https://cjpetersonwrites. com/series-books**

**C.J.'s Stand-Alone Books & Anthologies She Participated in can be found: https://cjpetersonwrites.com/stand-alone-%26-anthologies**

**Sands of Time Trilogy can be found: https://cjpetersonwrites. com/series-books**

**The Adventures of Chief and Sarge Children's Books can be found: https://cjpetersonwrites.com/chief-and-sarge**